RHIANA

An Urban Fantasy

ANN GIMPEL

CONTENTS

RHIANA
CIRCLE OF ASSASSINS, BOOK THREE

Urban Fantasy

By
Ann Gimpel

Tumble off reality's edge into a twisted world fueled by lore and magic

Copyright Page

BOOK DESCRIPTION, RHIANA

I'm one of the old ones. I've lived many lives, done many things. I've been called sorceress, witch, and far worse. Mortals have hung me, burned me, staked me out, and left me to die. What a pack of fools. I'm immortal, and their petty attempts were laughable.

So were they when I stopped their puny, pathetic hearts. The thrill of ending someone never gets old, no matter how unbalanced the contest.

When I want a break from everything, Dorcha—my bondmate—and I bide with the Circle of Assassins. I never mean to stay long, but the years have a way of slipping by.

While I find peace within the Circle, Dorcha becomes restive. She never used to mind being the only unicorn, but she's grown silent, withdrawn. The place within me where I feel her energy is often empty.

We need a nice juicy assignment to get things back on track, a mission worthy of our skill. Excited by the prospect of free-flowing blood and the crusty stench of battle, I searched for her, but she was gone.

Worse than gone, my link with her was buried beneath layers of unicorn enchantment. Could I find her? Sure, but she didn't wish to be found.

Between Covid-19 and the California fires, I've had a lot of time to dream up ideas for books. Watching too much *Blacklist* and *Warehouse 13* and *Stranger Things* probably didn't help. And the last season of *Supernatural*. I will miss Sam and Dean...

Meanwhile, a concept shaped up for me. Assassins have always held a fascination factor. Death is a job for them, but what kind of people are they beneath their knives and guns and poison? Toss a few bond animals into the mix, and the bones for a darkish urban fantasy series took shape.

Within its pages, you'll discover men and women who found their way to an age-old profession. Every king worth his salt had a court assassin, and so has every ruler from olden times to modern. If you're shaking your head saying such things can't happen today, just take a look at "suicides" that are swept under a whole bunch of rugs. Oddly enough, the victims of those suspicious deaths had stories to tell, stories someone wanted silenced—forever.

Rhiana has bigger problems. She's lived so long not much excites her. Between boredom and a restive unicorn, she's tempted to burn down a world or two.

1880 London

Calliope music swelled through the huge canvas tent. Its harsh spirited notes usually excited me, but not today. Our act would be on in a few minutes. We were popular because of how real my unicorn's horn looked. More than popular, we'd made a big enough name for ourselves we headlined every circus we were part of.

Pfft. The horn looked real because it was. My challenge was making certain we snuck off under cover of darkness so no one ever saw Dorcha for what she really was. She had a cushy stall in the stables, but she never used it. My excuse was she needed special food. Delicate stomach, and all. No one questioned me since horses are notoriously prone to colic.

Aye, it was a carefully balanced web of lies with me pulling the strings. I'd picked this spot, time traveling into the past to get away from everything. Dorcha was never on board with this particular plan, but I'd coddled her as days followed others, assuming she'd eventually stop bitching.

I may have miscalculated. Her complaints were more strident than they'd been six week ago when we first arrived.

"I'm done." Dorcha stamped a hoof. "This is absurd. Demeaning. You're an elemental mage. Why are you wasting your time entertaining stupid mortals?"

Breath whistled through my teeth; I wound a long whip made of magic and moonlight around one arm. Dorcha understood it was part of my costume. I'd never dream of hurting her with it. If I did, I'd feel the bite of her horn. Unicorns are more lethal than I am. That horn can cut through damn near anything, leaving destruction in its wake.

"Shall we talk about this after the show?" I added a smidgeon of compulsion to my question.

"It's what you said yesterday. And the day before that." More hoof stamping.

True enough. I'd made a point of taking us hunting after the shows in question. Usually fresh blood did the trick, mollified her, but she was canny and had my number.

The canvas flap covering our lean-to next to the big top swung open admitting a blast of cold, sooty air. London has always been a dirty town, and all the coal stoves didn't help.

"Who the hell you talking to?" John stuck his shaggy head inside the flap.

"Myself."

"Och, they say it's the first sign you're headed for Bedlam. You're on in five. Get mounted up and ready." He sidled closer and snaked a hand out to grab my ass. I pivoted beyond his reach.

"Someday, you'll appreciate me, darling. I'm who got you

this special spot," he reminded me like he did every time he got close enough to exchange a word or two. He had booted the previous occupant of the lean-to, but only because he was intent on seducing me. I gave it another few weeks. He'd tire of my excuses and move another candidate into position. Maybe she'd be more grateful than I'd been.

"Yes, yes, now get moving." I flapped a hand in his direction. My five minutes had shrunk to three. John limped away. His story was an elephant had broken his foot, but I suspected he'd fallen when he was drunk. Or tripped over something.

I slid a long woolen cloak off my shoulders, draped it over a hook, and vaulted to Dorcha's back. "We'll get through this, and then we'll leave," I told her.

Power stabbed me as she tested my words for integrity. I hadn't been lying, but I'd be damned if I knew where we'd go next. After a quick glance to make certain my costume covered everything essential, I kneed her softly, and we trotted to our place next to the entry for performers. People milled this way and that, everyone cooing over Dorcha and giving her pats.

She liked that part, but she'd rather die than admit it. Inky black with a lush mane and tail and delicate hoofs, she was beautiful. Her coat so black it shimmered with notes of blue when the light hit it at a certain angle.

The leading strains of our signature song began to play. We galloped into the arena to cheers and clapping. I wasn't under any particular illusion. Magic ebbs and flows around us. Mortals are drawn to the feel of it even though they're not certain what the attraction is.

I leapt to my feet and balanced on the unicorn's broad

back as we continued to canter around the big top. The ringmaster did his "ladies and gentlemen" gig announcing our act. The first fifteen minutes were ours. I went through a series of gymnastics atop the unicorn. Standing, kneeling, astride, sidesaddle position, handstand. My gauzy costume billowed. The many necklaces I wore clanked together, as did long hoop earrings.

Dressed like the Romani in a colorful tunic and trousers, I even kept my feet bare like they did. Traditionally known as horse people, the Rom had magic too. Nothing compared with mine, but it made more sense than dressing up like a Mongol.

Thundering hoofs announced the rest of the riders were joining us. They cantered this way and that, keeping Dorcha and me in the center of an ever-changing circle. I'd choreographed this particular number to maintain distance between Dorcha and the other horses.

Mortals might not know what she was, but equines have sensitive noses. They understood damn good and well Dorcha wasn't one of them. One of the other horses got too close. Dorcha bared her teeth and hissed.

"You're not a cat. Stop that," I told her.

"She will respect me."

"She probably has no idea what you are." I left it at that. Some creatures have archetypal memories. Horses aren't one of them. Nothing like Dorcha in their minds or memories to relate to. She might look like them, but they weren't fooled.

The music shifted to the final number. I jumped upright again. The crowd loved all of us standing on our mounts as they galloped wildly past, churning up dust and dirt.

We swept by acrobats and a man on stilts as we exited the

tent. I lowered my body until I straddled Dorcha, and we trotted across packed dirt to a river. She had a bridle and reins, which I held loosely. They were for show. I let her be as she sank her snout into the water and drank.

"Why do you hate it here?" I asked.

"Why do you like it?" she countered.

Her question wasn't rhetorical; she really wanted to know. *"It's different. A break from the Circle of Assassins and endless assignments. We don't exactly fit in there, either."*

"Better than here."

The unicorn straightened her graceful neck, nostrils flaring. I tossed a leg over her rump and landed next to her. Cold mud squished between my toes as I wound the magical whip around one arm and quashed its sparkling aspect.

"Is she real?" A street urchin of maybe six or seven with dirt-caked clothes and a grimy, snot-streaked face crept close.

Dorcha whickered and turned toward the little girl, ears pricked forward.

"Real enough," I said.

"Ooooh. May I touch her, missus?"

"Come nearer slowly. She'll let you know," I replied.

Eyes wide with wonder, the child edged forward, clearly afraid but willing to brave the horrors of Hell if she could get close to Dorcha. My bondmate was in a generous mood because she stood quietly while the girl stroked her nose.

"Wisht I had a carrot for you," she murmured.

I dug an apple from my trousers and handed it to her. "Feed her this."

"All at once?"

I fished out a knife I keep strapped to my ankle, split the apple, and said, "Do it this way," as I showed her how to offer food with an open hand. As soon as the apple was gone, the child slipped away, merging with lengthening shadows while afternoon ceded to evening.

I'd have asked her where her parents were, but London teemed with street urchins. This one appeared resourceful. She'd probably land on her feet if she didn't get sidetracked into a brothel.

"Feeling better?" I asked Dorcha.

"A little," she admitted.

Taking hold of her reins, I walked us to the small private enclosure where we'd waited for our turn to perform. The show was still going strong. If we were going to leave, now was as good a time as any. No one had touched my cloak, but I'd spelled it to burn any hand except mine. Grateful for its soft warmth, I tugged it around my shoulders and tied it into place.

"How about a walk on the shore?" I asked softly.

"Which shore?"

"You pick." I was so grateful her anger had run its course, I could afford to be generous.

She sent images cascading through my mind. They made me smile, and I built a quick teleport spell that incorporated time traveling elements. A short while later, we came out on a desolate section of the Washington coastline with the Pacific Ocean on one side and the Strait of Juan de Fuca to the north. Crags, wind, and beastly weather effectively sealed this spot off from casual visitors. I'd kept us well in the past to avoid modern scourges like hang gliders, helicopters, and people with fancy climbing equipment.

Dorcha cantered this way and that, tossing her head. The braids I'd put in her mane untwisted. She hated being decked out like the other show horses. For a time, I sat on a flat rock enjoying watching her kick up her heels. Salt spray scented the air with an astringent sweetness.

The tide was coming in, waves crashing and booming. I raised a hand in greeting to my old friend, Arianrhod. I couldn't see her, but she had to be in Caer Sidi, her special world, overseeing both tides and moon. I'd liked her earthy, no-nonsense approach, but most of the other Celtic gods were real pricks. Especially the men.

I inhaled deeply, willing myself not to go there. I'd been enjoying Dorcha's choice of beaches, and I didn't want to sully it with nasty recollections. Instead, I shuffled possibilities. If Dorcha truly put her hoof down about not returning to London and the circus, where would we go next? I'd figured we were good for a few more months there.

Timing was everything, but my clairvoyance skills have never been a strong suit. Something was bound to happen. It always did. Some random event would send us scurrying away from London. The last time we'd hustled out of somewhere had been because Dorcha killed a rude stallion who'd tried to mount her. It wasn't funny—at all—but it still brought a smile to my face. I knew exactly how she felt.

I'd have stuck around to defend her honor were it not for the impossibility of explaining how her horn—supposedly a prop—had exacted so much damage. We'd been in Prague then, around 1840. Eventually, we would run out of places and eras, but it wouldn't happen for a long while. It's only been since maybe 1970 that communications have become sophisticated enough to make starting over harder.

A black unicorn and her five-foot-ten-inch mistress with matching flowing tresses exacted notice everywhere. I tone things down with a glamour to make me appear less exotic—and less threatening. It smooths the cant of my cheekbones, adds femininity to my frame, and turns my bronze eyes with their moss-green centers a deep blue.

In times long past, those like me controlled every element. The Celts, damn their black souls, decided we wielded too much power, so they split new elemental mages into earth, air, fire, or water mages. They left the rest of us—the original elemental mages—alone, but none of us believed they wouldn't come after us too.

A flicker of anger licked at my innards. I ignored it. Revisiting the pyre of my fury wasn't wise. I'd thrown my power against the gods. Best I'd achieved was a draw—until another of them showed up. Eventually, I'd tired of being slapped down. Besides, I'd have to hunt for them now to continue the fight. Most were long gone from Earth. No one believed in them anymore. Or in me.

The specter of endless life weighed heavy.

I've hit sketchy patches before. Ones like this where I flounder about hunting for meaning and not finding anything but a cosmic joke. Dorcha wasn't happy, either. It ran deeper than the circus being a total waste of our talent.

The water had taken on an iridescent quality, maybe from the sun's downward trajectory. Regardless, it was alluring. Dorcha pawed at the sand with her front hoofs and walked into the water. Taking a dip in the sea held appeal. I slithered out of my cloak, trousers, and tunic, piling rocks on top of them to keep the wind from blowing everything away.

Already on my feet, I ran lightly across the rocky beach and into the water, following Dorcha's path. The bottom dropped away; I swam into the surf, welcoming the slap of waves as I cut through them. Living in the now, welcoming cleansing saltwater scrubbing away the smells of the circus, my world grew smaller and more manageable.

Moments were important. Good moments like when Dorcha let the street urchin pet her. All we needed was to find a spot where there were more good moments than bad ones. A tall order. Even in the Circle of Assassins, mages squabbled with one another. Grigori, head of the supernatural hit squad, kicked folks out from time to time.

A brisk whinny turned my attention to Dorcha treading water fifty feet away while Nereids crawled all over her. Faeries of the sea, they have gossamer wings, masses of hair in every shade of the rainbow, and fishtails like the mer-people.

A lissome nymph with violet hair, black wings, and rings on every finger dove off Dorcha's back and swam my way. "Greetings from Poseidon," she announced in a high, clear voice. "He welcomes you to his realm."

Oh-oh.

Selecting my response carefully, I inclined my head. "Tell him I wish him well, and we shan't remain long."

Her rosy lips parted in a slight smile. "You know our liege."

"That I do." I left it at that. If the Celts were dicks, Poseidon was a straight-up bastard. Arrogant and arbitrary, nothing was ever his fault. He slung shit at his underlings, expecting them to suck it up for the privilege of remaining his subjects.

"His favorite assassin left," the Nereid went on. "He will pay you handsomely to locate and return her."

"Be sure to thank him for his faith in me, but I'm in the

middle of another job. Dorcha and I were taking a break, or we wouldn't be here at all."

I flipped over and began stroking for shore with the Nereid pacing me. She could swim rings around me, but her tail gave her a strong edge. My toes touched bottom; I switched from swimming to plodding through the water intent on dressing and getting the fuck out of here.

Poseidon's methods were legendary. He'd hunt me down if his messenger didn't return with the right answer: that I'd drop everything and do his bidding. Not that he couldn't find me no matter where I went, but I wouldn't make it easy for him. Technically, I worked for the Circle, which meant all assignments were handled by Grigori. It gave me an out—if I chose to play that card.

I wrung water from my hair and chucked it over my shoulders. Funneling magic to dry myself, I trotted to where I'd left my clothes.

"Lovely as ever, my dear," rang from behind me.

Fuckity-fuck. Poseidon hadn't waited for the Nereid to return. He'd been listening to our conversation, and now he was here to do his damnedest to keep Dorcha and me from leaving. Eh, probably not Dorcha. I was who he was interested in. And I knew damn good and well where his escaped mage was. Hiding in plain sight and transformed by magic to ensure she'd never be captured.

Swathing my mind in strong wards—so he couldn't pluck thoughts from it—I aimed for an airy tone. "Give a lady a spot of privacy to dress."

"What for? I'd rather enjoy the view. Besides, it's not as if I haven't seen everything before."

Great. Mr. Tact-and-Diplomacy was in full bloom. We'd

had a fling centuries ago. Emphasis on "a fling." I'd never been tempted into a rematch. He was as boorish and inconsiderate in bed as out. Keeping my back to him, I pulled my trousers up still damp legs and settled my tunic over my head. The cloak came last, and I relished its soft folds.

Dorcha cantered close. "Ready to go?" she asked brightly.

My, "Sure," collided with Poseidon's, "Not done with her."

After wringing more water from my hair, I turned to face him. He hadn't changed a bit. Tall with a full head of silver hair that spilled to his knees, he was handsome in an imperious sort of way. The trident staff I remembered was held loosely in one hand. He's always favored robes. Today's was pale blue sashed in white with embroidered tridents.

"Sorry about your assassin, but hire someone else," I said.

"You'd be perfect," he insisted. "Being an assassin yourself and all." His voice took on a wheedling note, and I tasted compulsion, thick and cloying, clinging to the words. "I can't leave the sea for long. When I do, my powers fade, but you can operate anywhere."

I shrugged. "You're a god. I'm merely a mage. Plusses and minuses all around."

"Come on, Rhiana. For old times' sake. This wouldn't take long. I'll pay you whatever you wish."

We had no "old times," not good ones. "I really am swamped."

"I can wait. Whenever you get to this is fine."

Nice wasn't working. I shifted tactics. "I'm not interested. Period."

Nereids had slithered up the sand, forming a circle around Dorcha and me. I had a feeling they meant to keep us here. If we'd still been in the water, it might have worked.

The next wave washed over my feet. If I tarried, the sea would come to us, and the Nereids' circle would hem us in. They only looked fluffy and harmless, but they did Poseidon's bidding because punishment for non-compliance was swift, sure, and deadly.

I vaulted atop Dorcha and married my power with hers. This should be a slam-dunk. She and I hadn't had a chance to hash out a destination, so I tried to take us back to London. She had other plans. At cross purposes, our magic crashed against itself. The craggy shoreline, which had begun to shimmer and fade, stuttered back into place.

"Dorcha. Leave off."

"I am not going back to that circus."

Water was up to her hocks. We were running out of time. "It's the easiest place," I argued having given up on telepathy. I needed all my power.

Poseidon was laughing uproariously. Yup. I bet he knew a thing or two about insurrection in his ranks. All his underlings hated him. Not that Dorcha was subservient in any way. The press of sea magic, dense with the scents of salt and seaweed, wafted around us.

I switched things up and visualized one of the Circle of Assassin guild houses. It would take piles more magic to move us there since it wasn't located on Earth.

Dorcha grunted something that might have been assent and opened her magic to me again. I used every trick at my disposal, but the Nereids' circle blocked our escape. With Poseidon's laughter as a backdrop, I gave up after my third attempt boomeranged back in my face.

Whatever he had in mind—like imprisoning me until I capitulated—wouldn't fly.

Dorcha reared. I wasn't ready for it and slid down her haunches, landing on my butt. Screaming horsey outrage at Poseidon, her hoofs thundered against his chest, driving him to the ground.

"How dare you?" Dorcha screeched. "Release us immediately."

He still had hold of his trident, and he tried to angle it to stab my unicorn in the belly. Fat fucking chance. I bolted to where he was pinned and kicked the staff out of his hand. I'd just declared a full-out war on the god of the sea. It was bound to end badly, but I didn't care.

❧ 2 ❧

Dorcha reared again and brought her hoofs down on Poseidon's chest. The crunch of bones breaking was welcome, but he'd heal as quickly as she dealt damage. The Nereids had scattered, gone as fast as they'd materialized. Without his attention directly on them, they'd deemed it safe to leave.

Something was seriously wrong, though. Poseidon could have merged with the sea. Over a foot deep in our boulder-shrouded alcove, it offered an escape hatch. Why hadn't he taken it? Dorcha had him pinned, sure, but it shouldn't pose a problem.

I gave the trident staff a wide berth and ended up with my feet at Poseidon's head facing Dorcha. Sparks shot from the staff, turning the water blue-black. "Why aren't you fighting back?" I asked Poseidon pointblank. "Or leaving?"

"Who cares?" Dorcha whinnied. "What he did was rude. It violates our code."

"Newsflash. He's not one of us," I reminded my bondmate.

"So? It shouldn't excuse him from treating us with respect."

"Why would he start now?" I muttered.

His head was underwater, but it wasn't a showstopper for him. Hell, he was probably stronger for it, not weaker. "Let him up," I told Dorcha.

"No." She showed me a mouthful of squared-off teeth.

"We need to leave. Now."

"He's not going anywhere," she retorted. "We can take our time."

The sixth sense that's always been my best friend sent a shudder down my back. Small hairs on the back of my neck prickled unpleasantly. "Dorcha. We have to leave. Now."

She raised her head and stared stubbornly at me. The shudder turned into a cascade of horror mixed with outrage. Too late, I identified the magic hurtling toward us. Dorcha splashed through water as Poseidon hightailed it to greener pastures. No more reason for him to remain. His henchman was almost upon us.

Fetid breath turned the fresh salt air sour. Scales the size of meat trenchers glistened and retreated.

"Kraken," Dorcha whinnied indignation.

I opened my mouth to tell her she should have listened to me but closed it fast. I could sling blame all I wanted later. The task of the moment was escape. I leapt onto her back, winding a few strands of power to make sure we didn't get separated. We were stronger fighting as a unit, and we had a common enemy.

No matter how much she and I fussed and squabbled,

when the rubber met the road we agreed on the important shit.

Power built within Dorcha as the Kraken's sinuous coils became visible. Damn. He was half again as big as the last time I'd had a run-in with him. Had to be the same one. No room in the universe for two like him. Black scales were riddled with mold, some so eaten away they resembled Swiss cheese. His head was dragonlike, snout elongated around triple rows of wicked-looking teeth. Small beady red eyes stared at us as he considered what to do next.

Not the brightest bulb on the shelf, the Kraken had survived by stealth and cunning and sheer size. Most everyone ran the other way—like we should have done.

His forked tongue flicked out scenting the air, his head on a level with Dorcha's. Behind murderously sharp neck spines, his coils wrapped around our spot in the rapidly rising water. Escaping from his physical body would have been simple, but the pulse of power, malevolent and poisonous, pressed in on us, following the same circle as his coils.

Yup. Poseidon had snared me. I should have known better than to stick around, which made it all that much worse. He'd baited the trap with himself. When I'd switched from excuses to no, he called in the big guns.

"What'll it be, Missy?" the Kraken slurred. The moment he opened his mouth, my stomach clenched at the smell. Rotten bits of goddess only knew what clung to his hundreds of teeth. A cross between above-ground graves baking under a tropical sun and decayed vegetation, the fumes made my eyes water. If my stomach hadn't been empty, I'd have heaved its contents all over the shiny coils.

"Oh gosh. I have choices?" I shot back all the while

conjuring magic to get the fuck out of here. The Nereids' enchantment had stymied us, but there'd been about twenty of them—and they'd been shored up by Poseidon and his fucking trident.

The Kraken's mouth opened wider before he sprayed me with spittle and said, "Choices? Not really. All roads end in the king's dungeon. Only a matter of how beaten up you are when you arrive there." His tongue lashed back and forth. Several sets of tentacled arms extruded from his reptilian body. He crossed the upper ones over his chest.

With zero warning, Dorcha charged. She didn't even lower her head until she was moving. Wisely intuiting driving her horn through his scales would be a losing proposition, she jammed it into his open mouth. When that unicorn decides to move, she's like greased lightning. If I hadn't lashed myself to her with magic, I'd have fallen from her back a second time.

The Kraken's expression was priceless. The top layer was shock anyone had dared to take him on. Once it ceded to fury, and he whipped his head back and forth to dislodge Dorcha's horn, it was too late. Every wriggle on his part gave her an opportunity to thrust her horn in deeper.

Embedded in the soft palate at the top of his mouth, she pushed the horn on through into whatever passed for brains inside his scaly head. The neat pile of coils fell apart, sloughing off to the sides.

Who knew what brain part she was killing off, but it clearly had something to do with coordination and muscle tone. I fed energy into the fledgling teleport spell encompassing the two of us. Knowing Dorcha, she wouldn't be any readier to go now than she'd been earlier. Locked in combat with the Kraken—and winning—had to be heady as hell.

Too bad.

We'd missed our get-out-of-jail-free card earlier. I wouldn't make the same mistake again. Without discussing anything, I tossed everything I had at a casting to take us away from all this. Dorcha might fuss and whine later, but I didn't expect major pushback.

The craggy shoreline that had appeared so inviting when we'd first arrived finally, finally stuttered to nothing, replaced by the blackness of a journey channel. Dorcha was breathing hard, her sides foamy with sweat.

"I had him," she panted.

"Aye, sweetling, you did, but Poseidon keeps tabs on all his minions. How much longer do you think he'd have given us before he swooped in with an army of who-knows-what to rescue his pet Kraken?"

"I had him," she repeated. "He was stupid and slow and—"

"Not much of a challenge?" I inserted sweetly.

The unicorn brayed laughter. "You win. And I am glad to be gone from there, but bards would have sung songs about me. My kin would have been purple with envy. 'Tisn't every day we fight such as him."

I cleared my throat. "We'd have had a far harder time escaping from Poseidon's dungeon," I told her.

"Have you been there?"

I shook my head. "Heard about it, though."

Dorcha culled through my spell before snorting and laying her gory horn on my shoulder. "You didn't trick me. We're going to the guild house."

Her accusation stung. "When have I ever lied?"

"Not lied so much as stepped over my wishes." She hesitated before adding, "You never used to do that."

Her words jabbed unpleasantly—because they were true. Since I didn't want to go there, I said, "Wonder if Ciara knows her old boss is looking for her?"

"Doesn't matter. We can tell her. She's been gone for a long while, so this can't be a new project on his part."

"Not new, but he could have spent the first half century or so waiting for her to come home." I switched topics. "Any particular reason you wanted to go back to the guild house?"

Dorcha whinnied. "To get away from London and that infernal circus." She poked me with the horn that was still on my shoulder. "I never want to perform again. Ever. Are we clear on that?"

I wound my fingers around her horn and moved it off to one side, and then I wiped my hand on my pants. "I'm not fond of prancing around for a bunch of mortals, either, but the circus is good cover for us."

"Only if you insist on dragging us to where humans are."

My spell developed a different feel, one that told me our journey was nearly over. I'd aimed for the forest surrounding the guild house. I wasn't interested in detailing how I'd spent the last few years, not right away. Eventually, Grigori would find me, but I was hoping it would happen after I'd been back for a few days. Normally, he didn't pay me much heed one way or the other.

My spell dissipated. Dorcha tossed her mane this way and that, whinnying like a mad thing. I was glad she was happy, but I had no flipping idea what we'd do next. None. Mortals jump through hoops, eat special food, exercise their fool heads off, to dredge a few more years out of their three-score-and-ten. Most would covet my immortality.

Each situation has plusses—and drawbacks. Humans don't have a chance to get bored or tired or disenchanted with everything. Maybe they flirt with unhappiness, but before it establishes a solid toehold, they're dead and gone.

Dorcha cantered off, losing herself in a thick evergreen grove. Good for her. I must be slipping to squander time comparing anything about myself with mortals. I leaned against a tree, considering how to sneak into the guild house. Turns out it was a waste of time.

"Rhiana!" Grigori's deep voice boomed. "Welcome back." Something about my expression must have tipped him off because he added, "You are back, right? Not just passing through."

"Blunt as ever," I said with a jaunty grin. Grigori is a werewolf, and an old one with powerful intuitive ability. Trying for unobtrusive, I cobbled a shield around my thoughts and took a good look at him. Dressed in jeans and a thick black woolen sweater, he topped my height by almost a foot. Red hair shone in the afternoon light. He had it sectioned off in tiny braids, but they hit him past waist level. His blue eyes were as shrewd as ever, but new lines carved tracks in his forehead and around his eyes.

"Usually, I like being ogled by attractive women, but you're taking the whole 'nice to see you again' thing too far," he said.

I rolled my shoulders in a shrug. "Manners are for mortals. I had no idea if you'd be here. This is far from the only guild house. Have you been ill?"

His russet brows shot up. "Now who's the blunt one?"

"Well, have you?" I persisted.

He nodded and made shooing motions with both hands. "Into the grove."

I screwed my face into a quizzical expression angling for more information. Didn't do me a bit of good. He hooked a hand beneath my arm and pushed me toward a grove of white oak trees. Keyed to his magic, they'd shield our conversation from curious ears. No easy outs. I could tell him I wasn't interested in whatever he had in mind. Or I could make it clear I had no plans to remain longer than it took for Dorcha to come to her senses about returning to either the circus we'd left or one we had yet to find.

I could, but was I heartless enough to say no? His joy at seeing me was so genuine, I had to at least hear him out.

He set a brisk pace. Once he understood I'd accommodate him, he let go of my arm. I'd come close to telling him I was done with the Circle of Assassins on other occasions, but something always stopped me. I'd been here very little, my visits so infrequent I was far from up to date on who even laid claim to inclusion in the supernatural hit squad these days.

The Circle made sense when Grigori organized it hundreds of years ago. It made far less today. Between weapons of mass destruction and religious types set on immolating themselves—and taking hundreds or thousands with them—the assassin trade wasn't anything like it had been.

Eh, that could be said about a whole lot of things. Feeling ancient and out of sorts and like an anachronism, I stepped through a gap between two stout tree boles. The grove's power snagged me, flooding me with bittersweet memories of better times. Or at least times I hadn't been so sour, so used-up.

Grigori circled to face me. "I've known you for a long time, Rhiana. What's wrong?"

"Nothing. Everything." Air whistled from between my teeth. "It doesn't matter. I'll figure things out. I always do."

He face took on a thoughtful expression. Grigori has an amazing amount of warmth for a werewolf. Many are cold and calculating, which might explain his lack of a pack affiliation.

"Let's spin this another way," he said. "The Circle has been beset from within. I put out a call months ago to you and those like you to return and fight."

Surprise rocked me back on my heels. "I never heard from you."

"Where have you been?"

"Here and there. Time traveling, mostly."

"Explains it," he said. And it did. Telepathy doesn't penetrate the time-space continuum. "Why return now?" he went on.

"Dorcha hasn't been happy for a long while. We left the, erm, place we'd been to visit a favorite shore. Poseidon sicced first the Nereids and then the Kraken on us."

Grigori grinned, showing elongated fangs. "Kraken, eh? Bit of a dolt. Probably how you escaped."

I shook my head. "It was Dorcha. She stuffed her horn into his mouth."

Laughter burbled from Grigori. "I'd have loved to have seen that."

"It was priceless," I agreed. "If I ever get around to carrying one of those cellphone things, I'd have taken a photograph. The Kraken is beyond stupid, and the look on his face screamed disbelief anyone could have bested him."

"Did Dorcha kill him?"

"Nope. I dragged us out of there before Poseidon showed up with some other atrocity. Which reminds me, he tried to hire me to hunt for Ciara. She still here?"

"Aye, she is. But she's been here seventy-eight years. Why is he only now wanting her back?"

"Who knows?"

Grigori clasped long-fingered hands in front of him. "You're always welcome in the Circle, Rhiana. I could use your assistance and your magic."

"What happened to you?" I asked again since he'd never answered me.

"Someone got to me, dosed me with a potion designed to kill the virus that made me a werewolf."

My eyes widened. "How is that even possible?" I followed my question with a totally obvious scan as I assessed the relative state of his health. "You seem okay now. Did you find an antidote?"

"In a manner of speaking, but it's a long story. This isn't about me, but about whether you can spare a few months working for the Circle."

I stood straighter, hearing vertebrae crack. I could say no, walk away, but what kind of associate would that make me? What kind of friend? Grigori hasn't asked a whole lot of me for several centuries. I've come and gone as the mood struck. Sure, I've tried to carry my weight when I was here, but I never had any compunctions about dropping out of sight and remaining gone.

"Do you want to talk it over with Dorcha?" he asked.

It was a logical question and how most bonded pairs functioned. When had she and I gotten out of the habit of talking until we agreed on a topic? My mind flashed back to something she'd said when we were traveling here. That I'd made a habit of stepping over her concerns rather than addressing them.

I sank into a crouch wanting to drop my head into my hands, but my inner turmoil wasn't Grigori's problem. From the looks of things, he had plenty of his own without borrowing mine.

"Do you?" Grigori pressed.

"Dorcha is who wanted to come here," I said dully.

"But you didn't?" He hunkered across from me.

The same tide of hopelessness I'd been fighting for so long I couldn't remember when it hadn't dogged me threatened to annihilate everything. I sucked air through my mouth. In. Out. In. Out. I'd be damned if I'd break down in front of Grigori.

He'd stopped asking questions, but I felt the weight of his gaze. "I'm here if you want to talk with someone," he said. "Not much I haven't heard."

"Thanks, but I'm managing," I replied stiffly.

"I might even believe you—if I didn't know you as well as I do." He rose, the leather in his scuffed boots creaking. "Talk with Dorcha. Figure out if you two are willing to commit time to the Circle. We'd welcome you with open arms. Aidyrth has missed both of you, but especially Dorcha."

I stood too. "Aidyrth can drop in on Fire Mountain and visit other dragons," I murmured, doing my best to modulate the bitterness in my tone.

"Surely Dorcha knows where her kin are." Grigori cocked his head to one side.

"Once, she did. Now I have no idea."

He placed a hand on my arm. "Start talking with your bondmate again," he suggested softly. "It's the only way to maintain the link."

Before I could craft a reply, he was gone. The tears I'd sat on stung my eyes. Like any relationship, the one between Dorcha and me needed tending. I'd begun to view her as a burden. Who the hell knew how she saw me? The beauty of the circus was it had offered us something to do as a team, except she'd believed it demeaning, worthless.

From the perspective of entertaining mortals, she was right, but I'd looked beyond that part. What I'd focused on was her and me joining our magic to create something beautiful. I shook my head and brushed tears off my cheeks with my fingertips. We'd never sat down and talked about any of it. She'd been angry, alienated. I'd been anxious to mollify her, so we didn't have to change anything.

If we'd hashed things out, I'd have been forced to face up to her unhappiness. Worse, I'd have known I was the cause. Shame and guilt joined my rudderless existence, mocking me for how inconsiderate I'd been. In my rush to avoid a confrontation—and institute needed changes—I'd alienated the one person I loved most of all through all worlds and times: my unicorn.

Fuck me. What a mess I'd made of things.

Determined to rectify what I could, I strode out of the grove and hunted for Dorcha through our link. At first, I assumed I wasn't looking in the right places, but this off-world location isn't all that big.

It didn't take long to sink in that Dorcha had left. It was why she'd insisted on coming here. Power is strong in this world, and keyed to her ability. She'd piggybacked on the Circle's incipient magic and beat a track elsewhere.

I clung to our link. She hadn't severed it, and she could have. Should I follow her? If I did, would it make things worse? Maybe she'd taken a break, gone off to think about things.

But why would she do that without me? We did everything together.

Sorrow mingled with guilt. I walked in circles, big ones, small ones, never letting go of my tenuous connection with my bondmate. Finally, I couldn't stand it anymore and raised my mind voice. *"Grigori."*

A black-and-silver werewolf ran toward me, shifting to his human form when he got close. He didn't say a word, neither did he take his gaze from me.

"If that offer to talk is still open, I'm ready," I said in a choked-off voice I scarcely recognized as my own.

The familiar feel of his power wrapped me in its threads. When it cleared we were in his quarters in the guild house. He'd known I wouldn't want to see anyone else, so he'd protected my privacy.

"Thank you," I mumbled.

He pointed to a chair. "Take a load off, Rhi."

I dropped into the indicated chair. Now I was here, I had no inkling where to begin, but Grigori has always been a decent listener. "Dorcha's gone," I blurted.

He nodded. "I know. I felt her leave while we were in the grove."

"Why didn't you say something?" I demanded.

"Not my place. For all I knew, she was going somewhere the two of you had agreed on." After pausing to take a measured breath, he asked. "Why'd she go?"

"So many reasons."

"But there's a main one. There must be," he pressed.

I winced. "She thinks I quit listening to her, stopped valuing her needs as much as my own."

"Did you?" His question was neutral, assuming nothing.

A sob wanted out. I quashed it and managed to mumble, "Probably. I can see how she might have thought so." Once words started, they kept coming. "The happiest I've seen her in forever was when she'd impaled the Kraken."

"Was she angry about you forcing her to leave?"

I considered his question. "Not really. She understood we wouldn't be a match for Poseidon's forces. And he would have launched a mob to save his Kraken."

"Aye, he would have," Grigori agreed and made a grunting-growling sound. "Never understood what he saw in the beast, but the Kraken's been around since Earth was naught but water."

"There's only one of them, right?" I asked the same question that had rumbled through my mind when the Kraken wound his coils around us.

"There have been others, but every time Poseidon and his sea witch sidekick spawned one, the original made short work of it."

"He was jealous?"

Grigori shrugged. "Hard to tell about these things. The Kraken operates at a primitive level, and apparently being the only monster was more appealing than competing with others for Poseidon's favors."

We'd lurched to a much safer topic than my failings with my bondmate. Grigori didn't bludgeon me with it. He didn't have to. "Should I go after her?" I asked.

"What do you think?"

"I honestly don't know. It's why I asked."

Grigori dropped a hand onto my shoulder. "The only one who can answer that question is you. The bond is still intact?"

I nodded.

"Most of the animals couldn't manage this, but she could break it with a thought. She didn't."

"Yes, I know, and I took it as a positive. Geez, she checked the teleport spell I employed to bring us here—to reassure herself I'd kept my word." I looked away from Grigori's penetrating gaze. "Made me feel like crap."

He squeezed my shoulder lightly before letting go. "Forever is a long time."

"What's that supposed to mean?" I winced at how surly I'd sounded and mumbled, "Sorry."

His form developed a glistening aspect, morphing from man to wolf. "Find a chamber. Get some rest. Join us for supper." The wolf's tail twitched from side to side.

"But I should follow Dorcha," I protested.

"Aye, but maybe not right away. Forever is a long time," he repeated.

The door to his rooms swooshed open, admitting another werewolf, this one female and in her human guise. She'd been somewhere north of fifty when she was transformed. Seemed late. Usually, weres like their human partners younger. Gray-streaked blonde hair hung in curls to shoulder level. Slender and medium height, her hazel eyes twinkled warmly. Billowy black trousers hung off her hips, and a patched green sweater covered her torso.

"Oops. Sorry." She stood in the doorway. "Should I leave?"

"No need," I told her and held out a hand, walking close enough to shake. "I'm Rhiana."

"Rhea Lockhart," she said and clasped my hand. "Grigori's told me about you and all the other truly old mages." Offering a self-deprecating grin, she added, "I'm a brand-new werewolf. It's quite the tale. If you're here for a while, I'd be happy to talk with you about it."

"Excellent," Grigori barked approval.

It confused me, but I had bigger troubles than figuring out why Rhea's willingness to confide in me was a good thing. I let go of her hand and started out of the room.

"Looking forward to meeting your bondmate," Rhea called after me.

Her words hit me like a gut shot, except there was no way she could have known about Dorcha leaving. I called, "Sure, she'd like that," over one shoulder before I started up the nearest stairwell.

I was on the top floor and trolling through rooms with open doors before I understood I was looking for a place to light for a while. Had Grigori magicked-up his suggestions, seeded them with compulsion?

It didn't matter. If he had, his intentions had been pure. I also wasn't concerned about him spilling the beans about the problems between Dorcha and me. Grigori was circumspect, trustworthy. Without those qualities, he'd have been drummed out of his position as head of the Circle of Assassins long ago.

My favorite room in this guild house happened to be unoccupied. Or maybe nobody had lived in it since my last sojourn here. In a corner and under the eaves, the roofline was slanted. Windows faced both north and east. The only furniture was a double bed pushed beneath the windows, a desk, and a chair. I kicked the door shut and sank onto the bed, drawing up my legs until I sat cross-legged.

Forever was a long time. I'd understood Grigori well enough when he said it the first time. My snarky question had been reflexive, and I respected him for not answering it. Were Dorcha and I done? Had we outlived our bond? It happened, not often but occasionally.

Alone with my thoughts, I didn't blame her. The London circus was far from our first. I'd been on a circus and carnival kick for close to ninety years. We'd flitted from one to the next with occasional breaks at one guild house or another. Once our tasks for Grigori were dispatched, back to the circus we'd gone.

Because I wanted to.

Full stop. I forced myself to examine every choice point. Each event leading to one more sawdust-and-calliope-saturated entertainment venue. I'd told myself it was the simplest way of hiding what Dorcha was so she and I could blend in.

But that hadn't been it at all. Between her magic and my own, we could have crafted a glamour to hide her horn. The sick, sorry truth was cavorting in front of an audience appealed to me. The more screams, cheers, and applause, the better I liked it.

"Yeah," I muttered, "I didn't just like it, I craved it. Adulation was like a drug. The more I had, the more I wanted."

So much so, I'd sacrificed my relationship with Dorcha, told myself one lie after the next until I believed my own hype. The unicorn knew differently, though. She'd never gleaned satisfaction from performing. The more we did it, the worse it grated.

She'd tried to talk about it, but I hadn't been receptive. Finally, she'd quit trying until the last performance. Was it too late for us?

I uncurled my legs and stretched out on the bed pulling a fluffy duvet over me. I didn't expect to sleep, but a tentative knock on the door roused me. One glance out the windows told me night had fallen.

"Yes?"

"Dinner in a quarter hour," a high musical voice called back. I was almost certain it belonged to a faery.

"Thank you. I'll be there." Until I said the words, I'd had no idea I meant to sit in the grand hall and dine with my fellow mages. I was certain to know many of them, and they'd all ask after Dorcha. Even worse, many of their bond animals would be present too. Everyone loved Dorcha, and they'd be clamoring to see her.

What should I say?

"Don't be an ass," I lectured myself and unwound my body from the bedding. I had time for a quick shower. As I stood under needles of hot water, life became simple. All I needed to do was reassure everyone the unicorn was fine. And she was, so I wouldn't be lying.

Another unattractive truth shaped up under the punishing rush of water. Here, in our native environment where everyone was magical, Dorcha was a star. Where I'd dragged us—circuses and carnivals—I was the star. Dorcha might be lithe and lovely and talented, but to mortal minds horses were props.

That's the fucked-up part about understanding something. Revelations are often too little and arrive too late. I shut off the taps and finger-combed my hair, aiming magic to dry it. A cursory glance at my clothes told me I should visit the guild house wardrobe.

I could drop my things off at the laundry while I was at it.

Since I wasn't thrilled about putting filthy, Kraken-smelling garments on my clean body, I wrapped myself in a generous towel, snatched up my soiled clothing, and wended my way down back staircases to the basement. The first mage I ran into was inside the laundry. A smiling faun, he took my dirty things and said, "Welcome back, Rhiana."

"Good to see you, too, Joss."

I waved an airy hand and trotted across the hall to the clothing locker. The Circle has clothing from virtually every era in many sizes. Because it was simple—and I was late—I selected an unadorned black robe, slipped into it, and sashed it in red. A pair of strappy flat sandals fit perfectly.

Ready as I was likely to be, I retraced my route up a flight to the main floor. The tempting smells of food wafted my way as soon as I opened the door to the main hall. Even if I hadn't known where the dining room was, finding it would have been as simple as following my nose.

Being back in a guild house felt soothing, right. So much so I didn't understand why I'd been in such a hurry to run away. I'd hoped to sneak inside the dining room unnoticed. Stupid of me. I had all of ten seconds before someone yelled, "Rhiana!"

My name swelled through the well-appointed room, adding to my sense of coming home. Round tables for two, four, and six dotted the chamber. Mages took turns preparing food, serving, and cleaning up. I started for an empty table for two, but several mages invited me to sit with them. It would hasten the inevitable questions about Dorcha, but all I needed to do was reassure everyone she was fine.

Guilt, my new best friend, sat heavily on my shoulders. I should be out hunting for Dorcha, not indulging myself with old friends and a pleasant meal.

Forever is a long time, echoed through my head.

Dorcha had left, not me. She needed space. Surely, a few hours wouldn't be the death of our bond. Was that true, or one more pleasant fantasy like those I'd spun about her getting used to the circus, embracing it?

I'd give this a couple of hours, renew old acquaintances, refuel my power with a decent meal, and then I'd be gone. Having settled on what felt like a reasonable compromise, I headed for a table with Grigori, Rhea, Quinn, and Ciara, mostly so I could make certain to whisper about Poseidon to her.

"You're looking rested," Grigori said, not sounding the least surprised. Ha. Proof he'd spelled me during our brief stint in his quarters.

"Thanks. I am." Turing to Quinn, I said, "Long time no see." He hadn't changed a bit, but then none of us ever did. An earth mage, he had copious amounts of dark hair and dragon eyes.

"Grigori's a persuasive old dog." Quinn laughed as the werewolf elbowed him. "I'm here until the current problem is resolved. You?"

"Thinking about it." I aimed for noncommittal. Food materialized on the table, and dishes made the rounds as we heaped our plates with rice, fresh-baked bread, and a seafood casserole rich with thyme and dill and cream.

I'd sat next to Ciara on purpose. While we were helping ourselves, I bent close. "Poseidon tried to hire me to hunt you down."

"Bastard." She made a face.

"Is this something new?" I kept my voice low.

"Nah. Eventually, he'll give up. Grigori and the faeries made a few alterations in my magic. The sea god will never locate me, but it's annoying he's still trying. Thanks for letting me know." A corner of her mouth canted downward. "And thanks for not accepting his offer."

"I would never—" I began, offended by her words.

She nudged me. "I was joking, Rhiana. What happened to your sense of humor?"

Had I ever had one? "Guess it took a hike." I tried for humor, but she and I were both uncomfortable. We didn't know one another all that well. A sea mage, her power sprang from the same source as a quarter of mine. With her fair looks and blue eyes, she projected a delicacy that belied her actual strength.

A Sidhe was making the rounds with spirits. I savored mead he poured into a crystal goblet. Conversation flowed around me. No one seemed to care I was quiet. Many bond animals roved through the dining room, visiting among themselves and occasionally checking in with their bondmates.

I missed Dorcha. She'd always adored communal meals like this one, plucking this, that, and the other thing off plates with her horn. No simple path from horn to mouth, though. Usually, choice bits ended up on the floor where she scarfed them up.

Grigori played the gracious host well, but then, he always had. A delicate dessert followed the seafood entrée accompanied by a piquant port. No one asked where I'd been. More surprisingly, no one asked why Dorcha wasn't making the rounds chatting mages up and stealing from their plates once their attention was elsewhere.

Grigori had alluded to a major challenge, yet it wasn't the focus of conversation, either. What had he said? That the

Circle had been breached. Perhaps not every mage seated in the spacious room was trustworthy. He'd never been shy about weeding out problems before. What was different now? How many had he identified, and what steps had he taken?

I stuffed a brick in it. I'd had ample opportunity to ask questions in the grove, except then his information hadn't had much of a chance to sink in. Rather than confiding in me, he'd encouraged me to spill my load of grief. He'd moved us to the grove to talk frankly, but the only element we'd discussed was me—and Dorcha.

Grigori was wise that way. He'd understood I wouldn't be any good to the Circle—or myself—if I couldn't get the problems with my bondmate squared away. After draining the last of a well-aged port from my goblet, I folded my napkin.

Intuiting I was about to leave, Grigori said, "That issue we discussed earlier, it can wait until morning. The night is well on its way to being spent."

I leaned against the padded back of my chair. He was telling me not to go after Dorcha for a few more hours. Probably decent advice, but I felt her absence keenly. Unlike some bonded pairs, we were rarely separated.

A trio of faeries flew toward me, an ornate harp suspended between them. I pushed my chair out from the table and reached for the instrument. They placed it into my outstretched hands, their wings beating so fast they were a blur. The diminutive mages were panting, as well they should be. Three of them moving the harp on their own was quite a feat. Crafted in the 1500s, it was heavy. Once, it had been mine, but I'd left it in the guild house because it didn't match my peripatetic time-traveling lifestyle.

My fingers caressed the shiny wood and flirted with the

strings. Grigori was transparent as hell sometimes, and he'd clearly instructed the faeries to locate the harp in some dusty basement, clean it up, and bring it to me as a diversion from setting out in search of the unicorn.

Rhea clasped her hands together. "Will you play for us?"

I nodded. Dorcha would approve of this performance. Too bad she wasn't here to appreciate it. She'd always kicked up her hoofs and danced a horsey version of a jig when I made music. I plucked strings and brought the harp back into tune. Built by master craftsmen, it was designed to last forever, all except for the strings. They were overdue for replacement, but I cobbled the rough spots over with magic.

Mages shouted out suggestions for songs. Play this, or play that. If I'd done them all, I'd still be here a week hence. I started with old ballads, my hands warming to the task after the first riff or two. The music made me smile. Hundreds of years ago, I'd dressed up as a man and been a traveling bard—with my unicorn. In those days, mortals still believed in magic. No need to hide what Dorcha was.

Tales of the bard and his unicorn had spread far and wide, and we were welcomed wherever we traveled. I'd halfway forgotten those days, but obviously the circus wasn't our first brush with performing.

I added a few love songs to my repertoire. Apparently, I'd always been an entertainer at heart. How could I have neglected the draw of the harp with its haunting notes? Had I lived so long I'd forgotten more than I remembered? It was possible. Someone refilled my goblet, once and then again. Between the warm glow from the liquor and the joy calling music from the harp, I felt better than I had in a very long while. More hopeful Dorcha and I still had a chance to patch things up.

The eastern windows were turning pink with the coming dawn when I set the harp aside. Mages had dragged their chairs close. No one had left through all the hours I played.

Grigori stood, faced me, and bowed. "Thank you for the music. Others have tried their hand at that harp, but it only plays for you."

I laughed, surprised I still could. "Sure and 'tis on account of I hexed it," I said in my best brogue.

"It knows its mistress," Quinn said and squeezed my shoulder before he and Ciara joined hands and walked toward the door. Were they a couple now? Amazing job on her part if they were since Quinn was the original love-'em-and-leave-'em guy.

Swathing the harp in a quick travel spell, I moved both it and me to my upstairs room. Joss had placed my freshly laundered clothing on the bed. I propped the harp near the door and hung the garments from hooks before stretching out on the bed and dragging an overstuffed duvet into position to warm me.

The same sense of peace, of coming home after a rocky journey filled me. I rolled onto a side and placed another pillow under my head. Returning to any of the guild houses always had this effect, but it never lasted. After a month—or a year or two—I grew restless, ready to move on. But Dorcha usually had too.

Why couldn't I hang onto the tranquility spilling through me?

Promising myself I'd come up with an answer, I drifted into what passes for sleep for my kind. We float, rather than sleep, but it has the same effect. I set strong wards, protections designed to rouse me in time to defend myself, and opened my mind to the ebb and flow of the universe.

I was part of everything, and everything was part of me.

Everything except Dorcha, a stern inner voice lectured.

"She's here too," I argued.

Really? Look again.

So I did, fully expecting to find our bond.

The floaty, peaceful place I'd built shattered around me. At some point while I'd been immersed in harp music, my unicorn had made a unilateral decision and broken the linkage binding us. She'd been sneaky about it. No fanfare, just a gentle slide away, which was why I hadn't noticed.

Until now.

I heard myself shouting, screeching, "Noooooooooo." Power shot from me, destructive enchantment that broke windows and turned furniture to piles of dust. I tried to stop, but once loosed my brand of ancient magic is a fearsome thing.

Out of my mind with grief and disbelief, it scarcely registered when a pack of mages burst through my door—and my warding. What were a few mages? I'd lost Dorcha. My love. My heart. My soul. I'd flatten the world. Nothing else mattered. Teeth bared in a snarl, I turned to face whoever had the temerity to enter my chamber.

Didn't matter who they were, I'd make them sorry they'd ever drawn breath.

Power slammed into me and flew from my outstretched hands. Driven by rage and anguish, I didn't care what happened next. Nothing mattered without Dorcha. My life was over. Except it would continue endlessly. A million years ago I could have thrown myself on the Celts' mercy, such as it was. Begged them to end me. If Arawn or Gwydion had been in a charitable mood, which hardly ever happened, they'd have enjoyed torturing me until my essence ran dry.

Every lamp in the room broke. Another window blew outward. Magic jabbed mercilessly from all sides as the roomful of magic-wielders sought to corral my outburst. I had no idea who was even here. My vision hazed over with anguish.

No one bested me. Ever. But that was when I was linked to Dorcha. Together, our magic had been unstoppable. Now it was just me, and a heartsick, disheartened me to boot. By the time I realized my spells were boomeranging back at me, slapping me upside the head, someone had dropped a cage over me. Bars circled me from head to foot, and the earthy scent of werewolf magic hung heavy in the air.

"You," I growled at Grigori.

"Me, what?" He layered power over the stuff holding me captive.

"You set this up knowing I'd be so engrossed in the harp's music I wouldn't notice when Dorcha severed our link."

His expression registered surprise before turning stern. "How long have you known me?" Without waiting for an answer, he kept on rolling. "When have I ever supported a mage or a bond animal walking away from a bond?"

"When it wasn't right," I gritted.

"Aye, when the mage or the animal was tainted, perverted. Do you or Dorcha fit that description?"

Fury cascaded through me. Gripping the bars of my cage, I rattled them. "You know better than to ask. Let me go."

"Give me your word you're done destroying the guild house," he countered.

"Oh, I'm done, all right. And I'll be gone too—after I've repaired everything."

Grigori motioned for everyone else to leave. Once the door swooshed shut behind them, he skewered me with his gaze and dropped a sound shield around us. "Not as private as the grove," he said, "but it will have to do. I need your magic, Rhiana. The Circle needs it."

"I'm no longer part of the Circle," I said dully. "No bond animal. Remember that niggling detail?"

"I believe she will return."

"Nice words," I mumbled, sunk in feeling sorry for myself

and not caring how pathetic it made me appear. I'd announced Dorcha's defection to the group who'd been crowded into my chamber. Word would travel like wildfire. Everyone would pity me. The specter of turning into an object of shame, of derision was almost as bad as my mate-less status.

The bars surrounding me clanked to the ground before vanishing. "I won't hold you against your will," Grigori said softly. "Such was never my intent. When I first broke through your warding, I tried to talk with you, but you didn't even hear me."

He was right. I hadn't heard anything beyond blood pounding against my eardrums. I couldn't bear to look at him. I'd failed. At everything.

He walked near enough to place both hands on my shoulders, holding me in front of him. I could have broken free, but I didn't have the heart. For anything.

"You face choices," he said. "You can pick up your toys and run away, wallowing in guilt and misery. Or you can be the mage Dorcha was willing to bond with all those hundreds of years ago."

"Better than a thousand," I mumbled.

Nodding solemnly, he said, "I rest my case. Somewhere along the line, things slewed sideways. My guess is a lot of little stuff became cumulative."

I started to protest, to whine I'd seen the light but Dorcha hadn't given me a chance to make things right. The harsh truth was she'd given me hundreds of chances, thousands, but my fondness for performing had blown every one of them. Why had I been so convinced she'd eventually appreciate the circus?

Because it was what I wanted. And my desires blinded me to hers.

I wound my arms around my middle. Everything hurt. My teeth. My eyes. Even my hair. Twisting from under Grigori's hands, I raced for the adjoining bathroom and puked what was left of my dinner into the toilet.

Always patient, he was still standing in my chamber after I'd flushed and rinsed my mouth with water from the sink. "I can't remain here," I blurted.

"Why not? It's as close to a home as you've had since I've known you."

"Everyone will know—if they don't already," I moaned. Christ, I sounded like a total ninny. Why did I give a flying fig who knew about Dorcha. I wasn't in the habit of hiding from reality.

"Why not stick around?"

"What for?" I squeezed my eyes tight shut before opening them and muttering, "Sorry. I have no idea who I am anymore."

"How could you?" he shot back. "This is one place where I'm siding with Dorcha. I could envision one circus, maybe a carnival or two, but how many years have you been working the circuit?"

"Did I tell you about that?"

"No. I culled it from your mind."

Shame heated my cheeks, making my guilt even more visceral. "Lots of years if you count all the circuses."

"I'm guessing all the time you haven't been here."

"Pretty much."

"Pick yourself up. Be the mage you were born to me. I

don't care about the Celts splitting up the elements you control. Nor do I—"

"I do," I cut in.

"Why? You had no control over it."

"It wasn't fair. They were jealous. We were nearly as powerful as them. It's why they cut the knees out from under those like me."

"They didn't alter your magic," he pointed out.

"No, but they made damn good and sure there wouldn't be any more elemental mages."

He held up his hands, palms out. "You can spend the rest of forever holding a grudge. Or you can let it go." He hesitated for a few moments and then added, "If you keep going as you've been, you'll waste the gifts you were born with."

"I already am."

"I believe in fate. It brought you here for a reason." His words were slow, relentless, and contained visible persuasion.

"Well I don't, and I won't be here long," I muttered and swept an arm to one side. "I will clear up this mess before I leave, though."

The sound shield tightened around us. "I could use your assistance, Rhiana. Help me root out traitors in our midst. I've already found four."

"What makes you believe there are more?" I shook my head. "You don't have to be kind to me. I don't deserve it."

"I was fading for months before I accepted something was wrong," he replied. "Things I normally would have noticed…" He shrugged, stopping before coming out and saying he hadn't been at the top of his game.

While I quested about for something to say, he went on,

"It's hard to admit this, but the spies I identified infiltrated the Circle prior to my illness. I believe one of them dosed me with whatever did battle with the werewolf virus."

I dragged my gaze up off the floor. His revelation had been like a bucket of cold water tossed over my head. "But it makes no sense," I sputtered. "You've run the Circle forever without problems like that."

He shrugged again. "Who knows? Maybe I've done it too long. Maybe I've grown complacent. Maybe the finely honed edge I've always counted on to sort things has grown dull. Your power is different from mine. You could move among the mages at this guild house and all the others with no one the wiser."

"What would I be looking for?" The question reluctantly left the safety of my throat.

"Anything that doesn't add up."

I narrowed my eyes. "I'm far from infallible. What if I'm wrong?"

"You wouldn't be making the final call. I'd do that. But it would save me a lot of time to have a roster of likely candidates pre-sorted."

My first bent was to tell him his faith in me wasn't justified. I didn't trust my judgment, so how could he? Before I could bend words into something that didn't make me sound totally ungrateful, he started talking again.

"Someone has decided the Circle is a burr under their saddle. They either want to annihilate us or take us over to use for their own purposes."

"It would never work," I said indignantly. "Mages would have to cooperate with their power being turned to evil."

"We already kill people," Grigori pointed out. "How different would it be to kill for the other side?"

"The bond animals would never agree."

"Are you certain they could tell the difference? Killing is killing. I'm not asking for a lengthy commitment from you," Grigori explained. "Just a quick pass through this guild house and the other five. Report back to me, and I won't ask anything further."

"I should hunt for Dorcha."

He grabbed my chin to force me to keep looking at him. "How would you expect that to go?"

He already knew the answer. So did I. Dorcha didn't want to be found. She'd kept the link intact long enough to determine her next moves. Whatever they were, they didn't include me. A harsh breath rattled from me. Whoever said truth hurts knew whereof they spoke.

"All right," I said.

"All right, what?"

"I'll look for traitors. I'm not sure how I can face everyone here. They all loved Dorcha, and they'll blame me for her leaving."

He angled his brows and kept looking at me. He didn't remind me it was my fault, but he didn't have to. No place was far enough to run from what I'd done. He'd been right about choices. I could skulk away and never raise my head in the company of mages again.

Or I could own my failings and do my damnedest to begin anew. Without my bondmate. It was the harder path, by a good big bunch, but if I ran away the light would go out of everything. I'd wander the paths of the cursed and eventually lose my mind.

And my magic after I stopped caring about anything.

He let go of my chin, and I felt him withdraw from my mind. I hadn't been shielded, so he knew my thoughts. "Will you be all right alone?"

I nodded slowly. "Not all right. I'm a long way from there, but I'm done summoning chaos."

"I have faith in you, Rhiana. I've known you since before I drew the Circle together. The kicker is for you to have faith in yourself. It's why you've needed more and more validation performing. When crowds are cheering you on, it makes up for the empty places you've worked so hard to gloss over."

A reluctant grin split my mouth. Traces of sickness lingered. "Will you be sending a psychotherapy bill over later?"

He smiled back, warm, generous, and vintage Grigori. "Now there's an idea, except the Circle isn't shy on resources."

"Only on loyalty. Maybe."

He punched my upper arm lightly. "You'll be the judge. My wolf and I will serve as the jury. Take it easy on yourself. Focus on right now. That jagged empty place inside?" At my nod, he went on, "Dorcha feels the same. No one can be bonded as long as the two of you without wreckage on both sides. Believe in her. Believe in yourself. She's keeping tabs on what you do next, waiting to see if you—"

"Pull my head out of my ass," I finished his sentence.

Grigori turned to go. Before he cleared the doorway, I called, "Thank you."

"No thanks needed," he said. The click of his bootheels echoed down the hall.

I turned in a full circle surveying the damage I'd wrought.

It made me feel sick and ashamed. Starting with the windows, I called magic, letting it flow through me as I patched broken bits back together, making them whole again with fire and air and earth. It took longer than I expected, a whole lot longer.

No one bothered me. After my performance where I'd rallied destruction, they were probably scared to go near me.

By the time I was done, I felt more settled, more like the old me. Using power to build and create was affirming in a way I'd nearly forgotten. I traded my borrowed clothing for the items I'd arrived in and stood next to the door as minutes ticked past. The afternoon was well on its way toward evening.

Could I leave the relative safety of my chamber? Once I did, I'd run into other mages. They'd feel sorry for me. Or worse. Some would believe I'd never been worthy of my unicorn bondmate, elemental mage or not.

"I can't hide in here forever," I mumbled.

Maybe just until tomorrow, one of my inner voices suggested.

I shook my head. Facing the music wouldn't get easier but harder the more time that passed. If I caved to excuses now, they'd pave the way for bigger excuses tomorrow. I'd made a commitment to Grigori, one I couldn't execute languishing in this room.

Nope. I needed to lay eyes—and magic—on my housemates to gather the information Grigori required. I sucked air deep into my lungs, blew out the breath, and repeated the action a few more times. Ready as I was likely to be, I opened the door to my room and strode through.

Grateful for my woolen cloak, I wrapped myself more securely in its folds but resisted the urge to draw up the hood.

Having made a promise to Grigori, I would carry it out. The upper floor was empty. Before I started down the stairs, I sent thoughts Dorcha's way. If she was paying attention—and wasn't too far away—she'd hear me.

"My heart. My love. I understand why you left. You took the best of me with you. Take what time you need. Watch my actions. If you can find it in yourself to return and give us another chance, I promise everything will be different. I was a selfish bitch. No more."

I stopped there. Grigori was right about me becoming the mage she'd bonded with long ago. I wouldn't grovel. I'd stand tall. If she didn't return, I'd keep going. Somehow. None of the other options were viable.

Spreading power in a subtle arc, I hunted for mage energy. May as well get this ball rolling. I should be through assessing the mages here in a few hours. Then I could move on to the other houses.

I had no idea what I'd do once I finished, but I was getting ahead of things. After locating several groups of mages, I experimented with what I could glean from a distance. Turned out the goddess wasn't in a generous mood. Other than determining the type of magic-wielder and who their bond animals were, I didn't get far.

Thinking about the bond animals gave me an idea. A tainted mage would have a tainted bondmate. No way around it. I wouldn't have to face the mages after all, so long as I located their animals. Out of all the bondmates, I trusted Aidyrth implicitly. A dragon, she was far older than me, and dragon honor is legendary.

I had to start somewhere. Before I talked myself out of it, I zeroed in on her location and hurried toward her, passing mages as I went. No one talked with me. Hell, they probably had no idea what to say. I've always been respected for my power; those who were jealous of me were like as not rejoicing in my downfall. Except nothing had happened to my magic. It burned brighter than ever.

Aidyrth must have felt me approaching because she swept me into a teleport spell when I was still a few feet away. When it cleared, we were in the grove. Crossing her forelegs over her scaled chest, she bugled, "Explain." Red and gray scales rattled against each other. Red wings folded across her back.

"My fault," I said. "Dorcha was tolerant. I hope she will return."

"What was your fault?" the dragon pressed.

I sketched out enough details to satisfy her. They hurt just as much this time as when Grigori had dredged them out of me.

Once we'd cleared the topic of Dorcha, I said, "I sought you out because I agreed to help Grigori flush out others who don't belong in the Circle, those who are here under false pretenses. Can you help me?"

"Why would you believe I could?"

"You know the bond animals as well as any," I told the dragon. "A tainted mage will have a tainted bond animal."

She blew a plume of fiery ash skyward. "Interesting approach."

"If you see faults in it, now would be a good time to tell me."

"I don't. If I'd paid closer attention, I'd have picked up on the four demons masquerading as shifters. Their bond animals knew something was amiss."

My eyebrows shot up. First details I'd heard about the

traitors, and I pumped the dragon for information. "Do you believe we harbor more demons?" I asked. They were known for their shapeshifting ability, and could turn into damn near anything.

"Probably," she said after a thoughtful pause. "I'll do some sleuthing. The ones who were here were well disguised. If their bond animals hadn't complained, we might never have smoked them out. Until it was too late."

Talking with the dragon had edged from uncomfortable to almost normal. Doubts about Grigori assigning me this task faded. Dusk had fallen, and I needed to get moving.

"Thank you for speaking with me." I bowed my head. The dragon loved Dorcha, and she could have told me to go fuck myself.

Aidyrth puffed steam; it's the dragon equivalent of a healing balm, and it wafted around me smelling of ash and cinders. "I've had my doubts about two of the bond animals for a while, but then I've looked at everyone with a bit of a side eye lately."

"Who are they?"

"I'll dig deeper with them—and a few others. I will let you know what I find."

"All right." I nodded. "Tell me which ones they are, and I'll skip them."

"A nighthawk and a civet."

Determined to start the long journey of redeeming myself, I strode from the grove. Eh, redemption or not, if anyone so much as looked cross-eyed at me, or mentioned Dorcha, I'd flatten them.

Turned out I needn't have worried. No one wanted to spend five minutes with me, let alone look me in the eye. I skipped the communal evening meal. I wasn't hungry for starters. Neither was I ready to flaunt my presence in a fellowship where everyone was bonded with an animal.

Everyone, except me.

I did take advantage of dinner, though. With mages drifting in and out of the dining room, it was a good opportunity to creep close enough to scan them with magic. Most of the bond animals were present, so it saved me a lot of legwork. Grigori had said my magic was different from his. What he'd meant by that was my power was so arcane most newer mages wouldn't recognize it straight away. Neither would their bondmates They'd feel the brush of my scrutiny, but it was gone before they made sense of what had just touched them.

I took my time, leaving big enough gaps no one could exactly compare notes. I also added a touch of forgetfulness, so describing the feel of my power would be impossible.

It was closing on midnight when I tapped on Grigori's door and told him my suspicions. The list wasn't long; only three mages hadn't met muster. Two had been bonded to the nighthawk and civet Aidyrth suspected. The third was bonded with another civet.

"When will you leave for the other guild houses?" he asked not bothering to downplay a sense of urgency.

"Right away," I told him.

"Excellent. I'll be here," he said.

"I should be back in a day, two at the most." Turning, I made my way to my chamber one floor up. The harp was where I'd left it, leaning next to the door. I gave myself five minutes to coax a haunting minor tune from its strings before I cobbled a teleport spell together and instructed it to take me to another guild house.

This was the only off-world site. All the others were scattered around Earth. Smaller than this one, each location held only a handful of mages, and mercifully they wouldn't have heard about Dorcha.

Maybe.

I wasn't running away from what I'd done, but neither was I anxious to have my nose rubbed in it. Aidyrth had been kind. Grigori too. Not that they'd let me off the hook, but they hadn't turned their backs on me.

Chances of me knowing many of the mages at the other houses were high. What would I say when they asked after Dorcha? I turned the problem this way and that as my spell worked its magic moving me to a well-hidden location in the northern Nevada desert.

Convinced I should stick with the truth, I finally settled on just saying Dorcha was fine. No reason to lay out the whole sorry saga time and again. Other than Grigori and Aidyrth, I'd never been especially close to the other mages or bond animals. Even if they found out eventually—and they would—I wouldn't be caught in a lie. Dorcha was fine, or as fine as could be expected. Grigori was convinced she was as ripped up as me. I hoped he was right because if she were, it might bode well for her returning.

Somewhere along the line, I'd decided not to look for her. It wouldn't do any good. She'd sense me and put more distance between us. Until she was ready to face me. All of our years together hadn't been terrible. We'd built a solid history until I got on my circus kick a hundred or so years ago. Even then, we'd probably spent at least 30 percent of our time at one guild house or another.

I'm a master at underestimating how long things will take. Moving from guild house to guild house pounded that point home. Not that I ran into any difficulties, but between teleporting and being thorough without arousing suspicions, a full three days elapsed before I was on my way back to where I'd begun.

My aim was true, and my chamber at the guild house—the one I'd wrecked and rejuvenated—shaped up around me. It was the middle of the night. I considered waking Grigori. While I was running the pros and cons of disturbing him, he walked into my room, shut the door, and dropped a ward around us.

"You were on the lookout for me."

He nodded. "I was getting worried."

I turned my hands palms up. "No problems, but everything always takes longer than I expect it will. I have good news. Of the sixty-four mages I scanned, everyone was what I expected. Their animals too."

"Sixty-four, you say? Means five are missing."

I thinned my lips into a scowl. "I can hunt for them."

"List who you saw."

Closing my eyes, I rattled off names, grouping them by guild house.

When I was done, he said, "You fulfilled your promise to me. I require nothing further unless you wish to help."

The specter of leaving the guild house alone rose to taunt me. Grigori had kept his word, though. He'd been clear my assignment had parameters, ones I'd fulfilled.

I rolled my shoulders back and looked at him but stopped shy of bothering with a truth spell. "Do you wish me to go?"

"Of course not, but we had an agreement, and I don't want you to think I'm taking advantage of it. Or you."

My next words surprised me. "I will see this through."

"Excellent. I'd hoped you'd see it that way. My wolf was convinced. So was Aidyrth."

Awk. They were talking about me. It made my skin crawl, and I turned away, ashamed.

"Aye, we discussed you," Grigori agreed, having helped himself to my thoughts, "but it's because we care about you." He hesitated for a long moment before adding, "You've always been closed off, a force unto yourself. I assumed it was part of being an elemental mage. Quinn is like that. Ciara too. We all need someone, and the Circle will be there for you."

"People will blame me about Dorcha. And they should."

"Maybe they'll be more tolerant of you making a mistake than you are," he suggested.

I flapped a hand his way. "It was way more than a single misstep on my part. Give me the five names. Maybe we'll get lucky and I'll know them."

"You do," he said and listed the missing Circle mages.

"Are they off on assignment?" I asked. When he shook his head, I inquired if he had ideas about their whereabouts. Whole lot of worlds out there, and I could be years hunting them. From the looks of things, Grigori didn't have that kind of latitude to whip the Circle back into shape.

"Any idea about their last-known whereabouts?" I probed.

Crossing the room, he withdrew paper and a pen from a drawer and began writing. When he was done, he handed me two sheets covered with his stark, spare writing. He'd listed the mages, their last known locations, and roughly how long since they'd been there.

"It's possible they have no plans to return," he said. "After we outed the four demons pretending to be shifters, word must have traveled. We weren't kind to them. No 'run on back to Hell and we'll forget all about this.'"

"It's worth a cursory search," I said. "At least we know who they are. If they show back up at any of the guild houses, we can hold them until someone takes a really good look behind their magic to assess if it turned dark."

A thought occurred to me. "What happened to the animals bonded with demons?" Breath puffed through my clenched teeth. "The bond must have been horrible for them."

An unreadable expression flitted across Grigori's features. "One complained, a hyena. I told him to try harder. Maybe if

I hadn't been so caught up in my illness I'd have listened better."

"You can't blame yourself—" I began.

"Oh yeah, I can. And I do. To answer your question, we managed to salvage all the animals. One was nip and tuck, but he pulled through."

"So that chapter had a happy ending."

"It did. I'm curious why the three traitors who are still here haven't made excuses and left."

It was odd. Remaining had grown fraught with the danger of discovery. "Have either of the civets or the nighthawk tried to opt out of their bonds?"

Grigori shook his head. "These are scarcely freshly bonded pairs. They've been together for a very long time."

"Unlike the demons?" I sought clarification.

"They were brand new by comparison," he confirmed.

I thought about it before suggesting, "You could have two different problems."

"It occurred to me after you left," he grunted. "Tell me your reasoning."

"Maybe they were in cahoots with the demons, but if they were it was an afterthought. No one could have tempted them to sign on with evil if they weren't unhappy with the way things were going."

Grigori settled on the edge of the desk. "Those months I was ill are a blur. So much escaped my attention. Just getting up each day took almost more than I had."

"You never did have a command structure," I murmured, thinking out loud.

"I still don't."

Something about his tone told me not to turn that stone

over any further. I rattled the pages he'd handed me. "Maybe me hunting down the missing five is a waste of time. We know who they are. You can put out the word they're to be detained if they show up."

The air around him lit with werewolf enchantment, turning shades of blue and deep violet. Moments later he said, "Done."

"Do you have plans for what comes next?"

"Other than returning to Hell and carving as big a hole in Satan's operations as we can?"

"It's possible someone hired him," I tossed out.

"Who would do that?"

I shrugged. "Whoever wanted to take over the Circle. Have you kicked any disgruntled mages out in the last century or so?"

"Of course."

"Maybe that's the list I should be going after."

He jumped off the desk, crossed to where I stood, and clapped me across the back. "Quinn pegged damaged werewolf virus as my problem within moments of laying eyes on me. You've identified another fruitful avenue."

I screwed my face into a scowl but didn't say anything. He'd been culling the ranks as long as there'd been a Circle, but we'd never had any of the bootees come back and bite us in the ass. Mostly, they were ashamed to have washed out. Grigori had always given the bond animals a choice if they wished to remain linked with the mage in question. Most couldn't run far enough or fast enough, which left the mage in the unenviable position of losing both the Circle and their closest friend and confidante.

I didn't have to pass go or collect two hundred dollars for

my line of reasoning to lead me to Dorcha. A bittersweet sorrow pulsed deep within me. I'd never in my wildest imaginings believed my bondmate would walk away. And I vowed to never take anything for granted again.

Grigori snatched the pages from my hand. After flipping them over, he picked up the same pen he'd used before and wrote another list, presumably mages who'd been removed from the Circle.

Crossing to the desk, I peered over his shoulder not surprised to recognize almost all the names. "Geez, I had no idea there'd be this many," I mumbled. Mages came and went. Some were off on one assignment or another. Some took breaks—not as many as me, but enough. A few decided the Circle wasn't their cup of tea and left on their own. The net effect was I'd never been certain who was in and who wasn't beyond the faces I saw at various guild houses.

"I went back 500 years," he said. "Resentment can simmer for a long while before it ignites, and I didn't want to miss anyone."

I pointed at a couple of names. "Costs a lot to hire demons. Neither of these mages were ever able to hang onto tuppence. Gambling if I recall, and Shanara had a taste for fancy designer aircraft."

He tapped the tip of the pen on the page before saying, "Going to leave them in. A lot can change over a few hundred years. We always took care of our own. They could have grown better at managing money without the Circle standing behind them."

"Doubt it," I muttered.

"It's a long list," he said, agreeing with my earlier

assessment. "Would you like another mage or two to split it with you?"

"Maybe." I cast a longing glance at the bed tucked under the windows. "Can we revisit this in a few hours? I haven't slept since I left."

"Of course. Find me once you're up. We'll finalize plans then."

After he glided from the room, silent on his feet, I shed my clothing. They may have been clean when I'd left, but they weren't any longer. I didn't have the energy to drag them down to the laundry, so I hung my trousers, tunic, and cloak on hooks and doused them in magic to freshen them up.

After a quick turn through the shower, I rolled myself into the duvet and sank into what passes for sleep for those like me. A series of images cascaded through my mind. Mostly Dorcha and me in happier times. An era when unicorns had roamed in herds, as ubiquitous as horses, warmed my heart. Mortals had worshipped them, leaving apples and carrots and buckets of oats. Silly fools. They'd assumed unicorns ate the same things horses did.

No one ever told them different. Not that unicorns wouldn't chow down on an apple, but seeing one with blood dripping off its horn and into its mouth would have put a whole different slant on things. Mortals might have viewed them as a threat rather than creatures to be revered and worshipped.

For a time, I gave myself up to the gentle rolling motion of being astride Dorcha in my dream. While we addressed adversaries this way, she hadn't let me pleasure-ride her often, so the times she invited me along for a romp were special. We moved from rolling pastureland to an imposing castle.

Crafted of dark stones, glass, and magic, it had been my ancestral home.

Unlike many of the mages in the Circle, I'd arrived already bonded with Dorcha, but then I'd been one of the original members when Grigori formed the Circle of Assassins. Returning to my dream imagery, Dorcha and I galloped across the bridge spanning a moat and on into the castle where I'd been formed of every element mixed with magic.

Elemental mages were created, not spawned.

Familiar furnishings flashed past. The floors were clear glass. It made transiting the building impossible absent magic. Between the comforting warmth of the unicorn between my thighs and familiar smells surrounding me, I sank deeper into trance.

Was I back in the Circle for good? Or was I only there long enough to lick my wounds and regroup? Was anything as prosaic as regrouping even possible without Dorcha? Tears flowed, rivers of them from my sea mage side. I tasted the salt on my tongue and smelled brine.

One more thing to clean up before I left. Usually on the compulsively neat side, I'd left a broad swathe of destruction since showing up in Grigori's realm. Maybe thinking about the guild house was the lynchpin, but the glass floors, paintings, sculptures, and wall-hangings disappeared, traded for the spartan lines of the guild house.

Grigori had always been more invested in necessities than artistic touches. No matter how anyone dressed it up, the Circle was a group of paranormal assassins. It was how we'd began, and how we'd end—if Grigori ever retired his creation.

Or if we were overrun by evil. When I clawed my way upward, gnawing through layers of trance, my fists were clenched. No one would co-opt the Circle, not while I had magic to fight them. Guess I'd answered my earlier question, the one about my commitment to the Circle.

I'd shown up here when I was needed—fate is funny that way—and here I would remain until Grigori no longer required m aid. The chamber swam into focus along with my tear-soaked duvet. Feathers are warm and toasty—until they get wet. After that, they're sodden and worthless.

After draping the comforter over the headboard and setting a flow of warm air to fluff and dry it, I donned my clothes. A quick trip to the guild house wardrobe produced a pair of warm, fur-lined boots. Far more practical than the strappy sandals I'd borrowed for dinner the other night, they'd see me through my journey as I located the mages Grigori had ousted from the Circle.

The smells of breakfast beckoned, but I wasn't ready to face anyone, so I settled for a detour through the kitchens to grab a sandwich on fresh, fragrant bread with cheese melted between the slices. Grigori had said to find him, but I opted for a stroll outside as I ate.

Mornings have always appealed to me. Something about a brand new day, full of hope and promise, is tough to resist. I was brushing crumbs from my hands and clothing when a familiar whinny drifted my way.

My head snapped up. Granted, I was feeling more upbeat than I had since Dorcha left, but it was no reason to hallucinate hearing her. Turning back toward the guild house, I was determined to locate Grigori and be on my way. Sleep had been an indulgence, but I hadn't been anywhere near the top of my game. The bit of rest would go a long way as I tracked down mages who hadn't been seen in hundreds of years.

I hadn't gone three steps when I heard the same whinny. Hope soared, hitting me in the guts like a runaway train. I sent power skittering in a wide arc. It vibrated warmly when it found my unicorn.

Awk. I winced. Maybe she was mine no more but had only come to say her goodbyes. Doing my damnedest not to get my hopes up, I faced the direction I'd located her magic and stood tall, waiting.

# 6

Hoofbeats headed my way, skimming the ground quickly. Whatever Dorcha had in mind, she wanted to get it over with. Maybe not. She's never been one to loll about. Once she had a direction in mind, she barreled toward it, afterburners engaged.

Resolved not to sully the moment with any preconceived notions, I emptied my mind of everything except welcoming energy. She came into view, her black coat glowing with the magical light dawn adds. I tried to remain where I was, but I couldn't. Driven by hope and joy and delight seeing the familiar grace of her movements, I pelted toward her and wrapped my arms around her neck.

"You came back," I whispered against her soft coat. "You came back."

"Oh ye of little faith," she whickered, nuzzling my hair with her velvety nose.

"I had plenty of faith," I protested, "until you severed our bond."

"Did I? Or was I somewhere you couldn't sense it?"

I buried my fingers in the silk of her coat, never wanting to let go. No wonder I'd never had a man in my life for longer than a moment or two. No one could compete with my love for Dorcha.

Reaching for my link to the unicorn, it pulsed warmly as if it had never gone anywhere. My head had been lying on her neck; I kicked it back far enough to connect with one liquid equine eye. I was curious where she'd gone, but it could wait. What I had to say couldn't.

"I'm sorry. Everything you said on our way back here was right. I'll never make those mistakes again. From now on—"

"Never is a long time." She blew warm air on my fingers.

A corner of my mouth twisted downward. "Grigori said much the same, except his version was 'forever is a long time.'"

Talking around the lump in my throat wasn't easy, but I had to know. "Are you truly back? Not just passing through to say goodbye?"

She dropped her horn onto my shoulder. "What do you think?"

"I don't know what to think, but what I hope is you'll give me another chance. You'll have to help me. Prod me with that horn when I'm selectively deaf."

"Like this?" She pricked me with the tip.

I welcomed the burn and the slow trickle of blood. "Exactly, or even more if I'm too pigheaded to pay attention."

"No more circuses," she said firmly.

"No more carnivals, either. If I have a yen to perform, I'll find an audience in one of the guild houses with my harp."

Because all my attention was focused on Dorcha, I didn't notice Grigori until he was only about ten feet away. A smile lit his austere features. "See?" he boomed. "Told you."

"What did you tell her?" Dorcha tossed her mane.

"That you'd be back."

She whinnied long and loud. "What? Did everyone assume I went off in a snit never to return?"

"I can't speak for anyone except me," I replied, "but I'm ready to close the chapter on circuses and unhappy bondmates. We begin anew. Today."

"Does she know what you agreed to?" Grigori asked.

"Not yet," I said. "She just returned, and we had more important ground to cover."

"I'm always eager for Circle assignments," Dorcha said.

"This one is...different," Grigori informed her. "Shall we?"

Intuiting he wanted us to finish this conversation in the grove I set a path toward it. Within its protective circle of trees, additional warding in place, he didn't lose any time. "I refined the list," he said and handed me sheets of folded paper. "Pared it down to a hundred or so. With Dorcha's magic on board, the two of you should make short work of it."

She whickered agreement and interest without asking any questions. I'd fill her in when we were en route. "Ready to leave anytime," she said.

Her words made me smile. She was always ready to lend her magic and her spirit to worthy projects. It made me even more ashamed of my love affair with the circus. Shit. What had I been thinking?

"Before you go," Grigori was saying, "drop by the dining room. Let everyone see you together. It should quell the rumor mill."

"What did you tell them?" Dorcha jabbed me with the business end of her horn.

"Tell them? Nothing. But when I sought our link and couldn't find it, I fell apart and laid waste to the world." I left out the part about Grigori building a cage to contain me and my renegade magic.

"I went home," Dorcha said softly. "Except home is a whole lot farther away than it once was. Nothing could have survived my transit between universes, not even our linkage."

"If anyone asks," Grigori broke in, "tell them it was a communication breakdown."

"They won't," I retorted. "They'll be so delighted Dorcha is here, it's the only thing they'll see." Unicorns are magical in the same way dragons are. Their power inspires awe and sweeps everything else out of the way. Dorcha hadn't visited her kinfolk since they moved two universes away. Had she gone seeking advice? Solace? Or had she simply wanted the reassurance of her own kind. We weren't so different in that respect since my last trance state dropped me in the center of my original home.

Unlike unicorns who'd put distance betwixt themselves and Earth, elemental mages had razed the castle I'd seen in my dream and hidden themselves in nooks and crannies of psychic space. I had no idea where any of my brethren were, and no easy way to find them. After the Celts' dick move to ensure no more of us were created, we'd blown up the ship rather than waiting around for the next shoe to fall. I'd resurrected our decision many times, examined it, and found it full of holes. Why we hadn't told them to piss up a rope and kept on keeping on never made sense. They'd threatened to end us all if we didn't comply, but we're damned hard to kill.

And there were more of us than them. Why had we folded like a pack of dog-eared cards?

"Rhiana." Grigori nudged me.

"Sorry. I was thinking."

"Come to the dining room in half an hour. I'll have the kitchen put a noontime meal together, and everyone can bask in Dorcha's magic."

Trumpeting from overhead told me Aidyrth was ahead of the curve, but then she always was. The dragon swooped out of the sky and skidded to a landing only a foot away. With the addition of her bulk, the grove was full to bursting. She breathed wreaths of steam around the three of us and beamed like a Cheshire troll.

"Go and catch up." I made little shooing motions, intuiting the dragon and unicorn wanted some alone time.

"Are you sure?" Dorcha whinnied.

"See you in the dining room in half an hour," I told her and hurried from the grove with Grigori just behind me. To his credit, he didn't hammer home, "I told you so."

"Your joy is contagious," he observed.

"And my relief. I'd girded myself to keep going, but it took every scrap of self-discipline."

"Why were you so certain she was gone for good?" He fell into step next to me.

"Because I was awful. If I'd been in her place, I'd have kicked me to the curb a long time ago."

He hooked a hand beneath my elbow, effectively stopping

me and turning me toward him at the same time. "If you knew, why didn't you stop?"

"Ever since the Celts subjected those like me to genocide, I shut down. We—myself and the other elemental mages—made irrevocable decisions. As I've sorted through them, we made a whole lot of mistakes. We should have stood our ground, fought back. Instead, we capitulated. All except me. I fought the Celts, but I didn't have a chance by myself.

"After I gave it up for a lost cause, nothing else mattered to me. I kept going, but my heart wasn't in much of anything."

"Except Dorcha."

A bitter laugh burbled out. "You see how well I finessed that."

"If you add magic and immortality to the equation, not much is irrevocable," he pointed out.

"In this case, it is. Those like me went to ground, hid ourselves away."

"You could find them if you put your mind to it."

I made a little shrugging motion. "One problem at a time. Let's save the Circle first, shall we?"

His grip on my arm tightened. "They're not mutually exclusive. You'll make quite the transit of inhabited worlds hunting for defrocked mages. Nothing says you can't search for your long-lost kinsmen along the way."

"What if they don't share my outrage?"

"Then at least you'll know."

I've always appreciated Grigori's wisdom and his candor. He has a no-nonsense approach that doesn't get bogged down in needless emotions. He loosed his hold on me, and we strode toward the guild house.

I hadn't intended to spend much more than an hour or so, but everyone's delight seeing Dorcha laid waste to my plans. Grigori must have called ahead because by the time we showed up, elves and fauns were carting trays of nuts and cheese and bread and crackers with the occasional fancy olive for decoration. An alcoholic beverage spiced with cloves and anise provided a perfect complement for the food.

Dorcha's magic is refreshing, soothing, inspiring. Unicorns are the only magical creature with an unsullied track record. None have ever joined the dark side that I know of. She and the dragon were the only mythical beasts in the Circle. Aidyrth was unapproachable for the most part. It took a strong constitution to meet her gaze, and her scales and spines were daunting.

Dorcha's silky mane and tail and soft hide invited touches and inspired trust. In her heart, she was every bit as bloodthirsty as any dragon, but she hid that side of her nature.

The sad, lost part of me was crumbling. A positive development, and one bound to expedite the tasks ahead. Why had I jumped to the worst possible conclusion about Dorcha? I hadn't even tried to come up with reasons I couldn't sense her through our link. Guilt and shame vied with one another. I'd been thoroughly disgusted with myself, hadn't blamed her for jettisoning me. Hell, I'd have ditched myself if I'd been able to.

Luckily, no one bothered me in the corner where I'd taken up residence with a generous goblet of booze and a tray of goodies. Occasionally, a mage stopped by to tell me hello, but they never stayed long. My power intimidates almost everyone—except Grigori.

Raucous squawking announced the arrival of two eagles. Quinn's and Ciara's. From the looks of things, they'd pair bonded. I was pleased for them. Had Quinn and Ciara cast their lot in together too? I'm a shitty judge of such things. If it weren't for the occasional booty call, I could do without men entirely. Women have never been my gig.

That's the thing about living as long as I have. I've tried everything at least once. Arianrhod had a crush on me. We'd gotten together a time or two—until the Celts decreed my kind were done for. After that, I declared war on them. Ari reassured me she'd had nothing to do with any of it, but I hadn't been in a forgiving mood.

Quinn hurried toward me with Ciara next to him. "Bet you're relieved," he said once he got close.

"It was a simple misunderstanding," I murmured in an effort to maintain my dignity.

"All's well that ends well," Ciara said. "Poseidon actually tried to hire you, huh? I've had a chance to think about that. Do you suppose he suspects you know where I am?"

I shrugged. "No idea. He can't find you, so what does it matter?"

"He needs to give up," Quinn growled.

Ciara's laughter collided with mine, bitterness squared. Apparently, we knew the lord of the seas better than Quinn.

"Giving up isn't his style," Ciara muttered.

"So? I'll provide a nudge." Quinn draped an arm around her shoulders.

She sent a sideways glance his way. "Bad idea. If something goes wrong, he could track me through you."

"Nothing would go wrong," Quinn bristled.

Seemed like a good place for me to insert a comment. Or

two. "Underestimating him is a mistake," I said firmly. "He almost had Dorcha and me. He's clever, and he thinks things through. Worse, he doesn't give a crap how many soldiers he sacrifices, so long as he accomplishes his goals."

Ciara rolled her pale eyes. "Poseidon is the last person I want to discuss. I've spent most of the years since I arrived here doing my best to purge him from my mind. The reason we came over to talk with you," she went on, "is we want to help."

"Aye, you have a lot of ground to cover." Quinn nodded. "Three of us would make it go quicker."

The eagles had made a full transit of the room. Flying close, Gwaihir plucked a bit of cheese off my plate and closed his beak around it. Three times the size of a normal eagle, he was Quinn's bondmate.

"Slipping, are you?" I inquired, directing my question at the bird.

"How so?" he squawked.

"It's not bloody or meat."

He honked laughter, sounding like a goose. "Aye, but it was there, and stolen food tastes so much sweeter than any other."

"Except something we've killed," the other eagle chirped.

I hunted around in my memory and came up with her name. Tory was Ciara's bondmate. As bonded pairs went, they were relatively new since Ciara had only joined the Circle about eighty years back.

"So how about it?" Quinn asked.

"Uh, how about what?"

"Splitting up the mage list," Ciara clarified.

"Sure. We could do that," I told them. "I'm grateful for the help."

A group of Sidhe had begun to play music. I considered going after my harp, but it was impossible to justify burning more time. "Hang on," I told Quinn and Ciara and their birds, "I'll pry Dorcha away from her fan club, and we can finalize our plans."

Quinn dragged a couple of sheets of paper out of his khaki combat vest. "Already did." He offered a rakish smile that intensified his profanely good looks. Peeling the sheets apart, he glanced at them and handed one to me. "These are yours."

"You did that without even consulting me," I protested, wanting to be pissed at him but not getting far. Something about the earth mage projected a fresh-faced appeal. It would have been like getting mad at a well-meaning friend.

"I did," he agreed cheerfully. "Time waits for no mage—and all that rot."

"Overbearing, isn't he?" Ciara punched his arm.

"But irresistible," he shot back.

"You only think you are," she retorted.

Leaving them to a lover's sparring match, I wended my way around tables. Most of them were empty since nearly everybody was grouped around Dorcha. She lived for these gatherings, occasions reinforcing how special she was. It wasn't all that different than my penchant for performing. If the topic ever came up again, I'd be sure to remind her.

The rise and fall of her voice suggested she was deep into one of the old tales. A born raconteur, she could spin one story after the next. She might have felt more positively about the circus if she'd been able to launch her storytelling routine. Horses can't talk, though. And keeping her true identity hidden had been important.

If the circus patrons had known her horn was real, right along with the rest of her, we'd never have had a moment's peace. Most mortals meant well, but poachers intent on snaring her horn for a wall ornament would have shown up in droves.

And she would have killed every one of them. She'd done it before. Nothing like leaving a trail of impaled dead to discourage the next would-be glory hound.

I waited patiently until she was done with an old Sufi tale, one about dual realities, before I picked my way through tightly packed bodies. "We should leave," I told her softly.

After a thorough shake of her mane she gathered journey magic. Before it yanked us out of the guild house I said, "Quinn and Ciara and the eagles are coming."

Power spiraled back into her, and she trotted across the dining room. Mages fell back, opening a path for her. I took advantage of it, stopping to talk with a few magic-wielders I'd known for a long while. Delight at the unicorn's unexpected return was universal.

When I'd told myself it didn't matter if Dorcha and I were here or not, I'd misjudged our importance to the fellowship of mages. Not an error I'd repeat. By the time I reached the table where I'd been, Grigori was there too along with Rhea, the female werewolf.

Were she and Grigori a couple? Moving in that direction? Eh, none of my affair. I pulled out the crumpled paper I'd placed in an inner pocket of my cloak and held it for Dorcha to read.

Grigori tapped my arm. "When Quinn asked if he could

tag along, I told him I was certain you wouldn't mind. Did I misspeak?"

"Not at all."

"Is there another list?" Dorcha asked, all business now she was done playing queen bee.

Quinn nodded. Dorcha stamped a hoof. "Let me see it. I might want to make some changes."

I smothered a smile and waited while Quinn smoothed over the other sheet, holding it up. He might have refused another, but he was smitten by Dorcha's charm—and she'd ladled compulsion into her request. Grigori came up with a pen. Smart werewolf, he intuited it would be needed.

A few minutes later, after scratching out names in one spot and adding them to another, we were ready. "Let's cover the likely spots on Earth, first," I said. "We can touch base every midnight at the Nevada guild house until we've burned through the obvious locations."

Quinn snapped off an approximation of a salute. "Copy that."

I snickered. "Christ. You sound like a soldier."

"It's what I was until Grigori called me into service." His answer held serious undernotes. Would he remain once the Circle was no longer in danger? We'd have that conversation, but not here.

"I'll spend the next few days in Nevada," Grigori said.

"Thanks." I nodded. "It will be simpler to keep you apprised of our progress."

"We'll be dragging any suspect mages back with us, right?" Quinn asked.

Grigori frowned and turned to me. "What do you think?"

I shrugged. "They're fallen mages. Allowing them to live

was…generous. No reason to waste magic transporting them. Unless it's a very unusual circumstance, I say kill and move on."

Dorcha neighed agreement. "Killing. It's the Circle way."

Rhea laughed, but it held emotional edges. "What a bloodthirsty crew. Good thing I had a few years to get used to not being human."

"You still miss it, though," I said pointblank.

"Yup. I do, but I'll get over it."

"Aye, you will." Grigori's tone was as reassuring as I'd ever heard from him. He's not the touchy-feely type. Or he hadn't been. Maybe his near brush with death had crafted a few changes.

"See you tomorrow night," Quinn said. Magic simmered around him, Ciara, and the eagles before they glistened, turned translucent, and were gone.

He'd had a field pack strapped to his body. I'd never seen him without it. Taking a moment, I considered if I'd need anything from the guild house. Not wanting to be left behind, the magical contrivance that had formed itself into a sparkling whip materialized in my right hand. This time, it looked more like a sparkly saber. I conjured a sheath with a waistbelt and buckled it into place.

"Nice." Grigori explored its power.

"Thanks. Might come in handy."

"Best of luck," Rhea said. After a brief hesitation, she added, "My wolf says you should hurry, that time grows short."

"She's one of the old ones, isn't she?" Dorcha asked.

Rhea nodded. "She says she knows you."

Power flickered from Dorcha's horn. For a moment, the

shape of a wolf hovered behind Rhea. "She does." Dorcha tossed her head.

I crafted a travel spell. Dorcha and Rhea's wolf could rekindle their association later. Maybe at the Nevada guild house if Rhea came along.

"See you soon," I told them and ignited my casting. I'd been willing to help Grigori and the Circle before, but having Dorcha back added a layer of joy to my actions—and my magic. No longer pushing myself to go through the motions, I looked forward to getting to the bottom of who was behind the perfidy aimed at Grigori and his Circle of Assassins.

"It's good to be back," Dorcha whinnied.

I didn't argue; she didn't launch into I-told-you-sos. All in all a solid beginning for us to rebuild trust and whatever else had broken between us.

✻   7   ✻

Ihave a methodical streak, so I rearranged our assigned names into potential geographical regions to make certain we didn't miss anyone and could be as efficient as possible. No one on this list of mages had retained their bond animals; Grigori had severed the linkage when he booted them from the circle. Some of our targets were shifters, but the connection between shifter and mage was far different. For one thing, they lived and died together. Breaking the bond wasn't possible. For another, shifters were born.

As I understood the process, they dreamed their animals from a very young age, and their first shift usually occurred sometime around puberty. In contrast, bond animals were an add-on once a mage reached his or her full magical potential. The animals could veto a particular pairing; neither were they obligated to stick around if their mage engaged in chicanery.

"New list?" Dorcha tapped the page where I'd been creating columns and checking off names.

"Same list. Different order."

"Where are we starting?" the unicorn asked.

"Russia?"

"As good as anywhere. Why there?"

"Quinn and Ciara are going to cover Asia. If we do Russia that whole quadrant of Earth will be finished."

"Possibly finished. Depends on what we find."

I made a few adjustments to my journey spell. Since we had no idea who'd gone where, probably the name list was a waste of time. We'd cover geographic regions and see what turned up, crossing mages off as we located them. The desolate vista of the Kamchatka Peninsula flickered around us. One deserted, rocky, ice-choked bit of shoreline was as good as any other.

The startled bleating of a pod of walruses made me smile. Rolling in blubber, they weren't as dumb as they looked. Dorcha cantered over, and they formed a circle around her. Everyone worshipped at her altar, mortals, mages, and animals alike. Matching their bleats and grunts, she asked about unusual events and mortals who didn't quite fit in.

Brilliant strategy. I'd have used magic to search for mages, a plan I deployed while Dorcha gathered information. My method had holes. Mages could conceal themselves, even from my probing, but animals always had the lowdown on everything in the immediate vicinity.

I wound a layer of warmth around myself since I wasn't dressed for how cold it was. The more I thought about it, the more convinced I became we should mow through every mage we located. They'd all been rotten, or Grigori would have tried to salvage them. I didn't fancy repeating our efforts the next time something like this reared its head, no matter if it was hundreds of years in the future.

The notion caught me up. Had I decided to stick it out with the Circle? I'd never stayed long, not even at the very beginning. Dorcha and I often struck out on our own, returning when we wished. But that was before the Celt bastards sabotaged those like me. I'd buried myself in assignments after that. The more and the bloodier the better. When even they didn't take the edge off my rage, I launched the circus junket.

It had been the beginning of almost losing my bondmate. Thank all the gods—except the Celts—I'd come to my senses in time.

Dorcha trotted nimbly toward me, her hoofs slipping a bit on icy stones littering the beach. The walruses lumbered toward the sea. Clumsy on land, they were grace incarnate once waves supported their bulk.

"We may have found three," she whinnied. "And not far from here."

I offered a terse nod. "Simpler to kill them. Do you agree?"

Surprise flickered across her equine features. "Maybe. Hard to say until we lay eyes on them."

I opened my mouth to argue they'd been found lacking once, but hung onto my words. Dorcha could pluck thoughts from my mind, so final decisions could wait until we took a look at our potential quarries. They might not match up with the fallen mages.

"We'll be ready, though," I told the unicorn. "Even if they aren't ex-Circle assassins..." I left it there. Much evil walked all worlds. I'd made a point of snuffing it out whenever I could. I'd love to point to my deeds and label myself altruistic, but I enjoy killing.

Not randomly, but I've played judge, jury, and executioner so many times I've lost count. The role enriches me, stabilizes me, reminds me someone has to be in charge of cleanup.

Dorcha was weaving a spell together. I leaned against the warmth of her flank and let it take me along, the feel of her magic as familiar as my own. I didn't want to dwell on the past, but I murmured, "Thank you."

"For what?" Intent on her spell, she wasn't mucking around in my head.

"Coming back. Giving us another chance when I didn't deserve it."

"You're important to me too," she said. "Ward us. We're nearly there."

Her warning was timely. The squared-off barracks of an Arctic village came into view. No one would ever accuse modern Russian architecture of being graceful, pleasing to the eye. Its totalitarian aspect was doubly apparent in spots like this where function trumped beauty.

"The ones we're looking for are living among mortals?" I asked softly.

"According to the walrus pod."

It seemed off to me. Most mages wouldn't willingly choose to share space with humans. On occasion, sure, but not as a regular thing. Very little daylight in the northern latitudes this time of year. Threads of twilight were forming in the middle of the afternoon, and the place we stood was mostly deserted.

Dorcha scraped a hoof across the frozen dirt street.

"They're beneath us," she said. A man walking past glanced our way. Clearly, he'd heard us but couldn't see anything. In the fine old Russian tradition of pretending everything was fine even when it wasn't, he picked up his pace and hurried by.

I set a path toward the edge of the settlement. Didn't take long. Squat multistory buildings constructed of what looked like concrete blocks had been arranged in neat rows with a shopping area encased in the center. The village sat in a declination between rolling hills. Mountains beyond faced the ice-choked sea. In summer, a constant rush of waves would pound on rocks, but now everything was frozen.

As I moved, I aimed for a light hand scanning with seeking magic. If I were too obvious, any mage in the area would pack up shop and run—or prepare for battle. We climbed up and over a band of jagged hills and down the other side nearer to the ice shelf extending into the Bering Sea.

Where the terrain on the town side had been relatively smooth, the ocean side was riddled with cliffs. Seabirds swooped and dove, buffeted by a brisk wind. A resident colony of seals were spread on the ice below. Finally, I found what I was looking for and walked into a cave bearing magical residue. The entrance was tall enough Dorcha only needed to scrunch a little.

Getting out of the wind was welcome. It howled around the opening I'd selected, but only a few stray puffs made it through. "We can hope this cave system provides a viable path," I said and tightened my warding. "Or we could teleport."

"We could have done that from where we stood," Dorcha groused.

"I know more now than I did then," I explained.

"I told you where they were," she insisted.

She had, and I'd believed her but wanted to allow my seeking spell full rein. It was still working, and, if it was correct, far more than three mages were somewhere beneath us. At least it confirmed my impression they wouldn't willingly share living space with mortals.

"Yes, you did," I agreed and kindled a mage light. A soft blue glow bounced off icy walls, reflecting colors like a prism. "Let's scout a bit." I started off following the natural line of the cave. It led to another as I'd hoped, and then one more, all the while angling downward. When I glanced at Dorcha, she'd made herself smaller, a handy bit of enchantment in her toolkit.

Footprints marked the dirt suggesting this was a well-used route, except I didn't know by whom. Those with magic would likely teleport in and out most of the time.

Dorcha tapped my shoulder with her horn. I stopped and turned toward her, waiting. "Do you smell that?" she whickered through warm air swirling around us. I'd noticed the temperate air current in the previous cavern and welcomed it.

Tilting my head back, I sampled the air once and then again. The faintest of elemental mage odors teased me. Was the slight breeze in the cavern tossing my own smell back in my face? Seemed unlikely. More likely one of the banished mages had been an earth mage or a sea mage. Air and fire mages had never been part of the Circle.

The next time I sniffed, I couldn't find it. So much for my

theories. "Yes and no," I told Dorcha not sure what to make of what I thought I'd smelled.

Edging around me, she moved faster than I'd been. I cut the flow of power to my seeking spell. We were far too near the other mages for me to have power on the loose. Where the upper cavern walls had been shrouded by ice crystals, it was warmer the lower we traveled. These walls weren't even damp.

Aw crap. Were we headed into Hell?

Whoa. Whole lotta ground between an Arctic cave system and Satan's realm. I hated demons. They made my skin crawl. Because I wasn't paying attention, I pitched into Dorcha's hind end.

Back to her normal size, she'd stopped at the transition point between a corridor and the next cave. I crowded in next to her to see why she'd quit moving. My mage light was still kicking out lumens. I muted it somewhat, so its telltale radiance wouldn't alert anyone.

A tall, slender robed figure strode toward us, the cowl drawn over his head. When he—she?—was maybe fifty feet away I jabbed whoever it was with power. I'd be damned if I'd sit here like a dolt waiting. Dorcha's horn flickered in tones of gold and red as she concentrated her enchantment.

The mage felt my prodding and straightened his shoulders. "By all the gods, Rhiana, has it come to this? You no longer recognize me?"

The results of my magical examination coupled with his voice were like a one-two punch to the midsection that stole my breath. I jettisoned my useless ward and ran past Dorcha as the cowl fell from Shane's head. He hadn't changed in the hundreds of years since I'd seen him. Still wraith thin with gobs of silver hair, stark cheekbones, and penetrating dark eyes, he looked like a cross between a faery and a ghoul.

I stuttered to a halt when a few feet separated us. "This is where you've been?" I demanded. "I thought you'd all left."

"Some of us remained here," he countered. "Others are gone for good."

Dorcha joined me nickering, "Thought I smelled him."

Shane cocked his head to one side. I recognized his expression. I'd become one more problem. No *Aude Lang Syne* for elemental mages. Power arced from his hands, circling my head. Intuiting what he had in mind, I tossed up a ward. "Like hell you'll wipe my mind," I growled.

"I cannot allow you to leave with a memory of me in place." His words were soft despite their implied threat.

I flapped a hand his way. "Who else is here?"

He shook his head. Hair followed the movement, fluffing around his slender shoulders before falling back into place.

"Okay. Answer me this." I tried a different tack. "Are other than elemental mages here?"

"Why?" He answered my question with one of his own.

I sketched out my problem ending with, "I've been part of the Circle of Assassins since before the Celts cut the knees out from under us. I can't stand by and let it fall apart."

Shane puffed out a breath. "Since you have no idea who's behind the attack on Grigori, your plan is to find every mage he kicked out and annihilate them?" Incredulity sharpened his tone.

"Something like that," I muttered. "Simpler than sorting through who's evil and who's not."

"They were all wicked," Dorcha spoke up. "Else Grigori wouldn't have banished them."

Shane's attention landed on her. I felt him assess our connection. A rare smile formed on his gaunt face. The ghoul aspect retreated a little. "Bondmates, eh. Must be interesting."

"It is." At least he'd moved away from slicing and dicing my memories. Encouraged, I said, "You could help us."

"Why would we want to?"

Interesting. He'd said we. Meant my erstwhile kin were still working as a unit. "Are you the only type of mage in this grotto?" I repeated a variant of my earlier question.

"Aye. Some things never change, Rhiana. When did we ever tolerate those with lesser magic?"

His words made me smile. I'd missed being part of something larger than myself. The Circle had made up for some of my loss, but far from all of it. The shades of power circling Dorcha's horn deepened.

"There are ten like him," she said. "And they are drawing near."

I'd been focused on Shane. He'd already declined to tell me more about his companions. Maybe it was enough to know they were here. I'd wondered about their whereabouts for far too long.

"Back to helping me," I said, "you might want to get back into the game."

"I don't think so," he replied. "You signing on with that werewolf wasn't especially popular."

"Yeah, but that was before you found someone bigger and better to hate," I shot back. Before he rehashed the bitter dispute around me and my Circle affiliation, I kept on talking. "Go ahead. Stand there and tell me you didn't want to murder every Celt. They robbed us of our home, our birthright. We had to scatter to avoid being erased from the magical world. I was fortunate to have the Circle to fall back on. All the rest of you dispersed like chess pieces on a tipped-over board."

"Did you even look for us?" Shane's words held an undernote of curiosity.

"Many times. The Celts didn't say they'd harm us, only that no more would be tolerated."

Shane's hands had been clasped behind his back. He dropped them to his sides. It made the fabric of his robe shimmer; it wasn't really black after all. Many colors had been woven into it.

"It's what they said." He sounded tired. "Did you trust them? The rest of us didn't."

I rolled my shoulders back. "I fought them. Me. And Dorcha."

"What'd it buy you?" he inquired.

"Nothing over the long haul," I admitted.

"We had to do something," Dorcha said. "Otherwise, they'd have gotten away with it."

"They did get away with it," Shane pointed out. "We talked about retaliating."

"And?" I stared him down.

"Nothing we could have done would have changed their minds. We couldn't kill them, so what was the point?" Bitter laughter rolled from him. "The irony is they're long gone and we're still cringing under the ice at the ass end of the world."

Back when I'd thought I was the only one left, I'd run aground battering my magic against the Celts enough times to give up. If there'd been more than Dorcha and me, the outcome might have been different.

"You don't know," I said stiffly, "because you didn't even try. I fought them for years—by myself."

Dorcha joined her power with mine, resurrecting my ward and draping it around her too. "The others," she said.

Now that she'd pointed it out, I felt them, their energy faint, subtle, shrouded. They'd formed a circle around us. One thing about elemental mages is we can't lie. We can dance around the truth, but outright lies aren't within our ken.

"Were you chatting it up with us to snare us?" I asked Shane.

He didn't bother with words. A curt nod was all the answer I needed.

"Why?" I snarled and jerry-rigged a teleport spell with Dorcha's and my magic.

"You belong with us, not with a ragtag collection of inferior mages. The unicorn is a plus I hadn't counted on, but we'll keep her too."

Dorcha's outraged whinny echoed off the rounded cavern walls. Her horn took on a redder glow. Had Shane forgotten how powerful unicorns were? How their horns meant death even to those like us?

Mages came into view gliding toward us. White streamers arced from their outstretched arms, effectively forming a power circle with Shane and us in its center. I recognized them all, men and women I'd cut my magical teeth with.

Dorcha neighed a challenge.

I knew what would come next, but I didn't warn Shane. My loyalties lay with my bondmate, and Shane should have known better than to threaten her. Relegating her to a "plus" and stating baldly that he'd keep her like she was some sort of house pet had been mistakes. Fatal ones. I poured power into my getaway spell. The proper moment to launch it was almost here.

Dorcha pranced, her neck arched. A small step to the left, another to the right just before she bolted right for Shane, head lowered, horn aimed at his chest. Nothing magical is faster than a unicorn out for blood. By the time he saw her coming, her horn had impaled his chest. Magic oozed out along with blood.

Power jetted from the other elemental mages, but I was well-warded and the blows bounced off Dorcha's hide. Shocked cries peppered with outrage filled the air. I loosed the casting to move us out of the cave.

"Not so fast," Dorcha yelled at me. "I am not done." My spell guttered, not dead, but not far from it as Dorcha withdrew her share of the magic I'd used to craft our escape.

After yanking her horn free from Shane's lifeless body, she cantered in a full circle eying the other elemental mages. "Anyone else up for telling me I'm a prisoner?" she inquired caustically.

No one so much as made eye contact. "As it should be," the unicorn announced, followed by, "Rhiana and I are going to walk out of here the same way we walked in. You will not impede our progress."

Since she had their attention, I added, "You should be ashamed of yourselves. The Celtic gods are long gone. You owe it to all worlds to raise the banner of our lineage and employ your power for good."

With blood still dripping from her horn, Dorcha executed an about face and set a brisk pace for the upper caverns. I trotted after her. Emotions took turns jockeying for position. Disgust at my kin for checking out trumped everything else.

A teensy part of me felt sorry for them. They'd allowed themselves to become anachronisms.

I tried to find some guilt for Shane's death but couldn't. Maybe his loss would jerk the others out of their self-righteous rut. If I let myself dwell on events in the lower cavern, I'd be crushed. I'd nurtured dreams of someday being reunited with my own kind.

Ha. It would never happen.

We reached the uppermost cave, the one with ice coating the walls, sooner than I expected. "Not much progress with the list," I gritted.

"Progress is relative," my bondmate said and placed her horn on my shoulder. "You've wondered about the other elemental mages forever."

"No more," I muttered. "They're not worth my time."

"No, they aren't," Dorcha agreed. "What happened to them?"

"I have no idea." Starting from scratch I reconstructed a teleport spell.

"Where next?" Dorcha asked.

"The Russian steppes. We'll stand in the middle and use seeking magic to lure whomeer we find."

In other days, other times, my life would have been forfeit for Shane's death. Not that I'd caused it, but our laws would have viewed my bondmate and me as complicit. In the midst of my journey spell, I shrugged it off. Not only could I not latch onto guilt, I also didn't give a fuck. Shane had signed his own death warrant.

"Are you sorry I killed him?" Dorcha asked in her usual matter-of-fact approach to everything.

"Once, I would have been. Not anymore. No excuse for

them abdicating responsibility for everything. They forgot what it means to be an elemental mage."

"Probably exactly what the Celts had in mind," Dorcha whinnied.

I draped an arm around her arched neck. Wise of her to recognize the best way to cut the heart out of anyone is to render their existence meaningless.

Grigori had told me to look for other elemental mages. Turned out, they'd found me. Or maybe we'd found each other. Fate was funny like that.

My casting faded, spitting us out on the grassy steppes of Central Russia. Outside of a herd of spooked sheep and a pissed-off herding dog, no one noticed our arrival.

I didn't waste time; we'd already done enough of that. Dorcha kept a path open to her power as we searched far and wide. Still keyed up from the brush with others like me, I pounced on the first hint of foreign magic and jumped back into the travel channel I hadn't totally closed off. We could have walked, but this was quicker.

If the mage in question looked cross-eyed at me, they'd rue the day they ever picked up a spell book.

8

After fucking with us, luck ran our way—for a while.

Dorcha and I make one hell of a team. We mowed through half a dozen mages. I recognized all of them from their time in the Circle. Guess Dorcha signed up for my worldview, which was may as well knock them out of the game while we had them front and center.

She'd said she needed to lay eyes on them, but we came out swinging and never backed off. There's something clean and elegant about ridding the world of garbage. I didn't bother with conversation. Probably should have. No way to know if they were part of the Circle's current problems.

Next time, I promised myself.

The creepy, uncomfortable residue from Shane's death had receded. Not that Dorcha should have had any doubts about me backing her no matter what, but today cemented any remaining holes in our bond. After consigning a dead druid and witch to magefire, we stood on the northern shores of Lake Baikal, Neither magic-wielder had deserved to live, but I'd be damned if I'd leave their magic lying about for the other side to harvest and redirect.

"We should get back," I said after doing a quick-and-dirty time adjustment. The Nevada guild house was roughly twelve hours off from our location. Should get back was an understatement since we were already a couple of hours late.

Dorcha shook her head and poured more enchantment into the roaring flames. She was correct. We had to wait until the fire was well and truly out. Otherwise someone could glean information about us from the fire's components. It wasn't a skill I'd ever mastered, but the Fae were gifted at interpreting magefire.

Dancing flames contain a mesmerizing aspect. They cleared my mind as they swirled and leapt. Magefire has its own timetable. It burns what it was instructed to, period. None of the nearby stunted bushes had so much as a charred leaf.

Distant howling had been a constant since we'd arrived here. Louder than it had been, it held a haunting quality. Wolves on the prowl are creatures of beauty. Intense and loyal, they'd make good role models for just about anyone.

Dorcha tossed her head, scenting the air. Surely, she'd smelled wolves the moment our teleport spell dropped us here. Following her lead, my nostrils twitched. I snorted. How could I have missed the alteration? Werewolves had joined the others.

Not many. Two, or perhaps three. The resident wolf pack was amazingly tolerant of non-pack. They had to be able to tell the difference. My fire was close enough to done, I drew water from the air and doused the remaining cinders. No more reason to remain, but I wasn't quite quick enough.

An enormous silver werewolf loped toward us. In a hurry, but pretending not to be. When he drew near, he shifted midstride into a substantial, broad-shouldered man garbed in ragged blue trousers, beat-up leather boots, and a faded green jacket zipped partway up his chest. His hair was close cropped and the same silvery tone his pelt had been. His squared-off jaw was covered with gray stubble. Odd eyes, one blue and the other green, regarded Dorcha and me.

I didn't bother comparing him with my list. Grigori has always been the only werewolf in the Circle. Until Rhea came along, that is. Dorcha wheeled to face him, her horn lowered in warning.

He stopped and bowed low. After he straightened, he said, "Hold, Madam Unicorn. Grigori asked me to check on you. Apparently, you're late for a meeting."

I narrowed my eyes. Grigori had severed his ties with his kinsmen. How did this werewolf know so much about his business. Furthermore, why would Grigori confide in anyone about any of us. Dorcha must have come to a similar conclusion because she whinnied. Harsh and shrill, she was letting him know it wouldn't take much to convince her to charge.

I took a step forward and stretched to my full height. I wasn't as tall as him, but neither was I far off. "Who are you?"

"Xander."

I didn't offer my name in return. "How do you know Grigori?"

He gave a curt nod. "Fair enough. No reason for you to

trust me. Thanks for dealing with them." He flicked his fingers at the ash pile.

I arched my brows, waiting. If he didn't pony up information quickly, Dorcha and I would be gone. Her horn was still in attack position, but she wasn't on the verge of springing at the werewolf like she had been.

A corner of the werewolf's mouth turned downward. I tried not to notice how well-formed his lips were, chiseled and dripping sensuality. "Grigori and I go back a long way, to before the Circle of Assassins was even a glimmer of a notion in his mind."

Grigori had lived in this region before he'd been turned. I remembered that much. Spinning one hand in a get-on-with it gesture, I waited. Dorcha trotted toward me and stood with her shoulder touching mine, still intent on the werewolf.

"Thought we needed to be gone from here," she said into my mind. The were would hear her, but her statement wasn't classified information.

"We do," I said aloud. Shifting my gaze to the werewolf, I said, "Either you're going to tell us. Or not. Which is it?" I activated a truth spell. It was obvious, and a clear invitation to spit something out. Or to remain silent if he hadn't been forthright.

"He and I were pack," Xander said.

The words pinged cleanly off my spell. All right. Fine. They'd belonged to the pack Grigori renounced. So what? "You've no more need of us," I said. "You delivered your message. We're on our way out of here. And you're welcome for them." I nodded at the smoldering ashes.

"I'm traveling with you," Xander announced.

"The hell you are," I retorted. "If you're all that close to Grigori, find him on your own."

Dorcha had a spell at the ready. She'd built it while I dredged information out of the werewolf. Not that I'd gotten much beyond his name. My words had scarcely left my throat when the jagged shoreline disappeared, traded for the darkness of a journey spell.

"What was that all about?" Dorcha asked.

I puffed out a breath. "Only two possibilities. He's who he says, and Grigori reached out to him."

"What's the other?"

More breath formed clouds in the cold air. "Word of our earlier, erm, exploits traveled, and someone tracked us."

"I thought of that," Dorcha nickered. "What I couldn't ascertain was why. Besides Xander wasn't even considering harming us."

I glanced at the unicorn. "You pilfered from his mind."

"Of course. I always do when I'm deciding if I want to kill someone."

My eyes may have widened. News to me despite all the years we'd spent together. "What'd you find in Shane's mind?"

Air burbled through her nose, making a popping sound. "If I hadn't known you for so long, I'd have chalked elemental mages off my list of acceptable magic wielders."

"Not exactly an answer."

"He viewed you as property and me as inconsequential. One step up from a pet dog or cat." The stream of air turned into braying, and she sounded like a donkey. "I'd have preferred to draw out his death, ensure he understood where he'd gone wrong, but we had higher obligations."

Shane's death hadn't been weighing on me, but after

hearing Dorcha's assessment I was glad he was dead. No one demeaned my bondmate without consequences. A stray thought reared up and forced me to examine it.

Had he manufactured mental content hoping Dorcha would do exactly as she had? "Maybe he was tired," I murmured.

"Doesn't excuse him." Dorcha clacked her teeth together.

I fanned out the fingers of one hand and touched them as I counted off what I knew. "That group of elemental mages vanished shortly after the Celts' proclamation. Means they've been hunkered in that grotto for centuries. Probably, they've downplayed their magic. At first, it would have been to ensure they remained hidden, but living without power became a habit."

I stopped to take a breath. "They must have been miserable. Shane saw a way out and took it. Kind of like what mortals call suicide by cop."

"Except you're almost impossible to kill," Dorcha mumbled and stamped a hoof. "Did he manipulate me? Force me to end him?"

"I don't know anything for certain, only it would be unlikely for him to underestimate you. We all had the same lessons about magical creatures."

"That unprincipled bastard." Another hoof stamp.

"What's done is done. If he was truly weary of everything, you may have done the others a favor. He'd clearly adopted a leadership role. With him out of the way, the rest of them will pick a more fruitful path. Hopefully."

Our spell was winding down. The dry sage-laden air of the high desert filled my lungs before we tumbled out in front of the guild house. Not as grand as the off-world one, this structure resembled a rustic hunting lodge.

Grigori ran toward us. "Thanks be to all the gods you're all right. I expected you hours ago. Quinn and Ciara are working the western US. They'd planned on South America, but wanted to be close if you weren't back in a few more hours."

"We're fine," I said, touched by his concern. He's never been the papa bear type. Perhaps his illness had wrought a few changes in his personality.

"Who's Xander?" Dorcha whinnied.

"Means he found you," Grigori said.

"Pfft, more than found us, he wanted to hitch a ride on our teleport spell," I said.

"Which you refused." Grigori looked as if he were squelching a smile.

"Of course." I launched into who we'd killed, wanting to get the reporting part out of the way.

Grigori's always been a decent listener. When I stopped talking, he said, "What'd you leave out?"

I rolled my eyes. Somehow he always knew. "Nothing relevant to the Circle," I replied.

"We found a herd of elemental mages," Dorcha told him.

Grigori's russet brows shot up. "And?"

"They're not worth breath discussing," I growled.

He nodded. "All right. None of my affair."

"Did you send Xander to look for us?" Dorcha asked.

"I did."

"Any idea why he wanted to return with us?" I pressed.

"Why don't you ask me?" another voice chimed in just before the silver werewolf waltzed through a portal that hadn't been there moments before. His tail plumed, and his ears were pricked forward.

"You followed us?" I shook a fist his way, my voice shrill with accusation.

"I asked nicely to come with you. You refused, so I resorted to other methods."

"What other methods?" Dorcha pranced in front of him, horn angled between the wolf's eyes.

Feeling protective of Grigori, I placed my body between him and the other werewolf. Grigori dropped a hand on my shoulder. "Appreciate the thought, but Xander made me what I am. Because I am his, he can always find me, but the reverse is true as well. I assumed you were somewhere reasonably near his pack, so when you were late and I couldn't raise you, I tagged him."

Xander skirted around Dorcha, aiming for Grigori. As he moved, he traded one form for another. Reaching Grigori, he wrapped his arms around him. "It's been too long," he said in Russian.

"I am no longer pack," Grigori reminded him.

"You will always be mine, pack affiliation or not."

Grigori ducked from the other man's embrace. "Not what you said when I refused to turn the Circle over to you."

"Eh, I was younger then. Full of hubris." He faced Dorcha and me and bowed much as he had on the shores of Lake Baikal. "Who do I have the pleasure of meeting?"

Even with Grigori's explanation, I still hesitated. Long enough, Grigori said, "Meet Rhiana and her bondmate, Dorcha."

"Elemental mage," Xander said smoothly. "I thought all of you left for less critical pastures."

"Some of us did," I replied stiffly, damned if I'd tell him jack about my run-in with Shane and the others.

"Come inside," Grigori invited.

"We really should get back to it," I mumbled.

"You just got here. Your power must be depleted. I insist on food and rest before you leave again."

I may have rolled my eyes. "What happened to the days when you booted us out the door with a job and didn't micromanage every aspect?"

"Aye, well they crashed and burned after someone tried to kill me."

"Kill you?" Outrage lined Xander's words. "And you didn't call on me? Why?"

Dorcha butted me with her shoulder and crossed the courtyard toward the front steps. I can take a hint. Whatever Grigori had to say to his maker didn't require an audience. I was perched on a barstool quaffing beer and eating cheese and salami and olives and crackers when the two werewolves strolled into the dining room.

Dorcha had taken one look at the selection of food and hightailed it back outside, presumably to hunt. I raised my flagon and thanked Grigori for making it easy to refuel. More footsteps announced Quinn and Ciara.

"You're back!" Quinn loped to me and swatted me across the shoulders.

"What happened?" Ciara asked and dropped a cracker into her mouth. Quinn handed her a beer before popping the lid on another for himself.

I was getting good at the expurgated version of events, so I walked them through where we'd gone. This time, I included Shane et al. As sea and earth mages, they had a a right to know their prototype hadn't completely vanished from Earth.

The eagles weren't around. Presumably, they'd joined Dorcha and were running game to ground.

"Aw crap. That's rough," Ciara said. "Were you and this Shane person close?"

I shook my head. "After all the time that's passed, I scarcely know any of them."

Xander pried my empty glass from my hand, replacing it with a full one. Because I didn't pour it over his head, he promptly dragged a stool over and plopped onto it. "Did you want something?" I asked.

"To get to know you better." He'd switched from Russian to English. "Grigori says you play a passable harp. It's an instrument I enjoy as well."

"The two of you talked about me?" I looked from one werewolf to the other, nonplussed.

"Time for us to make up plates and find our room," Quinn announced.

"No need," I told him. "Besides, I haven't heard what you and Ciara accomplished."

"We did much the same as you," Ciara said between bites of cheese and crackers. "Found a few and did away with them. Would have been convenient to have Dorcha's horn. We had to kill the old-fashioned way, and it slowed us down."

Grigori chuckled, but without mirth. "I should have done more than liberate their bond animals when I kicked them out of the Circle."

"Yeah, it would have helped," I told him.

Between Quinn and Ciara and me, we'd dispatched a dozen, but the list held over a hundred names. Maybe killing all of them was a waste of time. It would be even more of a production, though, to determine who was complicit in the scheme against the Circle.

And so I was back to where I'd begun. Kill first and don't bother with questions.

Rhea strode into the room, beaming broadly. "I'm so glad you and Dorcha are back," she told me. "Grigori was worried about you."

"He never used to worry about anyone," I mumbled, realized I sounded like an ingrate, and added, "Sorry."

"Sure I did," he corrected me. "You never knew about it, though."

I'd had enough, so I dropped to my feet and pushed the stool back beneath the bar. "Give me an hour, and I'll get back to it."

I headed for the door. While Grigori's concern was a welcome change, still it annoyed me since it added one more layer to an already difficult task. Xander caught up before I crossed beneath the lintel. "Walk with me for a bit," he suggested, the words laced with compulsion.

I didn't want to be overtly rude to Grigori's sire, or whatever werewolves called their makers, so I waited until we'd cleared the dining room and the great room beyond before I turned to him. "I'm in the middle of a job, and I'm tired. Spit out what you want so I can address it and move on."

"You intrigue me."

I blinked stupidly, sure I hadn't heard him right. "But that's absurd. You've met me exactly once for a few minutes when my unicorn was considering killing you."

"We all have to start somewhere."

"You're nuts." I tossed my head to avoid looking at him. I had Dorcha. I didn't need anyone else, no matter how well built they were. No matter how light played in the silver of their hair. No matter how their earthy scent, replete with pine and rain-wet earth soothed and inflamed at the same time.

"No. Not crazy," he replied, sounding amused. "What I am is old and alone. Two qualities we share. Grigori told me I was wasting my time, but I can be stubborn when I come across someone special."

I crossed my arms under my breasts. "How often do you stumble across special?"

"Never. It's why I have to at least try."

I'd been prepared to mock him. The males I've known fell in lust several times a month. His interest in me couldn't run deeper than a stiff cock.

Unsure how to respond, I regarded him. He met my gaze before going on, "While you rest, consider allowing me to accompany you and the unicorn when you leave to hunt. You'll find me competent and resourceful. Our magic should slot together nicely."

"It's not only up to me." I was grasping at straws.

"I understand. Once you leave to rest, I will talk with your bondmate."

"You'll do no such thing," I sputtered.

"Oh but I will—unless she refuses to listen."

Raising my mind voice, I called Dorcha. Damn Xander to fucking hell. A small part of me was flattered, but the rest was determined to put this puppy to bed before it turned into a thorn in my side. I could barely deal with myself some days. Last thing I needed was a love interest.

"Hunting," drifted back to me.

"I need you here," I insisted.

After a short pause during which she scoured my mind, she replied, *"The werewolf can come with us. I have no objections."*

Xander dusted his hands together. "That excuse fell apart. What's your next move?"

Trapped between fury, embarrassment, and unexpected flickers of sexual heat from all the pheromones he was pumping out, I didn't trust myself to speak. Turning on my heel, I stormed down the hallway. To his credit, he didn't laugh or shout anything about winning this round. He also didn't follow me. Wise of him. Wasting magic to salve my pride was stupid, but the mood I was in, I'd have let him have it.

9

I hadn't expected to sleep, but I passed into a deep trance right after I located a bedroom, taking care to lock the door. It was foolish. No lock can keep anyone magical out. When I rolled to a sit, at least a couple of hours had elapsed. I did feel better, more balanced, but I was disappointed Dorcha had hung me out to dry.

Like as not, she hadn't understood what was at stake. In her equine mind, another magic-wielder would make our task that much quicker. She was correct, if he didn't have ulterior motives.

Grudging respect surfaced. He could have been coy. Instead, he'd showed his cards—most of them—and handed the next move to me. I took a quick shower and slithered back into my dirty clothes. They stank of blood and every type of mage we'd done away with. No need to be clean to return to the field.

A soft knock sounded on my door as I was tying my

boots. I sent a reflexive burst of magic to see who it was. Grigori's distinctive magic pulsed back at me. Was I relieved or disappointed? The question wasn't simple to answer. To avoid dealing with it, I called, "Come in."

He closed the door behind him. "Ready to go?"

I nodded. "Thanks for the respite. I could have done without, but it was welcome."

"Eh, you were dead on your feet. That run-in with your kinsmen couldn't have been easy." He skewered me with his blue eyes, and I shrugged. That ship had sailed. I'd moved on.

He set his mouth in a terse line. "You're tough as old leather, Rhiana, but soft places reside beneath. You slipped up and showed them when Dorcha was gone."

"Your point?" Before he could answer, I blurted, "If this is about Xander, stay out of it. He hasn't done anything wrong, but he's not my type."

"Do you have a type?" Grigori raised a red brow.

I couldn't help myself; a chuckle burst out followed by a couple more. "Sure. Unicorns are my thing."

"Then you won't mind Xander tagging along with you and Dorcha. I have no idea why you and Quinn and Ciara decided the only good banished mage is a dead one, but the path you've chosen will take longer than I had in mind. And it has one serious drawback."

"Yeah. Already considered it," I told him. "It leaves us with a vacuum where information is concerned."

He nodded. "Aye. You're going to have to either pirate information from their minds before you kill them, or get them to talk with you. Either path adds still more time. You probably already know this, but werewolves are skilled mind-readers."

"So's Dorcha," I countered. "Why not send Xander with Quinn and Ciara?"

"You know the answer to that," Grigori replied.

"Um, yeah. He wants to come with me." I pursed my lips into a scowl. "He made that abundantly clear last night."

"He's used to running things, but he's agreed to play off your lead."

"And that's supposed to make me feel better?" I made a face, and then felt foolish for acting juvenile.

Grigori crossed his arms over his chest. "How you feel is none of my concern. You have a task to do. Grab some food and get moving. If things go well, we'll be done with Earth in the next twenty-four hours, and then you can move on to the borderworlds."

He was gone before I could argue. I plodded out of my bedroom and sent streamers of magic behind me to make the bed and clear up any residual mess I'd left. I wasn't especially hungry, and I resented being painted into a corner. Grigori had assigned me work partners before, but none of them had made it obvious they were sticking around because I fascinated them.

I'd have skipped breakfast, but it was bad for my magic, so I choked down nuts, an energy bar, and a large cup of coffee. Remembering how cold it had been at our last locations, I grabbed a warm coat from the guild house wardrobe and set a path for outside.

Dorcha and Xander were standing in the courtyard chatting it up thick as thieves. His boots were the same, but he'd changed into tan pants that showcased his long legs. A green fleece shirt was topped by a well-worn leather vest. He raised a hand in greeting. Dorcha nickered at me. Didn't seem to be the time to rebuke them for plotting behind my back. They weren't. Not really, but Xander was wise. He was worming his way into Dorcha's affections, so I couldn't use her as an excuse to shut him out of my life.

The "my unicorn doesn't like you" justification was a nonstarter.

"Where are Quinn and Ciara?" I asked.

"Long gone," Xander replied. "They had farther to travel than us today, so they got an early jump on things."

On the heels of his words, I remembered they had South American in their gunsights. "We're finishing up with North America, right?" I held Dorcha's gaze.

"Grigori said it was up to us," the unicorn whinnied.

I chewed my lower lip, not exactly looking at Xander, but sizing him up. "We've never worked together—" I began.

"He'll figure it out," Dorcha cut in. "He's been the head of a werewolf pack since before Grigori was made."

Shit. Aw shit. Between sleeping and chatting with Grigori and stopping for coffee, I'd left far too big a window for Xander to make an impression on Dorcha. "Hope you're right," I mumbled and set a spell in motion to move us to the center of the US. From there, we'd fan power in an arc looking for our prey. We could have done the same thing from our current location, but our accuracy wouldn't be as solid for the East Coast.

A small, petty part of me considered telling Xander he could get there on his own, but Grigori had added him to the team. Leaving teammates to fend for themselves was tacky.

Fine. I'd get through this. Xander would weary of the game soon enough, and then it would be Dorcha and me again. Power ricocheted from hand to hand. "Ready?" I asked.

It was rhetorical, but snatching someone into a journey spell without any warning was rude.

"Never readier." Xander sounded jovial.

Good that he was having fun. I wasn't. I can't shield my thoughts from Dorcha, but I did from him. So far, she hadn't asked what was wrong with me. We'd worked with other mages—and their bond animals—hundreds of times. Why was I so twisted out of shape over Xander?

My spell dumped us in the middle of thousands of acres of wheat. Since it was winter, the fields were barren, but farmers weren't out and about, either. After scraping burned stalks out of the way, I initiated a search to the north and east and jotted Xs in the dirt in the rough direction of what I sensed. Dorcha used her horn to make notations. Xander added marks too.

I counted twenty-five, a respectable haul if most had been connected to the Circle. "We could each take a few," I suggested.

A surprised snort from Dorcha revealed how unusual my proposal was. We usually stuck together when we worked.

"I only bite when I'm provoked," Xander jested. The image of a wolf formed behind him, vanishing almost as quickly as it had arrived.

His tone lightened my bleak mood. I'd driven myself into a fine old funk, and for nothing. It wasn't as if Grigori had sent a babysitter along to keep an eye on me. Xander had probably hatched up this arrangement with Grigori to ensure he'd be included.

Left to my own devices, I'd have turned him down cold.

I'd been using a broken off wheat stalk to draw in the

charcoal-streaked dirt. Circling a group of Xs, I said, "Let's start here. Lot of targets."

"Works for me," Xander said. "I'll manage the magic to get us there."

It played hell with my control freak side, but I mumbled, "Okay," and jumped astride Dorcha. The warmth of her calmed me, reminded me why we were here. What was it about the werewolf that rattled me? No excuses for my power. It's on a par with anyone's, including the gods'.

I didn't want to relax into his journey spell, but his power was enough like Grigori's, I found myself enjoying the ride. And kicking myself for letting my guard down. We emerged in the frozen tangled wilderness of northern Wisconsin in the midst of hundreds of icy choked lakes. Glad I'd had the presence of mind to borrow a jacket from the guild house, I zipped it to my chin and tugged the hood into place.

A cross between a yodel and a wolf's howl emerged from Xander. What was he doing? Warning our quarry? Before I could ask, the air thickened with the smell of werewolves. Some dropped through portals; others loped close. All of them dipped their heads to Xander. I took it as a gesture of deference. The air around him developed a liquid aspect, and the werewolves acquired an attentive aspect, ears pricked forward, before they packed up and ran to the north.

"What was that about?" I asked.

"Saving us time," he said.

I shook my head. "Uh-uh. Not how this works. I didn't want you along in the first place, and I'll tell Grigori to make other arrangements if you're not more forthcoming. Why'd you summon them, and where are they off to?"

"I want to know too," Dorcha chimed in.

Breath puffed from between my teeth, forming a fine mist in the cold air. The unicorn hadn't totally drunk the Kook-aide, if she was demanding answers to the same questions as me. Still astride, I sank my fingers into her pelt, warming them.

"Fair enough," Xander agreed. "I sent them to alert their brothers and their brothers' brothers. They will search Canada and the Arctic."

"And then what?" I spun a hand impatient to get to work.

"They will do the same things as us," he replied. "Locate mages, determine if they are on the list you and Quinn developed, and act accordingly."

"Is that a fancy way to say they'll kill them?" I pressed for details.

"It depends. If they're not an immediate threat, and pulling information from their minds was simple, they'll release them."

"You should have discussed this with one of us, first," I told him.

His surprised expression was genuine. "Why?"

"Because we're working together. You know, on the same side, batting for the same team. Did you run this little sidebar past Grigori?"

He shook his head. "How could I have? I only just now thought of it myself."

Anger simmered. Before it hit a boil, I jumped down from Dorcha and planted myself in front of him. "I get it you're trying to help, but teams have leaders for a reason. When it's just Dorcha and me, we don't stand on formality, but when we work with other mages, there is one."

I blew out a breath. "In this instance, it's my team not

your pack. You took advantage of your relationship with Grigori to bulldoze your way in, and—"

"You're absolutely correct. Apologies." He'd said the right words, but they didn't appease me.

"Call them back." I jerked my chin upward.

"Can't put that genie back into the bottle. Sorry."

"Why not?"

Dorcha prodded my upper arm with the side of her horn. "Hash it out later," she said.

I unclenched my jaw before I broke a tooth. "No more unilateral troop deployment," I told him. "If you want to pull shit like that, sign up for someone else's group. Not mine."

The unicorn hooted a warning. No horses in this frozen wasteland, but I bet there were snowy owls. I sent magic scudding in a circle and growled, "Fucking great." While Xander had been recruiting werewolves to his bidding, our presence had been detected. Magic surged toward us. I picked Fae and Sidhe from the mix. Maybe a Druid or two, but their power is so pallid, it's sometimes difficult to pinpoint.

Dorcha faced one way; I set my back against her rump and faced the other. When I glanced about for Xander, a wolf stood in his stead. Hackles ran the length of his back, and his fangs were bared. Obviously, he was used to being in charge, issuing orders as natural as breathing.

What in the hell had he expected? That I was a total pushover, and he'd slide into his commander-in-chief role without me batting an eye? Mages strode toward us. I upped my estimate of their numbers as they drew near. The dozen I'd thought we faced had grown to at least thirty.

"What in the hell are all of you doing out here?" I shouted.

A Fae I'd known long ago ambled closer. "Still dancing to Grigori's bidding, eh?" he taunted.

"When it coincides with my needs, Torin," I replied.

Clad in only a thin pale-blue robe, he tossed a mane of violet hair over his slender shoulders and regarded me from milk-white eyes. Seer's eyes, except he wasn't blind. Deep red wings were folded across his back. He flapped a hand my way. "Go. We didn't request your presence."

Dorcha wheeled around until she faced him, horn at the ready.

With nothing but instinct driving me, I asked, "Why do you have it in for the Circle?"

I'd expected staunch denials. What I hadn't anticipated was ringing laughter. "Took you long enough to figure it out," he chortled. "Our planning spans better than a hundred fifty years."

I leveled my gaze his way. Could I have gotten lucky? Struck pay dirt and located the epicenter of Grigori's problems?

"Eh. Sometimes I'm slow on the uptake. When did you decide to take on the Circle?"

"You never did listen well," he sneered. "I just told you."

I sidestepped past his barbed comment. "Care to share why?"

"Grigori was always too self-important and full of bullshit. He fancied himself better than the rest of us, but his magic was inferior. Even worse, he knew it and pretended otherwise. Did you know his own pack kicked him out? Didn't faze him so long as he had a bunch of underlings to order around."

A low menacing growl emerged from Xander. Torin redirected his gaze and spat in the dirt. "Great. Another one.

Grigori didn't use to be in the habit of adding weres to the Circle. I always figured they were too smart to put up with his crap."

The other mages were edging steadily nearer. I extended both hands and turned in a slow circle. "Stop. Right. There." I infused compulsion into my command. It should have been the end of it, but they kept on coming. More slowly, but how were they still moving? Nothing wrong with my magic. Sparks shot from Dorcha's horn as she tested the mages nearest her.

A high, shrill whinny dripped with disgust. "You sold your miserable hides to darkness."

No one contradicted her.

"How widespread is this...?" I floundered about searching for a word that fit.

"What you should be asking," Torin said smugly, "is if the Circle is our only target. I'll save you the trouble. The answer is no."

Xander's hackles had edged up another inch. He was growling louder.

"Why?" I asked.

"Your time is over." Torin shook a clenched fist to punctuate his statement. "Ours is just beginning. A new breed of mage will rise to meet the needs of a new era. Good and evil are anachronisms, tired old constructs. We scrapped everything, built our strategy from the ground up, and—"

Xander sprang. While Torin had been boasting, the werewolf had crept close enough to drive the Fae to the ground. One snap of his jaws separated Torin's head from his neck. Blood spurted, coating Xander's muzzle, head, and shoulders. Unlike the Fae blood I was used to, this held black tinges courtesy of whatever deal he'd cut with demons.

Maybe demons. Who in the hell knew what had transpired. Torin, always a braggart, had been in a chatty mood, but Xander had enough and had cut his fountain of information off at its roots.

Wild whoops filled the air. The other mages mobbed us. Three against thirty are shit odds, but I couldn't blame this fight on Xander. They'd have attacked no matter what. I sent lethal magic flying in a wide arc. Dorcha charged, head lowered, as she gored one mage after the next.

They wisely decided she was a bigger threat than Xander or me, so they surrounded her, jabbing and chopping until her black fur was clotted with blood. I couldn't kill fast enough to keep them from hurting her. Fury drove me, anger at the damage mages I'd known were inflicting on Dorcha.

Rearing, she used her hoofs to trample and her horn to impale. Still, mages kept coming. Shit. Thirty had been the tip of the iceberg. I heard the snap of Xander's jaws as he dispatched mages who'd been poisoned by cheap rhetoric.

I'm far from an alarmist, but we weren't exactly winning this battle. Hell, we weren't even holding our own. For every mage we killed, three more sprang up to take his place.

"Now would be the time for reinforcements," I shouted at Xander.

"Thought you'd never ask." His jaws were full, so he resorted to mind speech.

Something swatted me from behind. I staggered, and, before I could recover, another blow pushed me facedown on the ice. Jagged shards chopped the fuck out of my face. I couldn't rise. Too much weight held me down. Grappling behind me, I shot power into where mages held me in place. It bounced back at me, turning my arms to a burning mess of agony. How had they redirected my power, using it against me?

The weight wasn't just on my torso. I couldn't move my head. Or my legs. What in the hell was going on? I heard Dorcha's frantic neighs and the wolf's snarls, and then searing pain battered the back of my head. I grabbed onto my fleeing consciousness with everything in me, but it left anyway.

❧ 10 ❧

I fought the sensation of twisting and falling and spinning end over end. Blacking out had been far easier than this. Instinctual, primal, my warding remained in place. More or less. If it hadn't, my magic would have peeled away. I've been in crappy spots before, but no one has ever gone after my power. Nausea racked me from more than the constant unpredictable whirling.

Elemental mages are legendary. Or we were. Whoever was behind the rude assault on me might not know what I am. If they did, they didn't give a crap. Used to other mages giving me a wide berth because I terrified them, I gritted my teeth. If there was a new game in town, it wasn't one I liked much. I splatted against something, jarring my spine before bouncing off and falling another few hundred feet.

It had to be illusion. I was caught up in someone else's spell. They'd captured my body, but I was proving a tougher nut to crack than they'd anticipated. The next point of contact was my head. Brains rattled from one side of my skull to the other; a headache bloomed behind my eyes.

When I caught a glimpse of my hands, they'd curled into useless fists. Nothing to fight against. Not that way. Most of my magic was hobbled behind my warding. Eerie laughter ebbed and flowed. Awk. Who was laughing at me? Who had the guts? When I got out of this, I'd...

Got to get out first, a stern inner voice reminded me.

Where were Xander and Dorcha? When I searched for their magic, I couldn't find them. Did it mean I'd moved to another plane? To a place where they weren't? Who had the power to finesse something like that?

Wasn't I the original twenty questions girl? None of them mattered. No one was going to bail me out. If it was going to happen, it already would have. Dorcha would lay waste to the world to save me. That she hadn't managed it was significant.

I took stock of my power. It was still in reasonably good shape, so I chinked a small hole in my ward to create a channel to fire through. Putrid black barbs stuffed into the opening, the stench horrendous. A tentacle waggled in a circular motion as it worked to widen the hole. With laser precision, I chopped it off and slathered power over the gap.

A muted groan suggested I'd caused someone pain. Good. Before this was over, I'd do a whole lot more damage. I hoped. Sealed into my bubble, I was panting. Sour-smelling sweat dripped down my sides. My brief respite from being tossed around like a rag doll stuttered to a halt, and I began rocking from side to side before I was turned upside down.

Bile splashed the back of my throat. I swallowed it. I'd be damned if I was going to puke all over myself, and, at the rate I was twirling about, anything emerging from my body could have ended up anywhere. Pushing seeking threads through my ward was tough. Fighting through its protective layers next to impossible. I could lob a javelin or two, making certain the ward closed behind each, but it would drain me quickly. No guarantees I'd hit anything, either. I pushed my palms against my throbbing forehead.

I'm an intuitive fighter. Defense comes naturally without fanfare. What was standing in the way now? Someone had made an end run on my power, but they hadn't stolen any. I should be more on top of this, but I didn't feel the slightest bit anxious. My earlier panic had ceded to resignation. Was I inhaling something designed to pacify me?

Too late, I tested the air. When the capsule—or whatever I was suspended in—chucked me to the right, all was well. To the left, a poppy derivative surrounded me. I couldn't smell it, but the difference was palpable once I searched. Paying attention to when to breathe wore on me, but my reward was a clearer head.

No closer to escape, at least I had a prayer of hatching a plan. One that might work. Could I teleport out of here? It was far too simple, but I tried anyway. It wouldn't cost me much. Predictably, my casting boomeranged back in my face, the pushback vivid enough to make stars burst across my visual field. The same laughter that had taunted me before was back.

Fucker. Bastard.

I welcomed anger rushing through me. If I couldn't teleport, my next move would be to break the bonds holding me prisoner. The poppy juice had been subtle, mostly hidden. Locating the tethers keeping me in the gyrating airspace was far more difficult.

I had to identify them all. If I missed even one, it would be enough for my enemies to hastily resurrect the ones I'd clipped. Next time, they'd be more vigilant. Eventually, I'd run out of magic, and then I'd be screwed.

Don't go there, I told myself and engaged in a methodical search. I covered my body three times, feeling my way with magic. The last run-through didn't reveal anything new. Was it good enough?

"Gonna have to be," I mumbled.

Setting blast points to coincide with the five spots holding me prisoner, I waited until I was certain they'd explode simultaneously. I had no idea where I'd end up, but so long as it wasn't here, I'd take it. No next moves until I was successful with the first one.

No reason to check again. The first couple of practice runs were prudent, but it was time to rock and roll. I took a deep breath to steady myself, realized it had been on the poppy side, and huffed it out.

"Steady." I spoke aloud and then did a silent countdown. No reason to warn my captors I was anything but nicely drugged.

Three. Two. One.

I dropped my ward. The detonation from my spell jerked me from side to side. The tether points give way one by one, but they were taking too long. I added magic to the last two, urging them to snap. The moment they did, I rolled into a teleport channel I had at the ready.

My lungs burned. My throat was raw. My head pounded. My vision swam, but I was free. Or I thought I was. On my knees, I sucked air like a drowning person and hoped to hell it wasn't laced with poison. My escape had cost almost all my magic. It shouldn't have. My usually sharp mind was a muddle. I couldn't figure anything out. When I reached for enough juice to complete my teleport, fumes mocked me. The same blackness that had encased me at the beginning thumped me in the back of the neck.

I fought, hissing and spitting, until I realized no one was there. I was blowing through my nonexistent magic. For nothing. Sheesh. What a dumb fuck. My eyes were heavy, so heavy I couldn't keep them open. Maybe I wasn't safe, but I'd moved beyond where anyone could reach me—or find me. If my enemies had been able to come after me, I'd have seen them by now. Consciousness ebbed, and then slipped beyond my control. No choices remained. I'd sort this out later.

I thumped back to sentience in the middle of a circle of werewolves with my body cradled on Dorcha's front legs. She lay on an ice-choked meadow with her head protectively over me.

"What? How?" My words slurred as I struggled to sit.

Dorcha held me in place. "Not so fast. You were very nearly beyond our reach. If Xander hadn't called in the local werewolf pack, I'm not certain we'd have been able to haul you back."

"But I rescued myself," I protested, my voice shockingly thin.

"Whatever you did helped," Dorcha said. "Reach up and grab my horn."

Lifting my arms was almost beyond me, but the minute my chilled fingers connected with her horn, she poured power into me. Sweet, heady, and oh-so-welcome, it reminded me of who I was.

Snatches of Torin and the never-ending cavalcade of

mages returned. "What happened to the rest of them?" I hoped my question made sense.

"Dead." Dorcha bit off the word.

It cost me to admit how clueless I was, but I asked, "Um, what happened to me? Why do I feel like I went ten rounds with Gwydion and Arawn?"

"Someone pounded a wedge between your physical and astral selves," Xander's deep voice sounded from somewhere off to my left.

"So my body never left here?" If I hadn't been clinging to Dorcha's horn, I'd have patted my tummy, hips, thighs, legs to make certain I was still whole.

"Correct," he replied.

It explained why I hadn't had access to the full spectrum of my power. And the sensation of unraveling that had plagued me. And why making sense of anything had been so elusive. Despite my earlier confusion, I was thinking now.

"If you killed them all," I said slowly, "then why didn't the spell holding me automatically terminate?"

"You know the answer," Dorcha whinnied.

I did. Now that I was coming back to myself, the stench of blood and guts sullied the clear northern air. With all the carnage, they'd somehow missed whoever nabbed me.

Letting go of her horn, I jimmied myself to a sit, leaning against her side. My butt was cold, but the rest of me toasty. All around me, the wolves raised their muzzles and howled. Warm, primitive, they were telling me I was pack.

"Thank you," I told them. My voice was stronger; it sounded more like me.

"Feel like talking?" Xander crouched next to me.

I nodded.

"Someone singled you out," he said. "What we need to determine is why. If today is any indicator, they're not going to stop until you're out of the picture. Do you have enemies?"

Laughter rolled from me. Verging on hysterical, I couldn't rein it in.

"What's so funny?" he demanded. A mystified look added creases to his high forehead.

"I've been killing for over a millennium. What are the odds I'd have enemies?"

A corner of his well-shaped mouth twitched. "When you put it that way…"

A snort followed the laughter, and I muttered, "Yeah."

"Dorcha knew right away what was wrong with you," he went on. "I've never worked with a unicorn before. Damn, she moves quicker than I do. She'd run half the enemy through with her horn before I got her to stop long enough to listen to me."

"He said we had to question them," Dorcha added as clarification. "Waste of time. I can always find you. I didn't need their feeble excuses to wade through."

I expected Xander to bristle at the rebuke. He took it in stride. "Meantime," he said, "I'd put out a call. Didn't know if any werewolves were left after the bunch I sent to Canada. Luckily, many rose to my summons."

"Why luckily?" I rolled onto a hip so I could look at him.

"We needed all of our combined magic to call you back."

"Your body was dying," Dorcha said softly. "I felt the life leaching from it. No matter how many dams I constructed, I couldn't keep you whole, not without your spirit."

"They took the part of you that held power," Xander spoke up.

"I don't require a primer on what's contained in my astral self," I said stiffly and winced at how rude I'd sounded. "Sorry. I'm not at my best. Thank you for marshaling your wolves to help me."

"Not mine," he corrected me, "but they recognize and respect my age and rank."

After a final round of yips and howls, the wolves separated into groups of twos and threes and ran into the forest. I rose to my feet. Stiff, sore, and humiliated I'd required such an august force to rescue me, I took stock of the piles of bodies scattered about.

"Did anyone get away?" I asked.

"No," Xander replied emphatically.

"After they snatched you, the steady stream petered out," Dorcha neighed.

I scrubbed the heels of my hands down my face. This had the feel of revenge. Who had I pissed off so much they'd want me dead? "Is this something different than the attack on the Circle?" I asked.

"It might be," Xander answered. "How much time have you spent there lately?"

"Very little," Dorcha replied.

Crap. The longer I stared at the problem, the murkier it became. "We need to determine who's behind all of it," I said flatly.

"Almost has to be related at some level," Xander muttered. "Evil calls to its own. Unrelated mages could have joined forces. Some hated Grigori; others hated you." He shrugged.

An unwelcome thought intruded, and I cast a pointed glance Dorcha's way. "We didn't leave Poseidon under the best of circumstances."

She whinnied shrilly. "Surely he's not holding the Kraken against us."

"What'd you do to the Kraken?" Xander asked.

"What else?" Dorcha looked down her long nose at the werewolf.

"You horn is strong, but his scales are impenetrable. I once broke a tooth on them."

"He made a mistake," I said.

"What?" Xander sounded impatient.

"Opened his mouth. Dorcha inserted her horn." I dusted my hands together. "End of story."

"For the love of Fenrir, you killed Poseidon's Kraken?" Incredulity underscored Xander's statement.

I shook my head. "We left before he was dead. At least I think we did."

"He wasn't dead," Dorcha neighed emphatically.

"But he's probably still pissed," I mused. "He wanted to hire me to return Ciara to him. She's a sea mage-slash-assassin who worked for him for a long while before running away."

"Seems like he should be able to find her," Xander observed.

"Grigori did something," I told him. "Changed her blood or her scent or something." I hesitated, and then added, "It's sad. She has family in the sea, but she can't ever see them again."

"Cut off from her pack?" Xander scowled.

I analyzed the problem from his perspective. Pack was everything. To never be able to be with yours again was horrendous. I'd hoped to accomplish more today. Walking among the dead, I turned those who lay facedown over and made mental notes about how they matched the list Quinn and I had split.

"We should get back to the guild house," I murmured.

"You're feeling better." Dorcha knew me well enough to not pose it as a question.

"I am. We need Grigori, though. He's talented at combing through facts and seeing connections."

"Goes with being a werewolf," Xander tossed out. He didn't do it in a "we're better than you are" manner. Maybe he was tiptoeing around me, attempting to stay on my good side. The notion made me smile inwardly. Not that I'm a bitch on wheels, or maybe I am, but remaining in my good graces is a lost art. After a while, no one even tries.

Other mages tolerate my moods for the sake of my magic. A quick internal assessment told me I had quite a way to go before I was back up to snuff. Shit. I was perennially recovering. Far better if I could grab the upper hand and hang onto it. Being forever on the receiving end of crap runs against the grain.

"I'll manage the spell," Dorcha said and snatched me into a travel channel.

On the surface, it bore sufficient resemblance to the place I'd been trapped, it gave me the creeps, but I forced myself to resurrect everything I could about my tipsy turvy prison. Maybe I'd recognize enough of a magical signature to gain clues about who'd kidnapped me.

"*We* must *be more careful*," Dorcha spoke into my mind.

"*I was warded. How much more care could I have exercised?*"

"*The ward could have included me.*"

"I can hear you," Xander said.

"We know," I told him. "It was kind of you to locate reinforcements."

"Nothing kind about it." He ran curved fingers through his cropped silver locks. "For the record, I'm never kind. I didn't want to have to explain losing one of his own to Grigori. Not while I was right there to protect you."

I started to blurt I didn't require his protection—or anyone else's, but the words died in my throat. I had needed his help. Without it, goddess only knew where I'd be right now. Not heading for the guild house for sure.

I looked around for the collection of moonbeams and gems and magic that I'd formed into a whip for the circus. It had been stuffed into a sheath hanging from a hip belt at the front end of this saga, and now it was missing.

Humiliation bit deep. "I, erm, know how they captured me. They have something of mine. My whip, except it's fluid, and I'd shaped it into a saber. Unless we get it back, I'm ripe for the plucking."

Dorcha wheeled to face me. "How'd you let them take it?"

"I was a little busy," I snapped. "You know, killing from every side."

Xander raked me with his gaze. "The sword. Right?"

I nodded dully. "It was crafted with my power to hold it together. It can lead the weakest mage right to me."

"Means it won't be hard to find." He snapped his fingers and exited from Dorcha's spell.

My protests that it was my problem, and I'd take care of it, echoed around Dorcha and me. Xander was long gone. I gathered magic, intent on following him.

"Don't," Dorcha said sharply. "He wants to make himself

useful. Let him. We have enough problems without worrying about magical flotsam and jetsam someone stole from you."

It grated, but I returned to my partial resurrection of being trapped. The longer I waited, the more the details would blur and grow harder to interpret. I was still deep in thought when Dorcha's spell spit us out half a mile from the guild house. She'd allowed me time to walk off any residual embarrassment before we faced Grigori.

He took care selecting Circle members. My perpetual absences must have disappointed him, but he'd never complained. I'd do better, justify the faith he'd always had in me.

We set off at a moderate pace. The guild house lights split the night, and we followed their glow. The dry sage-laden air was cold, but nothing like where we'd come from.

Quinn ran toward us. "Knew I sensed you," he panted.

I stopped. No reason for Quinn to run full tilt hunting us unless something had gone wrong. Dorcha neighed, and Gwaihir dropped from the skies landing on her broad back.

"Grigori is worse again," Quinn blurted without preamble. "Ciara is with him. So's Rhea. Her blood isn't helping. Where's Xander? That's who I've been waiting for."

"Unfortunately not here," I answered, unwilling to disclose how incompetent I'd been. Losing an item crafted with your own magic is at the top of the no-no list. A total rookie mistake, and one I'd have avoided if I hadn't been so full of myself, so certain I was beyond direct attack.

"You have to say more than that," Quinn pressed, his rushed speech underscored by worry. He's usually laconic, laid back. His current departure from the norm formed a start contrast and emphasized how worried he was.

"Did you summon the White Fae?" I asked.

He nodded tersely. "First thing I did. They're with him now."

I bolted for the guild house. I wasn't Xander. Neither was I a healer, but I'd stand by Grigori's side and raise all the power at my disposal if it would stave off disaster.

Dorcha galloped past me, Gwaihir still on her back. She'd beat me to Grigori, but her horn holds restorative qualities.

"We can't lose him," Quinn was saying.

"We won't," I reassured him and hoped I wasn't talking out of my ass.

11

Xander and I had nothing in the way of a special connection, but I raised my mind voice anyway. Skimping on details, all I said was he was needed immediately. I didn't say where, either. He was resourceful. He'd figure it out.

If he heard me.

It was a big if. I'd seen enough of Xander in action to understand he was one of the werewolves' super alphas. I didn't actually know if they had such a thing, but the moment he issued a summons, werewolves in the area responded.

Damn Grigori's pride. If he'd presented his original problem to the werewolf council, someone would have had a fix, or at least promising ideas. Could we hustle him back to the off-world guild house? He'd taken up residence there when he was diminished because his magic lasted longer away from Earth. The same could be said of all of us.

Inside the guild house, I followed Quinn, although I didn't

need to. I could just as easily have found Grigori from his occasional anguished howls. Not loud, but laced with pain, they tore at my heart.

He lay on the infirmary floor in wolf form surrounded by White Fae with Rhea's body curved protectively around him. More Fae were arriving, so they must have sent for reinforcements. It underscored how serious Grigori's condition was. With his head resting on his extended front paws, he barely twitched an ear at our arrival. Dorcha and the two eagles stood off to one side, wanting to help but staying out of the way for now. Too much magic can work at cross-purposes and do more harm than good.

Ciara detached herself from a trio of White Fae and hurried to Quinn's side. "He's worse," she murmured. "Just keeps sinking."

Not wanting to muck up whatever the Fae were doing, I kept my power muted and poked around the edges of Grigori's prone frame. Clumps of fur lay next to him, looking as if they'd fallen out. How could he have deteriorated so rapidly? I hadn't been gone for more than maybe fifteen hours.

Ask the right questions, I instructed myself. How he'd turned from vibrant to the heap of fur on the floor wasn't relevant.

My first scan hadn't picked up much, so I deepened my perspective and looked again. Breath caught in my throat. I must have gasped because Quinn grabbed hold of my arm. "What'd you find?"

I yanked free of his hold and shook my head as I repeated my examination of the power eating away at Grigori. My cheeks warmed; they must be splotched with red. Confession time had arrived, but explanations could wait. Shouldering into the midst of the healers, I said, "I know what's wrong. Give me space to work."

Dorcha clumped forward, her hoofs clacking on the hardwood floor and blue light swirling around her horn. Having heard my pronouncement, she was doing her own assessment. A shrill neigh exploded. She bent her head, running her horn up and down Grigori's gaunt form. He wasn't much more than fur and bones.

I wove power in with hers, an antidote to what was eating away at him, and hoped I'd caught it soon enough. Moments slithered past, and then still more as he hung suspended between life and the abyss. What happened to werewolves? Did they revert to the human they'd been? Did the wolf leave? Or was it trapped in the mortal's body.

The White Fae added momentum to my efforts, funneling their magic in one at a time once they figured out what I was doing. Dorcha's horn served as a touchstone for my unraveling task. The scents from our various magics swirled through the air. Fae smell of flowers and freshly cut fields with a piquant undernote. Depending on which element I'm channeling, my scent changes. Today, I cycled through every element.

Whoever had sicced this spell on Grigori was fighting back. I'd undo a piece, only to have it resurrected. Where in the hell was he? He almost had to be close to be this effective. Or maybe he was triangulating off me since I knelt next to the werewolf, hands raised as power flowed through me and into him.

I'd been hopeful at first. Once I understood whoever had stolen my magical whip was siphoning magic from it and using it to destroy Grigori, I'd been certain I could defeat them. That certainty ebbed the longer we struggled. The werewolf wasn't any worse, but we hadn't gained much ground. For every step forward, we slid back an equal amount.

The rate limiting factor was always magic. Whose would give out first? Since I was fighting my own power, it was a total crapshoot. How was whoever had stolen my working still dredging anything out of it. It fed off my magic, and I was here.

I cycled through and invoked the earth element, motioning to Quinn. Using our shared magical element as a private communication vehicle, I said. *"No time for explanations, but someone stole something I'd crafted with magic. They're using it against Grigori, and they have to be close."*

"I'll find them," Quinn growled and sprang upright from where he'd been kneeling next to me.

A furious spate of familiar snarls from elsewhere in the guild house suggested Xander had located my whip. If he'd been tracking the thief this whole time, they'd led him on quite the chase. Quinn, Ciara, the eagles, and a few of the Fae bolted from the room. I couldn't leave my post. I literally held Grigori's essence in my hands, and I would not release it until I was certain he could survive on his own.

Dorcha's horn was a critical element, so she couldn't leave, either. Together, we stood vigil over Grigori. No wonder Rhea's blood hadn't made a dent. This wasn't about werewolf virus. Her entire focus was on Grigori, her heart in her eyes. She loved him. Did he know?

With no warning, the force I'd been fighting ever since I understood what was going on crumpled. Because it was part and parcel of my own energy, I felt it depart in my guts. Any connection I'd had to the whip had been severed once it was stolen, but someone had done a bang-up job copying my style. Realization is a funny thing. The obvious had been staring me in the face, and I hadn't seen it until now.

Another elemental mage was behind the theft, and the attack. Dorcha had only killed Shane. We'd left the others, hoping they'd make better choices. If this was an example of what a "better choice" looked like, the others in Shane's troupe needed to relocate to a borderworld. Either that, or lose their lives.

With nothing to counteract it, power from Dorcha and me flowed into Grigori. He opened both eyes and lurched to his feet growling, shaking Rhea off in the process. "You." He faced me on shaky legs.

"Yes, it was my magic," I admitted.

"Why?" he growled louder.

"Another elemental mage stole my whip and used the magic in it against you."

Before I fell all over myself apologizing, a ruckus in the doorway snapped my head around. Xander, Quinn, and Ciara had hold of Dimitri with a combination of hands, teeth, and magic. I'd been damned sloppy with my whip, but right on about an elemental mage being behind the attack on Grigori. I bolted to where they stood and unwound my whip from where Xander had draped it across his shoulders. Without a constant infusion of power from me, it had reverted to its original form. Once I had it in hand, I doused it with the unmaking spell. My days of crafting useful artifacts and leaving them lying about were over.

"I've known you all the years of my life," I spat at Dimitri. "Why?"

"You murdered Shane." Dark hair streamed down his

back. Green eyes burned with defiance. Garbed in patched trousers and a moth-eaten woolen shirt, he looked more like a beggar than a mage.

Dorcha skidded to a halt six inches from Dimitri's polished boots. "You're wrong," she neighed. "I murdered Shane. You're next. How dare you steal from Rhiana."

"You murdered Shane because she ordered you to. I know how these bond animal things go." Dimitri angled a smug look at the unicorn.

Dorcha hooted equine laughter and pointed her horn at his chest. "You know nothing. No one orders me about. You weren't paying attention when your elders taught you about magical creatures."

I held up a hand. "Don't kill him yet," I told Dorcha. My mind jumped from one possibility to another as I fought an unwelcome suspicion my kinsman was somehow wrapped up in the plot against the Circle. Peppering him with questions would be a waste of time, though.

"Strip his mind. You're more efficient than me," I told Dorcha.

"I already did," Xander informed me. He'd shifted back to his human form while I was dismantling the spell holding my whip together.

"Good. You and Dorcha can compare notes once she's done," I told him.

We didn't need Dimitri alive. Not for long, so Dorcha wasn't gentle. The magic she aimed at his head must have hurt, but he barely grunted. Grigori had positioned himself between Dorcha and me. I felt his power—thank all the gods he still had some—as he tapped into Dorcha's information flow.

He was still growling, hackles raised, when she sank her horn into Dimitri's chest. Iridescent light shimmered around him as magic spilled out; his body slumped to the floor. Several of the Fae dragged him toward the door.

"Magefire is too good for him," one called over a shoulder.

"Aye, but we want him well and truly gone," another said.

I closed my teeth over my lower lip. From not knowing where any of the other elemental mages had gone to killing two of them was quite a leap. I should feel worse, but all I felt was pity for Shane and fury at Dimitri. He'd stolen from me and used my power against a friend. Back in the day, we'd had a set of laws. What he'd done was punishable by precisely what Dorcha had meted out.

Death.

Except it should have been slow, and he should have suffered more.

I knelt next to Grigori but kept a respectful distance and bowed my head. "I am so sorry," I told him. "This was my fault. I was careless, and you paid the price."

He shook his shaggy head and reclaimed his human form. I could have risen, but I remained on my knees. "You saved my life," he said.

Lifting my head, I met his stern blue eyes. "I try to clean up my messes, but there's no excuse for this one. Not really."

"You learned something." He pointed at the debris left from my magical riding crop.

"No kidding."

"I couldn't wrap my head around why my blood didn't help him," Rhea said. "It never occurred to me a different type of problem was in play. And it should have. I don't know enough about magic yet, but I should have trusted my scientific training."

"Get up." Grigori said gruffly, so I did.

Dorcha bumped me with her shoulder. Blood still dripped from her horn. I draped an arm over her neck. "You okay?"

She whickered. "No. His mind was a cesspit. How are you even related to someone like him?"

I shrugged. "Years pass. People change. Apparently, he changed a whole lot."

Grigori snapped his fingers and led the way from the infirmary to the great room. He walked a bit stiffly but seemed none the worse for his go-round with the rough side of my magic.

Dimitri always had a dark side. He'd figured out a way to hurt someone I cared for and destroy me at the same time. Sooner or later, I'd have figured out what happened, and I'd have been devastated. Dimitri was banking on Grigori being dead by then and me never being able to forgive myself. For all I knew, he was behind separating my physical and astral bodies. If that were true, he was counting on me being dead too.

Trays with finger food and flagons of mead and ale lined a long table at the back of the great room. Grigori waited until we'd helped ourselves and were seated before he asked Xander and Dorcha what they'd seen in Dimitri's mind.

The werewolf and unicorn exchanged a pointed look.

"Do not titrate any of it," Grigori ordered in stern tones.

"I'll go first," Dorcha said.

I flirted with taking a bathroom break, but it was cowardly. Even if I skated out from under hearing Dorcha and Xander's accounts, my memories of my people would never be the same. Today had sullied everything good. Eh, not everything, but I'd never view elemental mages in the same light. Maybe the Celts had been right to cut us from the fold. If what I'd seen earlier was any example, we didn't belong in the mage lineup any longer.

"Rhiana." Dorcha sang my name, turning it into something beautiful.

"Uh-huh," I mumbled.

"This is important for you to hear."

"Not going anywhere," I reassured her, but she'd been in my mind, and she understood how ambivalent I was.

"The others began by blaming the Celts," Dorcha began, "but over time they found it simpler to blame you. They knew where you were, for one thing. And you were but one, where the Celtic gods were many. At some point, one of the mages in Shane's circle had a run-in with either Satan or one of his princes."

"A prince," Xander cut in."

Dorcha's horn bobbed up and down. Dried blood flaked off it, leaving crimson shards on the thick ivory rug. "Elemental mage and prince works fine. They started at each other's throats, but for some unknown reason ended up trading descriptions of their enemies.

"From there, they discovered they had a common enemy. Demons hated the Circle, and the mages hated Rhiana for abandoning her family."

"But I didn't," I protested.

"Since when do facts count?" Grigori spoke up. "If someone wants to vilify you, facts get in the way. After enough time passes, memories fade and any convenient set of details will do."

"Handy Rhiana was part of the hated Circle," Quinn growled.

"It gave them common goals," Dorcha agreed. "The demons took things a few steps farther and made it a point to hunt for ex-Circle members. They assumed, and rightfully so, some would be disgruntled enough to seek revenge."

"Between rogue elemental mages and previous Circle of Assassin members, demons augmented their ranks in ways they're familiar with," Xander added. "They employed everyone they'd recruited as cannon fodder, preserving Satan's spawn at every opportunity while pretending to be on the front lines with everyone else."

"How come no one wised up?" I mused aloud. "Elemental mages aren't stupid. Surely, they recognized they were being manipulated."

"Maybe they didn't care," Grigori suggested softly. "The ones I kicked out of the Circle were weak. Elemental mages stopped believing in themselves after the Celts said they were done. They needed demons as much as Satan needed them."

"A brotherhood born of mutual need and seeded by hatred," Quinn muttered and shook his head.

"It was right under our noses, and we never guessed." Ciara sounded disgusted.

"Do either of you have anything to add?" Grigori looked from Dorcha to Xander.

"Aye. You're a long way from being done," Xander said. "We've made a small dent in their ranks, but they'll regroup. By now, they've figured out Grigori is after every mage he banished. They've gone to ground. Further efforts to find them will take much longer and force us to look backward, when what's needed is forward thinking."

At least we had a better handle on who the enemy was. Shame riddled me that elemental mages had signed on with such sketchy partners. We'd been a proud magical race with a glorious history. From what Dorcha and Xander had said, their hatred of me had been the lynchpin pushing them to join the dark side.

"It has to be more than that," I mumbled.

"What has to be more than what?" Grigori probed. He's always had ears like a lynx.

I straightened my slumped shoulders. The shadow of my kin's perfidy weighed heavy, but their sins weren't mine. "I'm only one mage," I said. "I can't believe I'm the only reason the other elemental mages signed a pact with Satan. I didn't burn any bridges when I left. I told everyone what I was doing. No one gave a shit. They were too spun out about the Celts' proclamation to pay me much heed."

"Think about the first part of what I said." Dorcha nudged me.

"The part where they swapped out hating the Celts for hating me because I was more accessible?"

The unicorn nodded.

"I still think there has to be more to it," I said.

"There might be," Xander agreed. "What Dorcha and I gathered was Dimitri's interpretation. Others may hold a different version." He focused his next words at Grigori. "What will you do next?"

"Protecting my mages is at the top of my list, but the Circle will return to business as usual. I'll begin accepting jobs again, and make it appear we believe the danger passed us by."

"Hoping to lure them?" Quinn asked.

Grigori nodded. "If they believe I no longer view any of

them as a threat, they're bound to move closer and get careless."

I winced. My carelessness had nearly been the death of him. Shit. I had to quit blaming myself. Redirection of the magic in my whip had been my fault, but I wasn't my brother's keeper. Decisions crafted by other elemental mages might reflect badly on me, but I'd had nothing to do with them.

I tipped back the rest of the mead in my mug. My plate was long since empty. All around me, mages had broken into small groups talking about getting back to normal. I had no idea what it even looked like. I'd been hanging around one circus or another for so long, I'd lost the feel of the ebb and flow of Circle life.

Dorcha and the eagles left. My bet was they were hunting.

I pushed to my feet, bid Grigori good night, and headed down the hall for the stairs and my chamber. Footsteps padded behind me, and I spun to face Xander. I couldn't be angry with him. He'd gone after my whip.

But I resented the fuck out of being beholden—to anyone.

"Let me walk you to your room," he said.

"Can whatever this is wait until morning?" I asked.

"No."

Something about his tone got my attention, and I resumed walking with him striding next to me. Even in his human guise, he moved with the grace of a wolf, light on his feet with a rolling gait.

We climbed the stairs, walked down another hallway, and stopped in front of my door. I pushed it open, and he walked in. "Close it behind you," he said.

Tired as I was, I sputtered, "Look. I didn't invite you in. Whatever it is you have to say, spit it out, and please leave."

The sensation of a sound shield banged against me. Alarm pushed my heartbeat up a notch. I dropped back into the hall, ready to pick another room. The guild house was full of them.

Xander shot through the door and grabbed my arm. "Christ, woman. I am not going to hurt you. We need to talk. For that, we need privacy."

"Why?"

"What part of privacy didn't sink in?" he countered.

Dorcha was close enough to come at a gallop if I needed her. If Xander meant me harm, I'd have sensed it sooner. Still reluctant, I edged into the room, pulling the door shut behind me. The sound shield plopped into place around us.

"Check your magic," he said.

"Why?"

"Are you always this contrary? Just do it."

Anger, my go-to place, burned bright. I folded my arms under my breasts, and said, "No."

nnoyance scoured me. "I am not one of your wolves to order about. Until you tell me why, I'm not doing anything." I hugged myself tighter.

"If you were one of my wolves, I'd check for you." His tone was soft, non-threatening. "I keyed in on a few unusual elements in that whip of yours. You destroyed the whole thing. I want to make sure you didn't accidentally create problems for yourself. Better to know now than when you're in the field and have need of all your power only to find some essential portion of it missing."

I dropped my arms to my sides. I was acting like a diva, a spoiled brat. "What exactly did you notice?"

"Small bits of each of the four elements."

My heart had begun to race at the possibility I'd screwed myself, no matter how inadvertently. I forced a few deep breaths and examined the problem. Sometimes the simplest answer is the correct one. I spoke slowly, deliberately as I murmured, "They probably came from Dimitri. He'd have needed a mechanism to coax the power in my whip to work for him, but I will check."

Grateful to have a possible explanation, I dove in. I'd exceeded my quota of errors for the decade over the past few days. Surely, I hadn't been stupid enough to wipe out some of my own ability.

Taking time to make certain I didn't miss anything, I combed through my magic, alert for holes in its weave. Perhaps a quarter hour passed before I switched my focus back to Xander. "I'm whole," I said. "Thank you for caring enough to draw this to my attention."

"You're welcome." The sound shield shimmered to nothing as he took it down. "Get some sleep. You look rough around the edges."

I cracked a grin. "You should see me on my bad days."

He shifted to his wolf form and glided to the door, which opened for him. I sent a jot of magic to pull it closed and lock it. I was sorry to see him go, but I buried the thought and slathered power over it. Like all truly old magic-wielders, his appeal ran deep. It wouldn't take much for me to let my guard down, and I didn't want to tread that path. We'd be associates working toward a common goal. When it was accomplished, he'd return to the Far East. Dorcha and I would remain with the Circle. Our paths would cross from time to time because of Grigori.

Maybe they'd cross. I'd managed hundreds of years as a tangential part of the Circle without running into him.

My clothes stank. I arranged them on hangers and set a cleaning spell in motion. Not as good as detergent and hot water, but it would make a dent in the smell. I could ask the mage in charge of the wardrobe room to launder them, but I've never encouraged anyone to wait on me. They'd be good enough for tomorrow. I'd figure out something better when I needed it.

After a turn through a dazzlingly hot shower, I toweled off and got into bed. Rather than rolling up in the duvet, I got under the covers, tugged the duvet to my chin, and doused the mage light I'd been using. Dorcha's touch skittered across my mind, light enough to not rouse me if I'd been asleep.

"Still up," I told her.

The clop of hoofs told me she was outside the door. It popped open, and she walked in. "Was the hunt with the eagles good?" I asked.

The door swung shut, and she made her way next to where I lay on the bed. "Very good," she replied. "Game is plentiful here. Humans are not."

"Perfect combination." I arranged a couple of pillows behind me and sat up.

"This could be going better," she said.

I didn't have to ask what "this" referred to. She was alluding to the last couple of days. "It could," I agreed. "Then again, it could also be worse."

"When I insisted on returning to the guild house—the other one—I had no idea I'd be plunging us into the midst of a war," she whinnied. "I'd apologize, but I've been having too much fun."

Drawing my knees up, I wrapped my arms around them. "If you'd known, would you have done things differently?"

She nickered softly. "Probably not. What about you?"

"We're needed precisely where we are. No one could have dispatched those elemental mages except you."

"They might not have been a problem if you hadn't surfaced," she pointed out.

"They would have been. Maybe not right away, but eventually since I was their scapegoat." I blew out a breath. "I've been considering remaining with the Circle after the current problems die down."

She pawed at the carpet, leaving a rent in its weave. "Excellent news. We need more unicorns. It's why I sought you out. I'm leaving to talk a few into helping us."

"So, you're returning to where you were when I was certain you'd broken our bond?" I was thinking out loud.

Dorcha nodded. "I may not be back for a couple of days."

"I'll be okay," I told her. "Xander's my new self-appointed protector."

"You could do worse," she said, nostrils flaring with amusement. Before I came up with a snappy comeback, she was gone, leaving colorful streamers shining in the air around where she'd stood.

I slipped back beneath the covers and tugged the extra pillows out of the way. "So I could do worse, eh?" I mumbled. Clearly, the werewolf had sweet-talked Dorcha into believing he was the greatest stuff since automatic rifles.

I made a good faith effort to search for connections between the enemies arrayed against us, but sleep snatched me away before I made much of a dent in anything.

I'D LOVE TO SAY I JOINED THE OTHERS FOR BREAKFAST, BUT I hadn't fallen asleep until close to dawn. Quinn, Ciara, and the birds were gone by the time I crawled out of the warmth of my bed and donned my slightly-worse-for-the-wear garments. They did smell fresher, a plus that almost offset their stains and rips.

At least I wouldn't offend anyone.

Everyone else was still at the guild house. Why had Quinn left? I'd thought we were coming up with plan B, or maybe it was C at this point. I felt whole, more like myself as I brushed out my hair and then hustled downstairs. The rich smell of coffee led me straight to the morning room off the kitchen, and I poured myself a cup.

Grigori, Xander, and Rhea were seated at a table in front of floor-to-ceiling windows that looked out at distant snow-capped mountains. Not all that different from the landscape in northern Russia, perhaps it reminded Xander of home.

Grigori motioned me over. I grabbed a couple of biscuits with something gooey melted over them and joined the werewolves. "Where'd Quinn and Ciara go?" I asked before settling in with my biscuits. The topping turned out to be caramelized sugar with nuts.

"Where's Dorcha?" Grigori replied with a question of his own.

"Went to get more unicorns," I told him around a mouthful of biscuit.

"Will they help?" Xander asked.

I shrugged. "Hard to say. Dorcha can be quite persuasive, but they left all of us behind for reasons of their own. Dorcha didn't go with them because of loyalty to me."

"She's always had an independent streak," Grigori pointed out. "If she hadn't, she'd never have left her herd for the Circle."

"Probably so. Now what about Quinn?" I pressed.

"He and Ciara left to rustle up Shira and Jake. Not Ciara, but the other three have expertise with explosives. They were going to craft a few bombs and drop them into Hell. Just to keep Satan on his toes."

"Who are Shira and Jake?"

"Shira is Aidyrth's new bondmate," Grigori explained. "Jake is a brand-new addition to the Circle, but Arrow, his wolf, has been part of our ranks for years."

"Mmph. Since when do we use bombs?" I patted the plate, disappointed to find the biscuits gone, and went back for two more.

"Since Shira came up with the idea." Grigori shrugged. "I'm open to newer techniques."

"Incendiary devices are scarcely new," Xander pointed out.

Before they leapfrogged into a discussion about bomb-making through the ages, I asked, "What happens next?"

"We all need to be in the same place to talk about it," Grigori said. "Everyone is returning to the primary guild house. We'll have an all-mage meeting after dinner this evening, so you have a few hours to do as you wish."

Rhea stood. "I'm going to practice a few of the moves you and Xander taught me. My wolf is excited to try them out. I'll be in the back garden."

Grigori nodded approvingly. "I'll let you know when I'm ready to leave. You can control the travel spell."

When she smiled, the years fell away, and she appeared almost girlish. "I'd like that. The more experience I have under my belt, the better I'll do. When I went on that mission with Aidyrth, I was woefully out of my league. Luckily, enough seasoned warriors were along I didn't have to do much, but I want to be more than dead weight."

After she'd left, Xander's neutral expression shaded to a frown. "How sure are you about her wolf?" he asked quietly. Clearly, the question was aimed at Grigori since I had no way to assess such things.

"She bears no loyalty to the Morak," Grigori said flatly. "I've spoken with her about them, and she holds them responsible for the initial failure of her bond to Rhea. When she went to them for help, they said she had to try harder."

"How can you be certain she hasn't softened toward them? Pack is everything," Xander insisted.

"It wasn't for me," Grigori reminded him.

"Aye, but you and your wolf have been an unbreakable team."

"Rhea and hers are moving in that direction after a cascade of early misunderstandings."

It was one way to put it. From what Quinn had told me, before the Circle intervened, Rhea and her wolf had been at loggerheads. Xander was well within his rights to question their bond, but this was none of my affair. I drifted back to the table with a few trays and helped myself to fruit and more coffee.

It appeared I had time on my hands, an unusual event for me. I perched on a stool at a different table, offering the werewolves privacy to discuss the renegade Morak pack. What had they done to merit the Draconian measure of being banished to another world?

Done eating, I carted my dishes to the serving table and dropped them in a bin holding other used plates. Not wanting to disturb Grigori and Xander, I headed out of the room.

"Where are you going?" Grigori's voice followed me.

"Back to the other guild house," I replied without turning around.

"I have tentative plans for us," Xander cut in.

I did turn then, resisting the urge to settle my hands on my hips and inquire caustically just what those plans might entail. I'd been a big enough bitch to him, I didn't need to compound my sins because he made me uncomfortable, reminded me of my femaleness.

If he hadn't left my room the previous night, would I have had the wherewithal to tell him to go? I wasn't at all certain. Standing facing him, feeling his bi-colored eyes assessing me, made me glad I'd taken the time to brush out my hair. And then I rolled mental eyes and kicked myself for being an idiot. In all my long years I'd never given two hoots what I looked like. And I'd be damned if I'd start now.

My breath might have quickened. My body definitely came alive under his scrutiny. Sex isn't one of my priorities. Maybe once, but not for a long while. Still, the rush of heat sweeping outward from my belly wasn't something I'd ever forgotten.

I rocked from foot to foot before remembering the reason I stood glued in place was he'd said something about plans. My mind had turned to mush. "What plans?" I mumbled, my words garbled because I had to remind myself how to talk.

This was why I avoided men. Exactly why. Dorcha took care of every need I had for intimacy except sex. Friend, confidante, and companion, she provided everything I required.

"They're up to you," he was saying. "I was hoping we could get to know one another better. Returning to where you first met me is a possibility; I could show you my home. Or we could travel somewhere warmer. Hop forward or backward in time." He smiled engagingly. "Do any of those sound promising?"

They all did. It was a problem. He could have asked if I wanted to sit on the floor and work on calculus equations. The important part was spending time with him, not what we did.

Oh-oh. I was on a slippery slope, one I'd slide down if I weren't careful.

I muted the arousal that had to be sheeting off me and aimed for a casual tone when I replied, "It's rare I have downtime, and it's been quite a while since I was in residence at the other guild house. I should take advantage of today to get things in order there and make a point of meeting some of the newer mages, so I'm not forever asking Grigori who they are."

"Excellent. Since we'll be fighting together, I need to know who they are too. And you can introduce me to the ones you already know."

Something about his words or his enthusiasm or his persistence made me laugh. "Are you always this relentless?" I asked.

"He wrote the book on work-arounds," Grigori spoke up, an indulgent smile lighting his usually stark features.

"Never takes no for an answer, eh?" I grinned back.

"Hey. I'm right here," Xander protested. "Talk to me, not about me."

My thighs were pressed together. Once loosed, lust wasn't about to retreat to a back burner, so I proposed a compromise that would afford me some time to myself. "Give me a few hours to get organized," I told Xander. "Meet me at the other guild house around five, and we'll take it from there."

"I'll see you then." Without bothering to rise, he took on a glistening aspect before a travel spell swept him away.

Grigori stood and walked to me. Hooking a hand under my arm, he led the way out of the morning room and through a set of double doors leading outside. Cold dry air was welcome with its hint of sage, and I breathed deep.

"I've never seen him like this," Grigori observed. "It's...interesting."

A little shiver traveled down my spine. I was delighted he wasn't a Lothario hitting on one woman after the next, but it made what was unfolding more complicated. Men who are players move on to greener pastures if they hear no enough times.

"He's not going to give up, is he?" I murmured.

"Not looking like it." Grigori hesitated. "We don't often mate, and when we do it's never outside our own kind."

"Why me?" I blurted.

"He's probably asking himself the same thing."

"But he can choose to walk away," I pointed out.

"Maybe he doesn't want to." Grigori let go of my arm. "Who can say why these things happen."

"Nothing has happened yet."

A corner of his mouth twisted downward. "And nothing will so long as you keep your guard up."

"Why didn't he make things easy and find a nice female werewolf?"

"Because something about you slammed through all his layers of insulation. Want to know what I think?"

I snorted. "You're going to tell me, anyway."

"Aye, I am. You know me too well. It's a lonely life, Rhiana, and a very long one. The chemistry between you is obvious. Don't bother denying it."

I waited, but he'd fallen silent. "That's all?" I demanded. "Long lonely life, and he rings my chimes?"

"And you ring his. See you at dinner."

I watched him lope away, quiet and graceful, and made my way back to my room. I'd meant to throw the bed together and leave. Instead, I snaked a hand beneath my top and rolled my distended nipples. Sparks shot outward, and I moaned softly.

I'd do this, but not here where I'd lay down a pheromone track half a mile wide. After setting the room to rights, I left the guild house and settled into an easy lope, moving deeper into the desert. I'd joined Dorcha in hunts before, so I knew the area well. Rickety cabins had sprung up in unlikely spots, all of them unoccupied. I followed a track from one to a deserted mining operation.

It was perfect. Far enough from the guild house no one would ever know I'd succumbed to my body's demands. Mages aren't exactly prudes, but neither are we like vampires who've turned public sex into an art form. After settling into a declination between two piles of tailings, I loosened my clothing and dipped a hand between my legs.

My distended nub throbbed a tattoo of long-denied need. I barely brushed my fingertips over it when a climax roared through me. It had been a long while, but I understood my body and alternated rubbing with stroking up each side of my clit.

I'd been teasing my nipples with my other hand, but I moved it between my legs and pushed fingers inside my vault.

Muscles snugged around me as I pressed on special places, ones that made me wild with desire. One climax followed another, each making me higher than the last.

Images of muscular male bodies, gorgeous asses, and oversized dicks with men jerking themselves off floated through my mind. The air grew slick and shimmery as I shed magic. After a while—a long while—my hands stilled. I hadn't had enough; it was one of the problems with sex and me. There never was enough, but the minutes I'd stolen would have to do. They'd take the edge off my desire for Xander, hopefully.

When I opened my eyes, a circle of curious rodents stared back. Drawn by my magic, they'd moved closer hoping for some of it to rub off. Squirrels, mice, rats, and marmots chittered softly. Not fighting, not trying to eat one another, they were lulled by the convergence of all four elements.

"Thanks for standing the watch," I told them. Putting my clothing back to rights, I scrambled to my feet. I'd teleport from here. No need to return to the Nevada guild house. I aimed for the room I'd used, the one where I'd left my harp. I'd take another shower and then visit the wardrobe room to don fresh clothes. What I wore reeked of sex, and the dirt and holes hadn't gone anywhere.

I'd ask Joss, the faun in charge of everything garment-related, if I could use one of the sewing machines to make some repairs before I washed everything. He'd cluck over me, and then tell me he'd prefer to manage everything himself. Probably made his life easier without a bunch of us cluttering up his workspace.

My spell ran true, but then they almost always do. The bedchamber shaped up around me. Unfortunately, it wasn't empty. Xander had pulled the room's only chair beneath a window and was looking outside. My harp was in his lap, and he plucked at the strings.

"Awk. What are you doing here?" I stammered, all too aware his sensitive werewolf nose would smell sex on me.

"Waiting for you. What else?"

"But you left well before me. I figured you had things to do. Our meeting time wasn't until five."

He nodded. "All true. Grigori invited me to come along with him and Rhea on the journey here. I had left, but I returned to travel with them. Her magic is coming along nicely, especially considering how young she is."

To cover my discomfiture, I resorted to questions. A time-honored diversion, they'd give me time to pull myself together. "How does that work?" I furled a brow. "She's newly come to magic, but her wolf has been around for a long while."

"Now that she's listening, and not pushing the wolf away, it will teach her. Eventually, they will reach a point where the partnership is balanced."

"Is that how it always works?" Feeling bold, I added, "Was that how it was for you?"

"Aye, but much like Grigori, I sought the werewolf bond..."

He had a pleasant voice. Deep and mellow, it was easy to listen to. I didn't know all that much about werewolves, and he was generous sharing knowledge.

13

A riff of harp notes filled the air, and then another, as he told me about his early years. The ones before he'd been turned. The village he'd been born in, about thirty kilometers north of Lake Baikal, was no more.

"Mortals didn't live very long," he was saying. "It was rare for anyone to celebrate their fortieth birthday. Over half my brothers and sisters died when plague mowed through our town. I'd just turned twenty, and, like so many young men, I questioned everything. Vampires and werewolves were commonplace. So were witches and other magical creatures. They didn't hide themselves away."

"Would you like some tea?" I asked when he stopped to take a breath and coax more music from my harp.

"Tea would be lovely."

"Back in a few." I ran lightly from the room. It wasn't exactly on my way, but I stopped by Joss' domain and traded my soiled clothes for fresh. The kitchens yielded a pot of hot water, tea leaves, a tray, two mugs, and a small jar of honey. I could have finessed everything with magic, but this was simpler.

Xander thanked me as I handed him a mug. His nostrils flared, and he murmured, "Mint, anise, and lemongrass. And you changed clothes. The others held such a delectable scent, warm and spicy, and—"

"Why'd you pick werewolves over, say, vampires?" I cut in not wanting to dissect the scents he'd identified on my clothing.

"It wasn't difficult. Werewolves work for good. Vampires are evil from the core out. They're dead, except they're still walking, an affront to the natural world."

I shrugged. I'd never thought much about it, but vamps had never been big favorites of mine. Of course, neither had werewolves—until I met Grigori.

"I figured I had time," Xander went on, "but I developed a fever and plague spots. That night I followed a werewolf pack and petitioned them to take me in. They smelled the sickness on me and ran off, leaving me to die. And I would have if my wolf hadn't taken pity on me."

"He returned?" I sipped at my tea, enjoying the herbal mix.

"He did. It was almost dawn. The fever was worse, and I was having trouble breathing. I didn't want to return to my village for fear of infecting others, so I'd accepted my fate. I'd watched enough people die from plague, I figured I'd be gone before nightfall.

"When a silver wolf nosed my side, I was certain I'd imagined it. High fevers do that. He started talking with me, and then I was certain I was hallucinating. So, when he asked me if I wanted to go through with the transformation, I assumed I had nothing to lose and told him yes.

"It was the last thing I remembered until I woke in a different place. He'd picked me up in his mouth and carried me. I still bear the scars, and he still reminds me how heavy I was and how I nearly dislocated his jaws."

"You were cured, though," I murmured.

Xander nodded. "I was. Human disease can't survive in werewolves." He chuckled softly. "It was the beginning of a steep learning curve. Thinking you want something, and actually getting it, are quite different."

"I can see where it would be," I told him. "I've always been what I am, and those like me were created not born. I do have one more question, though."

"Fire away." He set his empty mug on the floor and strummed the harp.

"Why do werewolves from different packs obey you? You're not their alpha."

"A good question," he agreed and stopped there.

"But not one you can answer? It's all right if I overstepped."

"You didn't. I assume you're aware of our council."

I nodded. "Now I am, but I had no idea it existed until rather recently."

"The council is comprised of twelve wolves, all from different packs. We're voted in. Because of my position on the council, other wolves do my bidding."

He'd left something out, like what his precise position on the council was, but maybe it was classified. Mages didn't bend over backward ensuring other mages understood their social structure and laws.

Xander was easy to talk with. We were getting to know one another, and even though he'd been clear about having ulterior motives, I was more comfortable with him than I'd been.

Light was fading from the day. "If you have anything you'd like to get done before dinner, now would be a good time," I said.

He set the harp down, propping it against the windowsill and got to his feet. "I've enjoyed visiting with you, Rhiana. Thanks for not kicking me out."

"Me too, and I did think about it."

"I know."

I'd been perched on the edge of the bed, and I stood too. "See you at dinner and for the all-mage meeting afterward."

He bowed low, a courtly old-fashioned gesture, took my hand, and brought it to his lips. "I'll look forward to it."

The place his mouth touched the back of my hand zinged with promise. His woodsy scent lingered after he left the room. For a time, I breathed it in, but then I left too. My original plan had been to get to know everyone in residence, an impossible task between now and dinner, so I settled for stopping at Joss' shop. If the guild house had a social center it was the wardrobe room. Mages gathered to chat about their day as they collected clean clothes and dropped off soiled ones.

When I arrived, Quinn was regaling a large group with tales of our exploits. Ciara stood next to him. "Rhiana was with us," Quinn announced once he saw me. "She was in a different spot than Ciara and me, so she'll have things to add."

"When did you get back?" I asked him.

"Maybe half an hour ago," Ciara answered.

"Who'd you kill?" a Sidhe called my way.

The question made me smile. We were assassins. Blood was our métier. I'd sat through plenty of group gropes where we relived particularly grisly murders and narrow escapes. They were our equivalent of ghost stories around a roaring fire.

"Dorcha was the real hero," I told them.

Cheers erupted, along with cries for the unicorn to join us.

"She's not here," I told everybody.

"Where is she?" Quinn angled a pointed glance at me, no doubt wondering if we'd had another falling out.

"Trolling for more unicorns," I told him.

Ciara clapped her hands together. "Marvelous news!"

"She may not find any who are willing to break from their usual pattern and aid us," I cautioned.

"Tell us about who Dorcha killed," another voice demanded.

For the next quarter hour, I detailed where I'd been and what had transpired. I'm certain the group didn't appreciate me glossing over some details. Occasional groans and "surely, there's more" confirmed my impression.

Dorcha loved these get-togethers. I've always been content to cede center stage to her, but I'd be lying if I said I didn't enjoy regaling the other mages with vivid depictions of spilled blood and guts.

"Are you doing all right?" a White Fae asked softly, concern shining through her question.

She had to be asking about the deaths of others like me. How to answer her? I opted for honesty. The others would sniff out half-truths. "For all the years I've wondered what became of the elemental mages, once Shane made it clear Dorcha and I would be prisoners under the ice along with the rest of his band, it infuriated me."

I pursed my mouth in a tight line. "Any mage can make poor choices. Enough of them, and they no longer deserve the right to levy power against another."

"Why didn't Shane understand how lethal Dorcha was?" someone else asked.

"I suspect he did," the White Fae replied.

"Suicide by cop?" Disbelief ran beneath Quinn's words.

"Something like that," I agreed.

Joss tapped an agate cylinder with a crystal wand, the signal dinner was ready. Soft pinging escalated in volume, and everyone migrated through the double doors. Mages squeezed my shoulder or my hand as they passed, recognizing I'd walked through my own personal hell and made sense of it.

The guilt that had nagged earlier returned. I should have been more broken-up over Shane. Torin, too. He hadn't always been a bastard. Dimitri was another story entirely. I was glad he was dead.

Ciara fell into step next to me. "I had a thought," she murmured.

"Always dangerous. What might it be?"

"The more I've turned things over, the surer I am Poseidon is neck deep in this. He hates both of us. Three if you count the unicorn who gored his pet Kraken. Usually, a single enemy is sufficient for Poseidon to wage war. So far, he doesn't know I'm part of the Circle, but a single spy could alter that."

"He has plenty of company," I told her. "The list of those arrayed against us is growing."

"You were with Grigori," she went on. "Any idea what he has planned?"

"Nope. How'd your project go?"

She drew me to one side. Mages flowed around us. Once we were alone, she lowered her voice and shielded us with the sound of running water. "It had its moments," she said, "but Satan is wise to either the feel or the smell of C4. We can't use it anymore."

"Aw crap. What happened?"

"We rustled up Shira and Jake. Turned out she had the makings for a few smaller bombs at her house, so we cobbled half a dozen together and set off, splitting up to cover more territory. Since there were four of us—and four bond animals, we each took a device."

So far, it sounded promising. I waited to see what she'd say next. Quinn joined us, slipping beneath Ciara's sound shielding. "I haven't even told Grigori yet," he said.

"It's okay," I reassured him. "He won't hear it from me."

"Quinn and I did okay. Planted our bombs, got far away, and detonated them, but we were using earth- and sea-linked power to push them to explode. Jake and Shira had to be considerably closer. Maybe demonkind smelled them."

"Maybe they were attuned to them since they were part of the forward guard who dropped the first batch of bombs," I suggested.

"Perhaps," Quinn muttered.

"Anyway," Ciara went on, "a group of demons managed to move Shira's bomb to a spot it didn't do any damage. Jake's blew up the crew trying to relocate it."

"Sounds like a win to me. Three out of four are rather good results."

"Jake and Shira don't see it that way," Quinn said.

"The bigger problem is we have to come up with some other way to knock holes in their ranks," Ciara added.

Xander strode toward us, clearly hunting for me. "Is this a private party?" he asked. "Or can I join in?"

"We were done," Quinn told him. "Good to see you again."

"You as well." Xander shook his extended hand.

Ciara dismantled her casting, and all of us hurried up the hall to the stairs and supper. It smelled divine now that I wasn't sampling the various scents through a waterfall. The dining room was full, and we selected a table for four toward the back of the large room. The last time I'd eaten here, I'd played my harp. The memory was bittersweet because Dorcha had been missing.

Bond animals wandered through the room helping themselves to choice bits from the buffet and off plates. Beyond the animals, no one milled around the buffet, so we made our selections quickly. Once we were seated with overflowing plates in front of us, Quinn poured flagons of mead. Raising his, he said, "Slainte."

I added, "To success," to his toast, and we all drank deep. I didn't start out liking mead. It's too sweet for my taste, but it has grown on me. I wasn't aware how hungry I was until I began eating. It's often that way for me. I've relegated food to the same place I consigned sex. Except I had to eat or my magic would wither.

Having Xander seated next to me felt comfortable. My initial skittish reaction to him had lessened, but not totally gone away. Letting anyone past my barriers would take time, maybe a lot of it since I've been adding to them all the years of my life.

Quinn is a natural-born storyteller. He walked us through his various trips to Afghanistan while we ate. Apparently, he'd spent a long while working exclusively with mortals.

"What made you decide to return to the Circle?" I asked.

He hooked a thumb at Ciara. "Grigori sent her to fetch me."

"I can be irresistible." Ciara grinned.

"That first night, I was convinced you dropped out of cyberspace to kill me." Quinn elbowed her.

"Who dropped a cage over whom?" she countered.

"Perfectly mated. Nothing like an argument to add spice to the mix." Xander drained his glass and reached for the bottle to pour more liquor for us all.

Empty plates floated to carts that wheeled themselves toward the kitchens. A few mages were still eating when Grigori loped through the room in his wolf form and jumped on a raised dais under a large bank of windows. Conversation died as mages focused on the Circle's founder.

Rather than the discussion I assumed we'd have, Grigori parceled out assignments. He'd adopted a broad-brush approach, but I saw holes in it. If all of us were successful—which was unlikely—we'd weaken our enemy but not wipe them out entirely anywhere.

While I was debating whether to open my mouth, Xander leaned close. "He and I discussed this."

Since he didn't seem inclined to add to his statement, I filed it away. Rising to my feet, I waited for Grigori to acknowledge me. He didn't right away, and it was starting to piss me off. Finally, he said my name, and I stepped forward.

"Where will you want the unicorns, assuming Dorcha was able to recruit a few." I didn't mention that if they were anything like Dorcha, they'd be as likely to come up with their own plan as to follow his.

As usual, Grigori was a step ahead of me—or he'd read my mind. "What makes you think they'd march to any tune but their own?"

I nodded and walked toward my seat, preparing to sit when he said, "What's really on your mind?"

"Nothing. We'll leave straight away. Dorcha can always find me." I'd never question Grigori in a public forum like this. He and I have had disagreements, quite a few, but we hashed them out in private. Plus, he was an exceptional tactician. Couldn't fault him for his planning or his execution. The only place he hadn't performed optimally was taking care of himself. Men weren't great in that regard.

Our team consisted of Quinn, Ciara, Loren, another earth mage, and me. Grigori had assigned all the elemental mages in the Circle to my group.

"Mind if I join you?" Xander asked me.

"Not only my decision," I informed him. "So long as everyone agrees, then sure."

Mages broke into their respective groups. We huddled in the same corner where we'd had dinner. Loren took his sweet time joining us. I've always liked his wolf, but Loren has rough edges. A whole lot of them. If I'd been Grigori, I wouldn't have tolerated his sharp tongue and foul moods.

"Any questions about our assignment?" I asked everyone. Loren was near enough to hear.

"Who's our team leader?" he asked from twenty feet away.

"Me."

"Why not Quinn?"

Before I flattened Loren, Quinn bailed me out by saying, "Her magic is considerably stronger than ours. Plus we're going after her people."

"Which is precisely why she shouldn't be in charge," Loren argued. "She probably still has attachments to some of them, and—"

"Enough." I snarled. Loren had finally made it to our table. "Two choices," I told him. "Don't come or live with me as boss of this team."

"Can Quinn be second in command?"

I gritted my teeth. No wonder Loren made enemies whenever he opened his mouth.

"Up to Rhiana," Quinn said.

Xander chose that moment to ask if anyone objected to him joining us. Predictably, everyone except Loren was enthusiastic. Mixed magics would make us stronger. I assumed Dorcha would be back at some point, but maybe not in time for our first skirmish.

"I don't understand what a werewolf will add to our efforts," Loren mumbled.

Xander growled low in his throat.

Ignoring both of them, I said. "We leave in half an hour. Be in the courtyard. It's very cold where we're going, so layer up. Otherwise, you'll waste magic keeping warm."

"What makes you think the elemental mages will be in the same place?" Ciara asked.

"They may not be, but they stayed there for centuries. We should be able to track them if they've left. Remember, we don't know if the others beyond Shane and Dimitri are part of the scheme to burn through good magic. I'm still not sure whether to believe what Torin told me about multiple targets."

"I'll strip mine information from them," Xander said, sounding as if he were looking forward to the project.

"See?" Loren sneered at me. "You're already protecting the other elemental mages. Grigori assigned us to end them, and—"

I rounded on him. "Not another word out of you. Grigori assigned my kinsmen to this group because no one else has sufficient magic to hold them in one place long enough to determine where their allegiance lies. I'm not in the habit of killing innocents."

"If you were in one of my wolf packs, I'd assign you latrine duty," Xander told Loren.

"Yeah, well, I'm not." Loren stared at the werewolf. I gave him points for guts.

Quinn pushed to his feet and walked behind Loren. When he got there, he placed a hand on either side of the other earth mage's head. Loren squirmed, but Quinn held him easily. "What happened since we fought at Hell's Ninth Gate?" he asked.

"Been having second thoughts."

"Where is your wolf?" Quinn glanced around.

"I can look for him," Gwaihir said.

The eagle spread his wings, but I shook my head. "We're leaving. Without Loren."

That got his attention. He shook free of Quinn and shot to his feet. "Grigori assigned me here. You can't countermand his orders."

It was a softer dismissal than he deserved, but I said, "Take enough time to consider your priorities. We'll return at some point. If you're feeling more like being part of this team, we'll include you then.

"See you in the courtyard in twenty-five minutes," I told Quinn and Ciara.

"And me," Xander said.

As if I needed reminding.

Done with Loren, who looked as if he wanted to kill me, I hustled from the room intent on gearing up for another trip to the Kamchatka Peninsula. What was Loren's deal? Did he have Mommy issues? Women issues?

Who cared? If we couldn't get along in the guild house dining room, problems would be inevitable in the field.

"You made the right choice." Xander caught up with me as I was stuffing a parka, hat, and gloves into a field pack. I've never relied on powders and potions, so I didn't plan on a stop at the alchemy lab.

"I made the only choice," I corrected him. "Ready to go, or do you need something from here?" I swung an arm wide to encompass rows of garments.

"My wolf thanks you, but his coat is plenty thick." Xander chuckled. After a moment, so did I. My question had been the equivalent of asking a dragon if they needed a fire to warm themselves. When he laced his fingers with mine, I didn't draw away, and we headed for the meeting place I'd designated.

Quinn, Ciara, and the eagles were there, but so were Loren and his wolf. Grigori too. "Loren is sorry," he told me.

"Are you?" I skewered Loren and dropped a truth net over him.

He winced. It was all the verification I needed. "Not sorry," he gritted, "but Grigori says I have to go."

I reeled in my spell and faced Grigori. "Will you force me to take him? His attitude is terrible. I can't trust him."

Loren's wolf growled at me and bared his fangs.

"Really?" I growled back. "You're going to be a dick too?"

Xander stood over Loren's wolf and forced him to back up several paces. The wolf's ears dropped; he tucked his tail.

"I've rethought this," Grigori said. "Loren come with me. Bring your wolf."

"But you said—" Loren protested.

"And now I'm saying something different." Grigori strode away.

For a few moments, I thought Loren was going to thumb his nose at a direct order, but his wolf trotted after Grigori. Maybe he recognized the werewolf as superior and didn't want another one up in his business like Xander had been.

Quinn snapped his fingers under Loren's nose. It got his attention where nothing else had, and he trudged after Grigori.

"Guess he doesn't like women," I tossed out, following it with coordinates for our destination.

"He's all tied up in knots," Quinn said. "I felt his inner turmoil when I had my hands on his head."

"Do you suppose the other side approached him?" Gwaihir cawed.

Quinn snapped his fingers once more. "Maybe that's it. He's quite the weak link, and isolated from the other mages. It would explain the conflict, and his wolf being absent during dinner. Bond animals are sensitive to evil." Power sheeted from him as he reached for Grigori to share our suspicions.

"See you at our target," I told everyone and built a travel spell.

Xander joined his magic with mine. It felt a lot like merging power with Grigori, so I didn't fight it even though I'd have preferred to travel alone. Maybe I should have tried harder with Loren, but mollycoddling isn't part of who I am.

"Do you have a plan for when we arrive?" Xander asked.

"Not really. I'm not expecting them to be where I left them."

"Then why are we starting there?"

"Do I have to justify myself to everybody?" I said tightlipped. Damn it. Why was I so fucking edgy?

He didn't say anything further. Neither did I. We'd play it by ear, the way I'd always done things. I should apologize, but I wasn't in the mood. Our mission was to kill elemental mages.

I never imagined I'd be a party to genocide for my own people, and I tried not to think about it. Go in. Get the job done. Sort the pieces out later.

We were almost at our destination when Xander asked, "Are you all right?"

I shook my head. "Nope. Not even close."

❧ 14 ❧

Xander didn't cluck over me. Didn't try to fix anything. He was smart enough to understand words didn't make much difference in impossible situations. My journey casting was winding down. It had thinned, and the howl of a raging blizzard battered my ears.

I'd aimed for the spot on the downward sloping ice sheets where I'd spied the cave entrance. It might be where we were, but visibility was about a foot. Wind tore at me, driving icy bits into my face and tangling my hair. I should have braided it out of the way. Too late to worry about it now.

Xander brushed against my side. He'd opted for his wolf. Wise choice given the crappy conditions. I'd never locate the cave entrance without a magical assist. Hell, it could be blocked by snow at the rate it was swirling and blowing. Eagles cawing announced Quinn and Ciara. They stomped toward us, changing from invisible to gray blobs to themselves.

I faced the hillside and fanned power in an arc. Trusting we had to be close, I expected a gateway to form, showing us the entrance. Usually, my expectations bear fruit, but nothing happened. I pushed more magic into my seeking spell and switched up a couple of parameters.

Meanwhile, Xander trotted this way and that, sinking into hock-deep snow as he used his nose, possibly trying to catch my scent or Dorcha's beneath the blanket of white.

Quinn quietly joined his power with mine. The addition of more earth-based enchantment did the trick. We clambered up fifty feet to reach the cave. Snow had blocked the way in, but it hadn't compacted and was easy to push through.

"We didn't have wind in the sea," Ciara muttered, fingers busy dragging her tangled blonde hair into a rough ponytail. I wasn't the only one who'd made the mistake of leaving my tresses hanging loose.

Being out of the wind was a plus, a big one. It howled like a banshee; more snow swirled into the cave, but this was 90 percent better than outside. I tugged my hair into a queue and slid the parka I'd brought over my shoulders, zipping it to my chin. The eagles cleaned snow off their feathers.

"How many elemental mages lived here, and for how long?" Quinn's tone suggested he was having trouble believing a superior magical race would settle for so little.

"Ten or twelve, and several hundred years," I replied.

The eagles squawked; Quinn whistled.

"They're not here now," Xander said.

I hadn't expected them to be. Their cover was blown. "The attractive part about this location was no one knew about it," I said. "It wasn't Shane's death that drove them from here but understanding full well I'd return."

"I never grasped why all of you vanished. Fate dealt you a shitty hand, but packing up and disappearing seemed extreme." Quinn arched his brows and looked right at me.

"It wasn't all of us," I replied. "I stayed and fought until I ran out of steam. If I hadn't been bonded with Dorcha, I might have made different choices, though. She kept me going long after giving up was the only logical choice."

"But what about the rest of your kinsmen?" Ciara asked. "We even heard about the diaspora in the sea. Poseidon said you were a bunch of cowards, but then he's always been buddies with Gwydion and Arawn."

"Celtic magic is part of what formed us," I told her. "When they announced they were done creating elemental mages, that we had too much power, rumors ran rampant."

"Like what?" Gwaihir cawed.

"Mostly that their announcement was only the first step, and more would follow, like them stripping parts of our power." I chewed my lower lip as I organized my thoughts. "The Celts understood the value of mages linked to the elements, so when they broke our backs what was left were those like you."

I aimed my gaze at Quinn and Ciara.

"Not that you're not wonderful," I hurried on, "but those of us who utilized all the elements worried we'd be stripped of some of them as time passed. The simplest way to avoid it was hiding."

"Were you the only one who didn't go to ground?" Xander asked.

I nodded. "I didn't realize it for a long while. Until one

day I hunted for my brothers and sisters and couldn't find a soul. The Celts never bothered me once I pulled the plug on my one-sided war against them."

"You lost your pack," Xander howled, the sound blending with the wind into a mournful dirge.

"One way of looking at it." I was back to business. Only so much can be accomplished chewing over old bones. "We're here to find them. I don't sense anyone but we're going to look before we set tracking spells in motion."

I strode through the descending system of tunnels and caves until I reached the large cavern where Shane had all but invited Dorcha to be the instrument of his unmaking. Side tunnels branched off, and we split up to explore where they went.

The scent of my people was strong, but it should be. Smell is the most primitive sense, and the one most closely related to emotions and memories. Images of earlier times rushed through me, places like this that had been full of those like me. We'd laughed and spun magic and never imagined any of it would change.

Except it had.

I'm not one to dwell in the past. Far from wallowing in bittersweet memories, I've gone to great odds to avoid them. Ergo, my treks through time to circuses where I could bury who I'd been and briefly become someone else.

Xander's statement about this place being deserted was true. We returned to the cave, ready to implement plan B. Part of me was tempted to leave my kin be, but it was precisely what Loren had accused me of: a soft spot where elemental mages were concerned.

"I did a little preliminary tracking," Xander said. He was

back in his human form, presumably because talking was simpler.

"So did we," Gwaihir swept a wing toward Tory, Ciara's eagle bondmate.

"They didn't stick together," Tory cawed.

"Of course not," I muttered. "Why would they make it easy for me?"

"How'd they know you'd be back?" Quinn asked.

"Because they're pack," Xander answered.

Even though he came from a different frame of reference, he wasn't far off the mark. We'd never alluded to ourselves as a pack, but once upon a time we'd been close-knit. I'd done my own sleuthing while exploring side corridors. "I found three paths leading from this place. Did anyone locate more?"

Seeing head shakes, I went on, "We'll explore them together. They'll be expecting company, so ward yourselves."

"They could have circled back, left false leads," Xander pointed out.

"We'll find out when we go after them." My pack had been dangling from a shoulder. I slipped the other strap over an arm. "The journey will take a while since all three tracks lead off world."

"I'd always heard it was where you guys went," Quinn said.

"Me too. Finding my people still on Earth was a surprise." And not the only one. That I still viewed them as "my people" qualified as a shocker. I'd written them off long before Shane and Dorcha's standoff.

"So it's possible this group joined the others via different routes?" Ciara arched a fair brow.

"More than possible, likely," Xander told her. He gathered

magic and explained. "Better if I control this spell. Werewolf magic won't cause nearly the alarm yours would."

The cave shuddered to nothingness, and we floated in a journey channel. Xander's magic was rougher, more primitive than what I was used to. It got the job done, though. Light came and went as we passed the bands that hold worlds separate from other ones. I shucked my pack to remove my heavy jacket. It was overkill here.

"Have you ever catalogued all the worlds?" Quinn's question came out of the blue.

"Have you?" I asked him.

He grinned. "I started once. And quit when the task took on impossible overtones."

"There are a lot of them," Ciara said. "Only a few are livable."

Xander made a course correction and cursed.

"What is it?" I asked and wove a few strands of magic in with his spell to track its progress.

"They anticipated being followed and threw diversions into the mix. Hope I didn't miss any."

I felt along the length of his seeking spell, backtracking, and found the places it broke into false leads. When I was certain, I said, "You didn't. I only found two spots."

"What do they have to hide?" Quinn mused aloud.

"They've been in hiding for so long, it's become second nature," I told him. "Bet they don't feel safe anywhere. Me stumbling across them must have been a shock, except they had to have sensed Dorcha and me approaching."

"True. Why didn't they hide then?" Quinn asked.

"Shane saw it as a way out." The more I'd thought about it, the surer I was he'd yearned for death for a long while.

"Bet he didn't float that boat in front of his buddies," Ciara murmured.

"Nope, he didn't. In this instance, he was only thinking about himself."

"Did you know him very well from before?" Ciara asked.

"Not well, no." I stopped there. I'd lay better than even odds I'd know all of the mages where we were going.

"Not far now," Xander cautioned. "Ward yourselves."

The problem with tracking someone is you come out precisely where they did. I'd have liked to have put some distance between our stopping place and where the elemental mages had emerged. It wasn't possible. If you don't follow the tracking vector to its endpoint, you risk never finding your target.

Luck was with us; we popped out onto a deserted vista of prairie grass spread across a sweeping dune. Waves pounded against a distant shore, and clouds floated in a pale-blue sky.

"I know this place," Quinn said.

"One of the worlds you mapped before you gave up?" Ciara asked him.

"Yeah. When I was here dinosaur shifters were guarding it. They made it clear no one else was welcome. When I reassured them I wasn't planning to homestead in their territory, they backed off and I never saw them again."

"How long ago was that?" I asked.

He frowned. "Long time."

"Before the Celts decided elemental mages weren't welcome?"

"Not that long."

Xander had been a few feet away, turning in a full circle.

"Odd," he said. "I don't sense anyone here. Not shifters. Not mages."

The chances of everyone being so well warded they wouldn't show up at all were thin. So far, we were spinning our wheels. I considered leaving, but what if that was what the other mages wanted us to do? Our power was capable of sophisticated concealment spells.

"We're digging deeper," I announced, "unless Xander has reason to believe his tracking spell went awry."

"It didn't. Once I found those broken crossroads meant to lure us elsewhere, I was alert for them." He sounded testy. Made sense. Werewolves who weren't exceptional trackers wouldn't last long.

Closing my eyes, I stretched my arms in front of me and gathered clues with my nose and ears and the feel of residual magic on my skin. "They were here," I said. "And not all that long ago."

Eyes open again, I began to map out a plan when the sound of distant drums turned into booming that rolled toward us. Xander growled, "Those bastards. They've been watching from behind wards."

Gwaihir and Tory leapt skyward. Excellent. We'd have aerial scouts, plus they were epic warriors, and we'd need every advantage. This had to be the world where the rest of the elemental mages had set up shop. Naturally, the group in the Arctic would know about it.

I hadn't, but neither had I made much of an effort to find out. The booms intensified, sounding like malevolent native drums. Beneath our feet, the surface bucked and heaved.

"Stop that," Quinn barked.

I didn't expect his efforts to make any difference, but the

earth quieted. I might hold all four elements in my arsenal, but his link to the earth was stronger than whichever of the elemental mages had set the quakes in motion.

The eagles squawked raucously and divebombed something I couldn't see. Reaching with magic, I felt a circle of power tightening around us. Instinctively, the four of us set our backs together, facing each of the four cardinal directions. Xander was still in his human form. I thought he might be stronger as a wolf, but it wasn't my place to dictate his choices.

"Lot more than ten or twelve," he said.

"All of them," I gritted. "This was their other hidey-hole."

"Same thing Gwaihir suggested," Quinn said. "Numbers aren't his strong suit, but he said many and from all sides."

The ground had stopped rocking and rolling, but tongues of water trundled toward us, no doubt lured by the sea-linked portion of our power. It wasn't much more than an inconvenience. "Don't waste magic countering it," I told Ciara.

"Not planning on it," she replied. "The sea is at least a kilometer away. Someone is blowing through scads of magic forcing it uphill to us."

Familiar magic pulsed around where we'd taken a stand. Mages came into view. I'd been right about knowing them. All of them. Being set upon by my own people was eerie, but I'd forced them into defending themselves by coming after them.

I didn't have anything white, but I raised my arms above my head and walked forward a few paces. Not so far I couldn't stage a hasty retreat and defend our position. "Stop," I shouted when they were 200 feet away.

They kept right on coming.

I tried again. "All I want is to talk."

Nada.

Fine. No one was in a chatty mood. I dropped back to my spot and channeled a blend of destructive magic. Dorcha would have been quite the deterrent, but she wasn't here. The eagles swooped and jabbed, catching bits of flesh in their beaks. I caught the familiar scent of elemental mage blood, sweet and musky. Our power flows in our veins, so our blood smells different.

"On my count of three," I told my team, "we will open fire. But our objective is that man. The one with long black braids and a red robe. We're going to capture him and move him away from here. Reuben has always been one of their leaders. If anyone knows about their involvement with demons or Poseidon or mages who've traded sides, it will be him."

"The birds can create a diversion," Quinn said.

Good enough for me. I'd come here for information, not to kill, but the mages wouldn't sit back and let us waltz out of here with one of their own. Ciara reached for the rivers cascading around us. Quinn connected with the earth. We felt ready to me.

"Three. Two. One," I counted down and loosed a volley of force dead center at Joro's chest. He crumpled into a heap, and the eagles closed in. The mages to either side tried grabbing Gwaihir and Tory and got pecked in the face for their trouble. Next, they funneled air channels to dislodge the birds.

Power burned where it slammed into me, leaving a trail of fire in its wake. I wrenched my attention away from Joro, and spun to face another well-known face. Better if I didn't think about my kinsmen by their names. It might make me hesitate rather than act.

I fought fire with fire, breathing in smoke as hair and clothing smoldered. Tiring of my lungs hurting, I chased the fire with a tidal wave of water borrowed from the channels swishing around my feet. Someone hit me from behind, knocking me to my knees.

"You killed Shane," he hissed in outrage.

"Nope. Dorcha did."

"Who's she? Your alter ego?" He hooked an arm around my neck, jerking my head back.

I clawed at the arm cutting off my air, and sent harsh power cascading into it. He grunted with pain, but his hold loosened enough for me to wrench his arm to one side as I broke the small bones in his wrist.

"She's my unicorn," I gasped. "Remember? The bond animal all of you pitched a hissy fit over."

"Likely story. Where is she now?"

Gwaihir landed on the mage's shoulders and drove his beak into an ear. He hissed with pain. Crap. My grand plan to move Reuben somewhere we could crack his mind for whatever secrets he held was looking less and less likely. The air was thick with smoke and magic, so thick I couldn't see where everyone was. Grunts and squeals and shouts rang around me, sounds of a battle in full bloom.

The eagle let go, circling for another point of attack. I voted for the other ear. Or maybe both eyes. Blind enemies were useless until they managed to heal themselves. The idea was sound, so I ran with it and formed fire into two javelins aimed right for his eyes. He sidestepped me at the last moment, staggering. Gwaihir took advantage of his misstep to snag an eyeball.

Crowing his success, he crunched it down and hovered, wings beating a slow death chant. Above the din, I thought I heard hoofbeats, and then I chalked it up to wishful thinking. Being half-blind hadn't slowed my opponent, but he was pissed.

Leveraging his bulk, he threw himself on top of me again. This time, he crafted a canopy to keep Gwaihir out. Fists pummeled me. I punched back, but I'll take magic over brute force any day. This time, I aimed for his knuckles, scraping the skin off them with rocks. Once I was down to the pulpy flesh beneath, I switched to fire.

He kept on punching me, keening with pain but not letting up.

With no warning, a horn protruded through his back, stopping an inch from my face before it withdrew. Fuck me. I'd heard hoofbeats after all. Crying Dorcha's name, I tossed the weight of the dead mage to one side and leapt onto her back.

Whinnies told me everything I needed to know. Other unicorns had joined the field. "Good work," I yelled. We spun to the side in time for her to gore someone with a flaming arrow aimed at me.

"What? You thought I'd miss out on all the fun?" Neighing crazily, she cantered into the thick of the fray.

I was where I belonged. On Dorcha's back fighting evil. If the elemental mages ranged against us hadn't lost sight of the bigger picture, why were they doing their damnedest to end us? It had to be more than retribution for Shane and Dimitri—if word of what happened to him had even filtered through to this lot.

Aw crap. It was terrible, but I tiptoed around the possibility we'd made a mistake. Loren was a dick, but he'd nailed me dead to rights about having a soft spot for my kinfolk. I had a hard time wrapping my mind around elemental mages embracing darkness, but they'd engaged us, refusing my invitation to parlay.

Surely, the refusal was significant. We've never been warriors, but neither have we shied away from confrontations when the need was great. The unicorns—Dorcha had brought two others with her—were a game changer with their horns.

So much so, I told her to wait until we were attacked before she killed anyone else.

"But I was having fun," she protested.

"Plenty of battles in the offing," I reminded her, not wanting to come out and say I didn't want to be the only elemental mage left in all the worlds.

Reuben charged through the murk with a bit of white linen clutched in one hand, screeching, "We concede. Stop before you finish what the Celts began."

His distress was genuine. Raising my mind voice, I called everyone off.

Quinn and Ciara joined me. Streaked with dirt and gore, they looked ready to be done. Gwaihir and Tory were still circling. Beaks dripping blood, they were in the mood for more carnage, but they'd stick with feasting on the dead. I jumped from Dorcha's back. She bolted off to gather the other unicorns.

They didn't answer to me, or to her, either. Magical solutions are often two-edged. They save the day, but they also have their own agenda. The only unicorn I'd known well was Dorcha, so I couldn't predict how easy these two would be to rein in.

Xander circled around Reuben from behind. The mage's attention was on the field where he was probably counting the fallen. By the time he saw the werewolf, Xander had snared him, knocked him out, and was culling through his mind.

I'd have just asked Reuben, but this was more surefire and didn't require a truth spell.

Dorcha returned with two silver-white unicorns in tow:

one male, one female. I bowed to them. "Thank you. Your assistance made all the difference."

"It always does," the male whinnied and pawed at the muddy ground.

Xander dismissed his spell and moved away from Reuben. A squirmy, uncomfortable sensation pricked me. Could I forgive myself if we'd ended most of the elemental mages for nothing? I bit my lower lip hard with stern instructions to stop imagining the worst. I'd killed the wrong target before. It went with the territory.

"Well?" I asked the werewolf after all of a minute had passed. "Did we do all of this for nothing?"

"They're guilty, all right." Xander glanced at Quinn. "Those dinosaur shifters were apparently a problem. Too ancient to kill or dissuade, they set traps and made the mages' lives miserable."

I was having trouble connecting the dots. "And?"

"You have some kind of council structure?" Xander raised a silver eyebrow.

I nodded.

"Some of them went trolling for help back on Earth. They cut a deal with Torin and his renegade mages to corral the dinosaurs. The quid pro quo was they'd help take down the Circle and other magic-wielders who clung to the old ways, and—"

Reuben groaned and staggered to his feet, holding his head. "We never thought we'd have to pay up," he grunted. "Most of Torin's group were on the weak side. Traveling this far taxed them, made them ill. We didn't expect they'd return."

"Where are the dinosaur shifters?" Quinn growled. "I may not have liked them, but I respected them."

"They should be free," Reuben said. "We had to maintain a constant flow of air and earth to contain them."

"We were never cowards," I told Reuben. "You should be ashamed of ousting the ones who lived her first. That's not how things work."

"We tried to coexist."

"Clearly, not hard enough," Quinn said.

The eagles flew near. Gwaihir landed on Dorcha. Tory circled the silver-white male before landing on his back. My guess was she'd asked permission.

Our work here was done. I'd be damned if I'd walk the field to see who was dead.

"You didn't ask for my advice," I told Reuben, "but I'm going to give it to you, anyway. The dinosaurs will be furious. You need to clean up this mess"—I swept an arm wide—"take the survivors, and find another place to live. It might not be a commodious as this, but at least it will be yours."

He turned and trudged to where half a dozen of his kin— and mine—had gathered fifty yards distant. No one else wanted to talk with me. Just as well because I didn't have anything to say to them, either.

Nothing more to do here. I was anxious to leave, so I could separate myself from the field of dead stretching to all sides. We agreed to meet at the guild house. Dorcha and the unicorns traveled separately, and the rest of us were well ensconced in my travel spell when Xander asked gruffly, "How are you?"

"Relieved."

"I bet," Quinn said.

"It would have been awful to be a party to killing your brothers and sisters for nothing," Ciara added.

It ran deeper than that. Since we were formed at the hands of the gods and not born, I shared a lot with every other elemental mage. The carnage we'd left behind would leave a mark on me, but I didn't know yet what it would be.

To divert myself, I dropped into tactical mode. "We did well," I told everyone, "but I'm not certain wiping out every mage who's part of this scheme is practical."

"Seems to be a lot of them," Quinn muttered.

"You don't need to kill them all," Xander said. "But they must respect Grigori and the Circle of Assassins and understand they are off limits."

I don't usually have a philosophical bent, but I tossed out, "What if we backtrack."

"What do you mean?" Ciara asked.

"Dark power never used to hold allure. Those who practiced it weren't respected. Satan has always had a tough time recruiting anyone with magic to turn into demons."

"Okay." Quinn made a come-along gesture with one hand. "Where are you going with this?"

"When did evil become enticing? What changed?"

Even though I'd posed the question, I floundered about looking for possible answers.

"Magic changed," Ciara replied. "Not how we practice it, but how it's viewed. When mortals believed in it, their energy fortified us. They even used to leave offerings on the shore for the sea gods." She smiled. "Of course, the Nereids stole most of them, but still, the warm fuzzy aspect was there."

"No more offerings," Xander agreed. "Also no more mortals seeking us out and asking to join our ranks."

I remembered what he'd told me about his transformation, but the seeking-out part was unique to werewolves. And maybe vampires, although most mortals weren't clamoring to join the ranks of the undead.

"I'm not seeing how we can change any of that," Quinn said. "Mostly, I've worked with humans in recent years. Depending on how dicey a situation is, they're a whole lot less curious about what tricks I conjure to get us out of it. At first, I figured they'd flatten me with questions, but it never happened."

I didn't see an easy way out. Did it mean we'd spend the rest of forever wiping out tainted mages? Satan's demons were one thing, but everyone else? Maybe I'd asked too big a question, but what we were doing had to make sense.

The birds were done cleaning blood off their feathers and stood next to their bondmates.

"Rhiana?" Xander was looking at me.

I shrugged. "I don't know. We can launch missions like this and return victorious for the most part, but are we really winning a war?"

"It's a good question," he said gruffly. "One worthy of finding an answer for."

The transition to the guild house courtyard was more abrupt than I would have liked, but I was tired. Not so much physically weary, but emotionally drained. Maybe I should have walked the battlefield and bid farewell to each of the fallen.

Bullshit.

I'd never adopted other than a business-as-usual approach to death. No reason to change things up just because the fallen were related to me. What happened to them was their own fault, a product of poor choices. I had more compassion for the dinosaurs who'd only been protecting their turf than I did for my relatives who'd muscled their way in.

Either we were the first group to return, or maybe everyone else had checked in hours ago. From the looks of the stars, it was the middle of the night. Grigori ran lightly down the steps.

"Debrief over breakfast," he said. "Everyone's back. Dorcha and the unicorns said you'd arrive presently."

"Losses?" Quinn, always on point, asked.

Grigori nodded. "Aye, we lost three. When we gather in the morning, we shall remember their bravery."

I didn't ask who. Ashamed I didn't want to know, I turned and walked heavily toward the house. This assignment had taken something from me. For the first time ever, I questioned whether death was the answer to problems. Over the short haul, maybe. But over the long term?

If new enemies bounced back up, taking the place of whoever had fallen, what was the point? Would we be fighting the same battles forever?

Because I was deep in thought, I wasn't aware of Xander behind me until I was up the stairs and nearly to my room. Turning, I mumbled, "Not very good company right now, even for myself."

"Which is precisely why I'm here." He tucked a hand under my elbow, walked us to my door, and followed me inside.

I stared at him, almost asked why he was in my room, but wisely kept my mouth shut. I was legendary at pushing people away.

"Thanks for not ordering me out," he said and hooked a

foot around the room's only chair before he dropped into it. I looked at the bed, but remained on my feet.

"I had time to think on the way back," he said. "What you did today would have been unthinkable in a werewolf group. Even those from disparate packs are still one family. Alphas mete out punishment—and sometimes death—but pack members never raise teeth and claws against each other."

"Your point?" I sounded surly, but I wasn't sure I wanted to hear more about how superior werewolves were.

"The reason consequences fall to the Alpha is because presumably they're strong enough to live with the loss of a pack member. Some manage. Others are consumed with second guessing their choice. Often they cede pack leadership to another.

"For a while today," he went on, "I hated you, didn't understand how you could kill your blood and move on to kill another."

"Because they'd have done the same to me," I said dully. "Or didn't you notice?"

"Of course I did." His tone was sharp. "I also reminded myself elemental mages aren't werewolves. You are related, but not in the same—"

I rounded on him, grateful to glom onto anger. It was a whole lot more palatable than my earlier misery. "Before you tell me how you managed to forgive me," I said my voice laden with sarcasm, "let me educate you. The Celtic gods made us. Depending on which of them were involved—and it was always more than one—some of us are as close as clones in our composition. It's one of the reasons we didn't get along all that well. Try looking into a mirror and arguing both sides of a point."

I was on a roll, and I kept on talking. "I was the only one who fought back. Do you get that? The only one who stood and fought the Celts after they cut us off. Once, Gwydion laughed in my face and said if all the others had been like me, they'd have made a different decision."

"Does it signify you were less attached to the other elemental mages?"

"I'm not sure what attached means. I never went out of my way to track them down. Before I set out hunting for our enemies, Grigori suggested I could also search for my long-lost kin."

"He's a werewolf, he would have said that. Pack is everything."

"To you, maybe," I countered. "Stumbling across Shane and his group wasn't exactly a peak experience. I was happy to see them. Until he made it clear my place was with them, and Dorcha was collateral damage."

Weariness washed over me in waves. I shook my head. "I don't want to relive any of this again. Moving forward is better."

"But you have to understand where you came from for the future to make sense."

He stood, walked to me, and put his arms around me. I wanted to pull away, but I craved the comfort he offered. I'd been running from everything all those years I'd dragged Dorcha and me from one circus to another. When I was performing, I didn't have to think about anything.

We stood like that for a long while. At some point, I tucked my arms around him. He kissed my forehead, and said, "Get some rest."

"I don't want you to leave." My words surprised me, but I didn't slather other words over them to try to take them back.

"Then I won't."

We let go of each other long enough to walk to the bed. I bent to take my boots off. He did the same. We were both filthy, but the bedding could be washed the next day. I wasn't ready to remove my clothes or suggest a shower. When we lay next to each other, I felt safe, cared for in a way I'd never known. As I drifted in and out of sleep, sometimes he was human, and sometimes his silver wolf was curled protectively around me, soft and warm.

Either light streaming through the windows or the rancid reek of the battlefield woke me. In his wolf form, Xander's amber eyes were open and trained on me.

"Thanks for keeping watch," I murmured, my voice thick with sleep.

"It was an honor." The wolf sprang lightly to his feet, licked my face, and shimmered to nothingness.

I blinked at where he'd been. Had I dreamt the whole thing? Bending forward, I touched the place the wolf had lain. It was still warm. Nope, not a dream after all.

My mouth curved into a smile. I pushed out of my clothes and walked to the bathroom intent on cleaning up. What an odd night. We hadn't had sex, yet I felt closer to him than I did to anyone except Dorcha. Out of the shower, I donned a robe and teleported to the wardrobe room for fresh clothes. While I was there, I apologized to Joss about sleeping in my clothes and making the bed dirty.

"Warriors never apologize," he told me and vanished.

When I returned to my room in fresh clothes and socks to retrieve my boots, the bed had been stripped and my discarded garments removed. A single red rose sat in a cut crystal decanter on the table. Beneath it was a slip of paper with an X on it.

Bending, I sniffed the flower, enjoying its fragrance. When I turned to head down to breakfast, Xander stood in the doorway. He'd changed too, and his hair was wet like mine.

I smiled. "Your wolf is quite the charmer."

"He likes you." Xander extended an arm and said, "Shall we? It will be a full morning."

I walked to him and laid a hand on his arm. "Why are you staying?"

"For you. I told you that before."

My cheeks grew warm. He had, but I'd figured he was just after a quickie, and then he'd be gone. "You want the real deal, huh?"

He nodded. "As close to it as we can manage."

My heart was full and my mind a jumble as we walked downstairs. I pushed everything aside as we entered the dining room. We'd make decisions today that would make or break the Circle.

Did Grigori know? He almost had to.

Xander and I filled plates from a buffet and found seats in the middle of the room. Everyone else was already eating. "Coffee or tea?" he asked.

"Coffee. Black."

He returned with our drinks just before Grigori walked to the dais and started talking.

❧ 16 ❧

I was on my third cup of coffee before all the groups, including ours, had checked in. Bond animals circulated through the room. Dorcha and the unicorns stood near the rear wall with the eagles perched on their backs.

We'd left a swathe of carnage a mile wide through mage-land, but we'd also posted a declaration of war. Rot had spread deep, affecting far more magic-wielders than I'd have guessed. I didn't have much of an excuse. I'd been buried in the past sucking down calliope music and sawdust, but Grigori and the other mages in the room had been as oblivious as me to the decay creeping right beneath their noses.

Easy to cast blame and totally non-productive. Grigori had been fighting for his life. For everyone else, it had been business as usual waiting for him to recover enough to sort through potential assignments.

"It doesn't matter how we got here," Grigori was saying. "What does is how we proceed from here."

Xander got to his feet and walked toward the other werewolf, taking up a position slightly behind him. I remembered his comment to me about how understanding the past was elemental to addressing the future, but he didn't contradict Grigori, merely offered support.

"Since this will affect us all," Grigori went on, "I'm opening a discussion. It's not how we normally do things. As you know, I usually parcel out assignments in the grove, but we're all in this together. Determinations we make today will have wide-ranging consequences, so this is the time to speak up. I'll start by offering my opinion."

He smiled crookedly. "This is a once-in-a-lifetime opportunity to rip my reasoning to shreds."

Loren rose. "Before you embroil us in planning, may I have a moment?" At Grigori's nod, he faced me. "I owe you an apology, Rhiana. If we set out in teams again, I want to be part of yours."

Nonplussed, I stood and stared at him. "What made the difference?"

He gave an uncomfortable shrug. "You did something I didn't believe you would."

"Not the time for protracted explanations," Grigori cut in. "Do you accept his apology?"

"Yes."

Before Loren could thank me, Grigori shooed us back into our seats. "The way I read the situation," he began, "we have three choices." He counted them off on his fingers. "One, we do nothing. Two, we form brigades and launch attacks until they give up or none of us are left."

"What's the third?" Quinn called.

Something about his expression suggested he already

knew what Grigori would say, but then Quinn spent years in military and paramilitary operations.

"It's my choice, but it will be difficult to pull off." Grigori hesitated. "Impossible if I missed a few traitors and they're seated among us."

The bond animals snarled, snapped, and stamped their hoofs, clearly ready to rip anyone not 100 percent loyal to the Circle to shreds.

"Door number three is we put the word out that I'm still ill, except this time no one expects me to recover. I've made it clear my final weeks will embrace solitude, so most of you"—he swept both arms to the sides—"have returned to the other guild houses. Werewolves, but not too many, have traveled here to hold vigil over my passing."

"Except we'll all still be right here," Quinn said, followed by, "Brilliant. It could work."

"You always did jump in feet first," Grigori commented, earning him an easy grin from Quinn.

"It's why you love me," the earth mage said.

"The thing about baiting a trap," Grigori went on, "is it can't look like one or smell like one. There are many places this scheme could run off the rails. We could be sitting here for weeks, waiting, while our enemy grows stronger.

"Therein lies the primary risk," he went on. "By not keeping up the work we just completed, we're allowing those arrayed against us a window to beef up their game. If they think I'm dying anyway, there's not much incentive to hustling things along. They can kick back and wait for the inevitable rather than storming the fortress."

"Maybe you're not dying." I got to my feet. "Maybe we put the word out you've lost your mind as a result of your previous illness. The Circle is in disarray as many of us have scattered in search of a cure."

"That's even better." Grigori nodded approvingly. "There's quite the appeal to swooping into chaos and taking advantage of it."

"Waiting would be a crapshoot," Quinn said and leveled a pointed look at Grigori. "After all, you could recover, and then we'd be back to the status quo."

"Come on." Grigori snapped his fingers. "Pick this apart. Before we walk out of here I want something bulletproof."

For the next hour, we fine-tuned my idea. Dorcha left the unicorns and stood next to me as the group batted suggestions back and forth. Xander and Grigori had their heads together. Power flickered around them, suggesting their chat was confidential.

"I discussed it with the others," Dorcha reverted to our private mind speech.

I figured she was referring to the unicorns. *"Discussed what?"*

"When we are done here, no one leaves this room who hasn't been vetted by one of us."

"It's a sound idea. I'll let Grigori know."

She tapped her horn on my shoulder and returned to the other unicorns. I wove through groups of mages engaged in spirited dialogue. Once I reached the werewolves, I waited until Grigori motioned me through what turned out to be a sound shield. I'd believed the visible magic was a conversation, but it ran deeper than that.

"The unicorns will check everyone's integrity," I told them.

"Good," Xander said.

"Doesn't mean someone isn't using one of the mages as a conduit to listen in," Grigori pointed out.

"Seems like something the unicorns would discover," I murmured.

"Aye, but then it's too late," Xander growled.

Grigori dropped a hand onto his shoulder. "Old friend. I refuse to live in fear. We will do the best we can to eradicate obvious leaks. If one resides in this room, we'll follow it to its end and silence whomever we find.

It would blow up our plan, but nothing is ever foolproof. Presumably, no one except another werewolf could listen in on the three of us. Xander pointed behind me. I twisted in time to see the unicorns already making the rounds of the room. Guess they'd decided not to wait until the meeting was over.

"Good thinking on their part." Grigori nodded emphatically.

I glanced at him, and then away. He carried the history of the circle etched into his bearing. He'd handpicked each of us. For him to have made not just one error but many must be devastating.

"Mages change," I said softly.

"Not the four false shifters," he muttered sourly. "Those shit choices are all on me."

"It happens. Some of my decisions weren't red-hot, either."

Raised voices snapped my attention to the rear of the room. One of the silver-white unicorns had hemmed in a faun with magic. At first, I was concerned it was Joss, but the coloring was wrong.

Joss cantered close but couldn't get past the unicorn's magic.

Grigori doused his sound shield, and we hurried over.

"You're wrong about me," the faun shouted, but his shoulders slumped. Even his horns didn't have as many curves.

Joss grabbed my arm. "He's my cousin. He hasn't been here long, but I asked him to work for me. He's naught but a youngster."

One glance at the unicorn, mane spiked into hackles and horn quivering with outrage, told me he'd found something. I'd never known Dorcha to make a mistake where evil was concerned.

"Look at this." The unicorn painted sideways strokes with his horn. A silvery mist wafted around the trapped faun. Within its layers, I saw both the faun and a long dark twisted cord extending from beneath one arm to some distant point well beyond the guild house walls.

"Noooooo," Joss moaned. "It cannot be. I helped raise him."

The unicorn's binding wall didn't stop Grigori. He stepped through and grabbed the faun by the shoulders, twisting him until they stood face to face. Except the faun was a good foot-and-a-half shorter.

"Explain!" Grigori shouted.

"I can't. I don't know where that thing came from." The faun shied away from the black rope and then ducked his head and tried to chew through it.

Grigori dragged him upright. Power augured into the faun as the werewolf mined his secrets. He wasn't gentle, and the faun staggered beneath the onslaught. Joss' grip on my arm tightened, but he knew better than to intervene.

"Joss," Grigori said in his front-and-center-now tone.

The faun let go of me and got as close as he could. "I am here."

Grigori and the unicorn still hung onto the unfortunate faun. "Follow that cord," he told me. "Once you're gone, the unicorn will sever it."

"I will send fire and magic up its length," the unicorn said.

"I shall accompany Rhiana. Better give us time," Xander spoke up.

"How much?" Grigori's question was terse.

Xander looked at me, so I took a stab at it. "Maybe half an hour. It's probably more than we'll require."

A loud cracking noise from behind me turned out to be Dorcha's hoofs on the wooden floor. "I'm coming too," she announced.

"Half an hour is too long," Joss said. "That thing is draining magic from my cousin. Whoever's on the other end knows they've been discovered."

"Good point." I tossed a tracking spell together. If they were sucking power from the faun, it meant they were still there, but they might not be if we didn't step on it.

Dorcha wove power in with mine. Xander looped an arm around my shoulders. No time to waste. As soon as I picked up the scent of sour enchantment, I ignited my casting.

Tracking spells are a variant of teleporting but with a specific item substituted for a defined location. Or, in this case, a specific twisted mage. Fury boosted my efforts. This was worse than the faun choosing evil. He'd been used, an unwitting victim.

"Someone went looking for the greenest mage in our midst," I told the others.

"We'll make them sorry," Dorcha snorted.

"Perhaps," Xander told her. "We could be playing right into their hands and walking into a snare not unlike the one we aimed to set for them."

"We're stronger. We'll win." The unicorn sounded certain.

Damn, I hoped she was right. I kept track of the markers that came with tracking spells. If I read them correctly—never a slam dunk—they'd tell me how close we were to our target. The black cord was fraying badly. Had Grigori chopped it at the other end to save the faun's magic, and his life?

"This could go either way," I said. "We might not hit an end point before the rope turns into a cinder."

"I can fix that," Xander said and gripped a segment of the unraveling rope as it flashed past. Once he had a good hold on it, he cut it behind us. The far end fell by the wayside but at least whatever was destroying it wouldn't affect the faun any longer. My tracking spell remained intact, attached to the portion Xander held onto.

The rope smoldered. Someone had upped the ante and was covering their tracks. Dorcha slathered magic around Xander's hands to keep them from burning. At least we'd pulled the plug on destructive magic traveling toward Grigori's end, hopefully while life remained in the hapless faun.

Bastards.

"Yeah," I muttered. "You haven't won yet."

Xander had his hands full managing the rope. I poured power into my tracking spell, urging it to hurry. Our travel channel shattered around us, spitting us into the midst of demonkind. I didn't bother to count how many. I've faced shitty odds before. Dorcha and I dove into the fray. I immobilized demons, and she speared them. Xander flashed into his werewolf and launched himself at the nearest demon, grabbing him by the throat. I'd have offered support, but four demons jumped me, dragging me toward putrid slime coating the rocky dirt beneath my boots.

The nasty reek of Hell wafted around me. So that was where we'd ended up. I'd seen more than enough of Satan's realm to last me for centuries. Weight bore down on me. Something settled into the middle of my back. Dorcha's outraged whinnies followed me down.

I was in a terrible position to fight back. Hell's fumes made my eyes water. A furious grunt was followed by, "You gored my friend."

"You're next," Dorcha squealed.

The pressure on my back let up a little. I reared back, smashing something with the back of my head. The satisfying crunch of scales breaking gave me the window I needed, and I spun around, lethal power at the ready.

I've mentioned how hard demons are to kill—for everyone but a unicorn. The bastard I'd head butted was sticking an eye back into a socket. Recognizing opportunity, I threw myself on top of him. We crashed to the ground, but this time I was on top. He stabbed my thigh with a talon. I grabbed his hand and bit it off at the wrist.

Ick. Ewwww. Demons taste horrible. Rank roadkill and a gluey sulfur element to their blood made my stomach rebel. I puked in his face. Dorcha charged from the side and drove her horn dead center into his throat. I jumped off and out of the way before she yanked her horn out. Good call on my part since more of the foul blood geysered. It hit me, but not full in the face like it would have.

I whipped around. First opportunity I'd had to look at where we were. All of Hell's caverns are the same. Demons milled around, but they'd backed off, leaving a respectable circle around Dorcha and me.

Crap. Where was Xander? I scanned piles of demon bodies before I got smart and used magic. Dorcha's battle cry, shrill and feral, echoed off the cavern walls.

"Where is he?" I shouted and shook a fist at the leering demons.

"I have him," a deep gravelly voice announced. It belonged to a burly demon with red-and-black scales and a swagger to his gait as he walked toward me.

"He doesn't belong to you." I planted my feet shoulder-width apart and balanced magic between my hands where it arced from palm to palm.

The demon pushed his shoulders into what might have been a shrug. "Depends. I might be up for a trade. What do you have?" Eerie laughter rolled from him. It made the fine hairs on the back of my neck flicker with disgust.

"We do not bargain with filth," Dorcha whinnied.

"We're not leaving him here," I told her, not bothering with telepathy.

The demon rocked from one hoof to the other, staring at me. "I see two choices. You'll do." He patted his member where it hung from his body. It thickened and rose, curving against his scaled belly.

"In a pig's eye," I snarled. I'd never been raped, and I wouldn't start here.

"Well then, your horsie will do, but she's not my first—"

"Shut up," I shrieked. I'd be goddamned if I'd play his stupid cat-and-mouse game.

"Leave," rattled through my mind.

Xander. At least he was conscious. *"Not without you,"* I told him. The demons would hear, but I didn't care. I tested my magic. It was still in good shape. The journey here hadn't taxed me unduly.

"Very sweet," the demon sneered. "First, you have to find him, and then you have to free him. By the time you accomplish anything, you'll have fallen into the same pit. And then I'll have all of you. Satan will be pleased."

Dorcha stamped her hoofs on the rocky ground.

I took stock of the demons littering the cave. Not the dead ones, but the others. Twenty or so were left, along with Mr. Bully-Boy. Dorcha flashed her head around and gored the nearest two. The others dropped back a few more paces.

Black blood dripped from Dorcha's horn. She reared, and, in a feat I'd never seen her perform before, she rode magic to the next closest demons, slashing one to ribbons with her sharp front hoofs while she gored the other one.

Two could play this game. I wasn't as efficient as she was, but I formed power into javelins and sent them flying. They wouldn't kill, but they'd disable. I aimed for eyes. Blind adversaries were as good as dead—until they resurrected their sight. No wonder Quinn had spent so much time as a mercenary. Dead mortals stayed dead. None of this halfway shit.

Dorcha killed three more.

The demon who'd taunted us with threats had lost his top-of-the-heap swagger. He grabbed a double-bladed axe from a rubble pile and headed straight toward me, swinging it. Goody, I love it when they get mad. Angry warriors stop thinking and make mistakes. I'd been in that spot enough times to recognize it.

A swoosh of unicorn power told me Dorcha was gearing up for something. I was still managing vectors for my javelins to maximize their reach when silver burst across my visual field. Furious neighing followed, along with raucous shrieks from eagles.

Woohoo! Quinn and Ciara and the two unicorns were here. Eagles too.

"Sloppy," Quinn yelled in my direction. "A dead dog could have tracked you."

"Best looking dead dog ever," I quipped, and then added, "Maybe I did it on purpose."

The demon with the axe had stopped dead. Not the brightest bulb on the shelf, he was obviously considering what to do next. Three unicorns put an entirely different slant on things since they were romping through his demon horde killing with precision and enthusiasm. Quinn and Ciara leveraged earth and water to hold the demons in place. Otherwise, they'd have fled before the unicorns gutted them.

Laughter burst from me when the twenty who'd surrounded us were reduced to eight, and then six. "Hold up," I shouted at the unicorns.

"Why?" Dorcha twisted her neck to look at me.

"We need Xander back. If we kill them all, we'll have nothing to bargain with." I sauntered to the demon commander. "Release my friend, and we'll leave."

"If I don't?" The question was surly, but his tone wasn't.

He actually sounded cowed. Might have been wishful thinking on my part, though.

"If you don't, then everyone in here is dead, including you. Plus anyone else we come across when we hunt for Xander. You heard me say it before. I'm not leaving without him."

He growled at me, his ugly face twisted with fury. Yeah. No one likes to lose, but this round went to us. I scattered fire about just because I could. Some of the dead turned into pyres, and the air thickened with rancid smoke.

"What'll it be, bud?" I laid it on thick, saccharine as hell. "We'll find our friend with or without your help. The only difference is this is your one opportunity to save yourself." I didn't mention the other demons since he didn't give a rat's ass about them. Hell was like that. Every fucker for himself.

A weak jolt of werewolf power pricked me. It had to be Xander. He was the only werewolf here. I threw my power open to Dorcha. "You're a better tracker than me. Follow that," I shouted.

She's quick, my bondmate. Glittery streamers had scarcely settled from her exit when she returned with Xander clinging to her back. He looked like shit, but I'd worry about that later.

"Finish them." A ululating battle cry rang from me and was taken up by my friends. The unicorns and eagles added neighs and squawks to our victory song.

Xander slid from Dorcha's back and staggered toward me. I wrapped protective power around him and set a teleport spell in motion aimed at the guild house. Plenty of firepower in the cavern to end a handful of demonspawn. Xander might not last long enough for me to be party to the endgame.

He sagged against me. His color was horrible, and his

breathing ragged. I held onto him. "Stay with me," I told him. "You are not allowed to check out."

"I was supposed to save you," he gasped.

"Ssht. Conserve your energy. We won. It's all that matters." Except it wasn't true. He mattered to me. A whole lot. I'd meant what I said. He had to pull through.

He lapsed into unconsciousness. I diverted a stream of energy into him, not at all sure what I was about, but determined not to lose him. The White Fae would know what to do. They'd had plenty of practice with Grigori. Plus, they were healers. It has never been one of my strengths. I cycled through the elements, checking after each alteration in my magic. A mix of earth and fire seemed to work best, so I cancelled out air and water.

Despite my efforts, Xander was slipping away.

Hoping to hell I was close enough for Grigori to hear me, I raised my mind voice and told him to meet us in the courtyard with the healers.

The journey took longer than I'd have liked, but I couldn't withdraw my power from Xander. Even with it, he kept fading, almost as if someone had sabotaged him in much the same way Grigori had been damaged—except faster.

Finally, when Xander's breaths had slowed to maybe one a minute, we dropped into the courtyard. Clumsy, inelegant, and almost out of magic, I broke our fall with my body. Grigori raced forward with a phalanx of White Fae.

"What happened?" he cried.

"Demons nabbed him." I sat on the ground, cradling Xander against me.

"Rhiana," one of the White Fae said sharply. "Let go. Now."

Nodding blearily, I did and watched them place him on a magical bier and teleport inside.

Grigori thrust a flask into my hand and barked, "Drink."

The alcoholic brew burned going down, but it cleared the cobwebs from my mind. Glimmers of my power started to return. I'd been so focused on getting Xander here, everything else had faded to insignificance. I took another swallow and urged the brew to work faster.

The courtyard sprang to life as the unicorns, eagles, Quinn, and Ciara bounded through a gateway.

"Mission accomplished." Quinn thwacked Grigori across the back.

"Perhaps one of you will fill in the details?' Grigori raised a russet brow, surveying the newly arrived.

"I assumed Rhiana already did," Quinn said.

I scrambled to my feet and shook my head. "Rough journey," I told him.

"Did Xander make it?" Ciara asked pointblank.

I nodded. "Barely. I am so not a healer."

Dorcha whinnied in solidarity and trotted to my side, rubbing her horn along my shoulder.

"Is it okay with you if Quinn and Ciara tell you what happened?" I aimed my question at Grigori.

"They weren't there the whole time," he reminded me.

"I was. I'll fill in any missing details," Dorcha whinnied.

"Thanks." I smiled wanly at the unicorn. "I want to clean up and sit with Xander in the infirmary."

Grigori cast a curious look my way. Making shooing motions, he said, "Go. Find me when you have a progress report on Xander."

For someone who rarely tipped her hand, my heart was in my voice when I asked, "He's still with us, right?"

"He is, indeed. I'd know if he passed over." Grigori favored me with a rare smile.

On that note, I trudged toward the house, too weary to bother with magic to teleport to my chamber. In the interest of expediency, I stopped at the wardrobe room and stripped. Joss wrapped a robe around me and handed me another one plus clean clothes.

"Thank you for believing my cousin was innocent," he said.

"No thanks needed. Is he okay?"

"Aye, but he almost wasn't. It was close."

I patted the faun's shoulder. I'd have liked to be more supportive but worry for Xander ate at me. After picking up my boots, I made my way up two flights to my room and stood in the shower until I couldn't smell demon stench. Steam from the bathroom wafted into the rest of the chamber and swirled around the red rose still in its cut-crystal vase.

Seeing it made me hurry with drying and dressing and brushing my wet hair into a queue. The bed was inviting, but I could sleep later. Sitting with Xander, infusing my slowly recovering stores of magic into him, was more important.

Two White Fae stood at the infirmary door. They moved aside so I could enter before taking up their post again. Xander lay on a raised platform in a room with many windows. Light from the fading day played across his form. He'd changed back to his wolf's body. It gave me hope if he was able to shift.

Rhea, Grigori's werewolf friend, stood off to one side fiddling with glass tubes in a rack. They appeared to be filled with blood.

"May I sit next to him?" I asked one of the Fae.

Wings beating so quickly they were a blur, she conferred

with several others. When she returned to me, she nodded. "Aye, but you must remain quiet and not interfere with our magic."

"Got it. I'll keep my power under wraps."

Her expression was solemn when she murmured, "This is delicate. Competing magic could turn the tides, and not in the direction we want."

Using my ability is instinctive. If Xander took a sudden turn for the worse, could I keep my oar out of the water? I pretty much had to. With firm instructions to myself I wasn't in charge here, I settled at the end of the platform and stroked the wolf's rough coat.

Did he know I was here? I started to check but then stopped myself. No magic. Not here, and not from me.

"I think I solved it," Rhea said. "Come look."

Several White Fae flowed around her looking at something that had to do with the glass tubes. Rhea had been some kind of scientist. She must be working on an antidote for Xander's woes.

"Might work," floated over to me.

"We have to do something," Rhea insisted. "There are risks, but if we do nothing..."

She didn't finish her thought, but she didn't have to. Things were grim in Xander-land. Did werewolves have their own healers? Would he be better off with his pack?

Would he survive long enough to get there? Our journey had really taken it out of him. Reining in my control-freak tendencies, I waited to see what those who knew more than me decided.

Rhea and half a dozen Fae formed a semi-circle around the bed.

"I'm sorry, but you have to leave," a Fae told me.

"Why?"

"This won't be pretty, and I know you, Rhiana. You'll have the goddess' own time not adding your magic to the mix. You cannot. You must not. If you have any doubt, you should wait outside."

Considering how little I'd been at this guild house, she knew me too well. I had doubts. Lots of them. After stroking Xander's flank one last time I got to my feet. The safest place for me was on the far side of the infirmary door.

No, I told myself, *it was safest for Xander.*

I'd have asked the White Fae to bind me so I could remain, but they'd need all their magic for Xander. One of the hardest things I've ever done was walking out that door.

Grigori stood in the hall, arms crossed over his chest. "Any news?"

"Rhea put something together. It has risks, but they're out of time."

He bit his lip so hard blood welled. "She's talented, and she's a werewolf. We must hope for the best."

Growling and snarling was followed by a heartrending howl. I started back inside. Xander was in pain, suffering. I had to do something. Grigori grabbed my arm. "Don't." He snapped off the single word.

On the verge of forcing him to free me, I reared back and gathered power. In a contest of pure magic, I'm stronger than him, but he stood against me to keep me from making a horrible mistake. Part of me knew it; a bigger part didn't care. Maybe the Celts had been right to cut us off at the knees. Holding great power isn't without risk or responsibility.

Grigori's fingers cut into me as I fought with myself. My

heart hammered against my ribcage, but common sense won the day. Panting from the storm that had passed through me, I withdrew the enchantment poised to slice through his hand.

"When did you discover you loved him?" Grigori's question was soft. He didn't mention I'd come within a hairsbreadth of raising magic against him, a sin that would have excommunicated me from the Circle.

"Not sure." My voice was thick with barely suppressed emotion. A pain-laced howl rolled through the air a second time, and then a third. "Christ, Grigori. We have to do something." This time, I grabbed his arm, holding on tight.

"We already did," he gritted. "We delivered him to those who can help where we cannot."

Tears pricked behind my lids. I'm not a crier, but I was hanging back while the mage I loved needed me. Grigori closed his arms around my shoulders. "He's tough. He's survived worse than this."

"But we don't know what they did to him," I groaned.

"Some things aren't our job to figure out." He held me, and I leaned against him. At some point, Dorcha, Quinn, Ciara, and the eagles joined us. When Grigori let go of me, I wound an arm around Dorcha's neck, breathing in her clean horsey smell.

The night was nearly gone when a White Fae beckoned from the doorway. She was smiling, and I took it as a good sign. "You can come in now," she said, "but not all of you."

"You and Grigori go." Quinn gave me a little push.

"Too many of us will tire him," Ciara said.

"I'm coming," Dorcha announced. "There's never been an evil spell my horn couldn't erase."

I girded myself as we walked through the barrier holding

the infirmary closed to all but those who'd been invited within. Because the last place I'd seen him was curled up in a ball on the platform, I didn't expect him to be on his feet. He looked a little haggard, but nowhere near as diminished as I expected.

"Your friends have been worried about you," Rhea told him.

Xander smiled. "Reports of my death have been greatly exaggerated."

Grigori strode forward and dropped a hand on his shoulder. "Since when do you borrow lines from Mark Twain?"

"Hell, I'll borrow lines from anyone so long as they fit, and that one does."

Dorcha glided close enough to rub her horn across his other shoulder and up and over his head. Power sparkled blue-violet the places she touched him.

He reached around and stroked her neck. "You should have been here earlier. Your healing doesn't hurt."

"What was wrong?" Grigori stepped back a pace and eyed Rhea.

She scrunched her forehead into a mass of thoughtful lines. "It's hard to know exactly since I lack samples of demon essence, but I believe they injected him with enough demon blood to sabotage his wolf."

"They were forcing a split?" Grigori gritted.

"Seemed so to me," Rhea replied. "So the first thing I did was have my wolf coax his back to ascendency. I needed time to craft a cure, and it was the only way I'd get any."

"Why didn't you call for me?" Grigori asked.

She shrugged. "No time, and I'm not at all certain two

wolves would have been better than one. I was proud of my wolf. She tracked Xander's down dark paths. She was frightened. I felt it, but she didn't give up."

Rhea rolled her shoulders back. "Once his wolf showed up, I went to work." She flapped a hand at the counter with tubes in a rack and round plates filled with something red. "The Fae were great getting me everything I asked for."

Dorcha lifted her head, done with her part of Xander's healing. "You are whole," she proclaimed.

"Same thing we told him." A White Fae stroked Dorcha's mane. "I appreciate you corroborating it. Unicorns were the original healers. We learned our skills from you."

Dorcha whinnied softly. The Fae surrounded her, stroking and cooing. The unicorn lived for moments like these, ones when she was truly appreciated. I was glad for her, and for Xander.

"Can he leave?" I asked.

One of the Fae turned toward me and nodded.

"Excellent," Xander said. "When I asked a little bit ago, they said no."

I extended a hand, and he laced his fingers with mine. "Where would you like to go?" I asked. "Are you hungry?"

"They've been feeding me," he said. "Let's walk a bit, share the new day."

When we strolled out of the infirmary, Quinn and Ciara and the birds circled around us. All their questions and attention were on Xander as they reassured themselves he'd make a complete recovery.

"Never got nearly this much attention in Russia," he joked.

"Probably a hell of a lot safer there," Quinn said.

"But not nearly as interesting," Xander replied.

The eagles swooped this way and that. "Tell your wolf to come out and hunt with us," Gwaihir pressed.

"I'd love to, but not right now. Perhaps later today?" Xander furled a silver brow.

"We'll look forward to it." Tory landed briefly on his shoulders before taking wing again.

"We don't want to tire you," Ciara said and beckoned to her bondmate.

Quinn picked up on the hint. "See you at dinner," he told us.

"Dinner it is," I agreed. Gratitude rolled through me that Xander was well and whole and would be at dinner. Fate could have dealt him a worse hand. Far worse.

We walked down the stairs and outside. Dawn had turned into midmorning. For a time, we strolled hand in hand in silence. Words wanted out. After attempting to keep them corralled, I gave up and blurted, "I wanted to be there for you, but I didn't trust my magic not to go ballistic. When your wolf howled as if you were being tortured, Grigori had to hold me back. I came within an angstrom of hurting him."

I shook my head. "It would have been awful I I'd raised my power against him."

"You didn't, though." Xander's deep voice was reassuring. After a pause, he added, "You managed the most difficult part. You brought me here."

It had been hard. No reason for him to know how many times I'd nearly lost him. Maybe he already did. "How'd they capture you?" I chewed my lower lip. "I feel guilty about not paying close enough attention. I looked up from a skirmish, and you were gone. I threatened to bring the roof down on the demonspawn, but their spokesman laughed at me."

Xander chuckled. "They're steeped in self-interest."

"Indeed. I finally got that slime guppy's attention by telling him I'd personally see to his destruction. By then, I was chucking fire this way and that."

I waited for more details. I'd asked what went wrong. He'd tell me if he wanted to.

We reached a creek and sat on flat rocks. The rush of water was soothing. He wrapped an arm around my shoulders. "Thank you."

"No need. I never leave any of my team behind."

"Not what I meant," he murmured. "You fed me from your essence. Without it, the demons' infusion would have taken over, separated me from my wolf." He blew out a breath. "What happened to me was my own fault. I got cocky, assumed they couldn't hurt me, and took chances I shouldn't have. I had a demon in a chokehold. I'd clawed his neck open, expecting the same shower of rancid blood, but someone had baited him with toxins.

"I knew something was wrong the moment I smelled his blood. It was still rank, but in a very different way. The fumes knocked me out. When I woke, I was chained to a wall with iron. Nothing I did made any difference. I reached for my wolf. With his help, maybe we could defeat the iron and shift."

Xander pulled me against him, fingers digging into my arm. "My wolf was a long way away. So far, I knew I was in trouble. I reached for you, told you to leave."

"Never. Not without you. I'd have turned that shithole upside down and inside out. I command earth and water and fire and air, and I'd have used them all to get you out of there."

"My fierce protector. No one's ever taken care of me except my wolf."

"Same for me, if you change out unicorn for wolf," I told him.

With his other hand, he cupped my cheek, angling my head so we faced one another. He touched his mouth to mine, gentle and tentative. I kissed him back, but there was nothing shy about my response. I loved him, and I'd almost lost him.

Curving my arms around his body, I held on tight while our kiss became inventive, full of bites and suckles and long, slow tongue sparring. My breasts were crushed against his chest, and my breathing quickened. Power sparkled around us as desire spiraled.

His lips were sculpted, firm. They felt as exceptional as I'd imagined. He kissed me as if we had all the time in all the worlds. I floated in a place as close to paradise as I could imagine. But then reality crashed into me, and I broke our kiss.

"Are you sure you're all right?" I asked breathlessly. "You nearly died. It's okay if we wait, and—"

"Do you want to wait?" His question held rough urgency.

"No, but I don't want to harm your recovery."

The silver wolf formed behind him and swiped my forehead with his tongue before withdrawing.

"What was that?" I grinned, still feeling the warmth of the wolf's tongue.

"He likes you and approves of our joining."

"I like him too. I petted him while Rhea was working up her antidote."

Xander stroked hair away from my face. "You're not a casual fling, Rhiana. We will mate, you and I. Once we do, there's no going back."

"Werewolves only have sex with their mates?" I was confused.

"Not at all, but I want you by my side and in my life forever. So the sex will be different."

"Different, how?"

"Not the point. Do you pledge your life to me?"

"Not fair. You should ask questions like that before you kiss me and addle my brain."

He cocked his head to one side. "You're hedging. Why?"

He was right. I wasn't sure how to answer him. "I love you," I said.

"Then it's settled." He bent to kiss me again.

I ducked away. "No, not settled at all. How will we do this?"

"What do you mean?"

"Will you expect me to return to Russia and live with you and your pack? How does Dorcha factor in?"

His forehead had been creased. The lines smoothed. "We will design our lives however we wish. I can move between my pack and the Circle, as can you."

"But I'm not a werewolf."

He shrugged. "They'll love you as much as I do, and they'll be fascinated by Dorcha. Did you plan to remain in the Circle? Grigori told me you weren't here often."

"My place is here. It took me a long time to figure that out."

"Everything you mentioned is incidental," he went on.

"You said you love me. Do you wish to join your life with mine?"

My heart did a funny little flip-flop in my chest. Would I run from him? Cut myself off from intimacy and caring like I'd done all the long years of my life? Or would I trust to an uncertain future where, for once, I didn't control all the variables?

He brushed my lips with his thumb. "I'm being pushy. Impatience when I want something is one of my failings. You can think about this, about us. Take all the time you need."

He was proposing an out. A slice of me sat back watching with interest. It would be so easy to glom onto the time excuse, except time wouldn't change a thing. I'd still be plagued with ambivalence. Not so different from battles, the only way out was through.

I nodded shyly. "Thanks for the offer, but time isn't the issue. I've never wanted anything more than I want to build a life with you."

His bicolored eyes lit with joy, twin fires burning in their depths. Power surrounded me, werewolf enchantment. When it cleared, we were in the guild house in his room. It had to be since the heady scent of werewolf was thick.

"Undress for me," he purred. "Take it nice and slow. I want to savor each bit of flesh, every one of your secrets as you choose to reveal them."

I felt self-conscious and tongue tied, but my arousal roared back hotter than ever. I couldn't stop smiling as I bent to untie my boots.

❧ 18 ❧

For each garment I removed, he mirrored my movements. It added spice to the game, made it doubly voyeuristic. Since it wasn't only me getting naked, I considered which part of him I wanted revealed next.

Shoes and stockings were only the beginning. I unfastened my trousers and let them slide to the floor. He untied loose pants that had been hanging off his slim hips. Where I had panties on, he was naked beneath the garment that puddled on the floor.

My gaze traveled upward from his bare feet taking in well-formed legs and thighs slabbed with muscle. The view made my throat thicken with desire. Most of his cock was hidden by his shirt, but generous testicles swung between his legs, and the bottom of a column of rigid flesh was a total tease.

Images bombarded me. Scenes of throwing myself on top of him and capturing the hot hard length of him inside me.

My thighs slicked with lust, and I slithered out of my panties, pushing the flimsy soaked nylon down my legs. Shivers racked me, but I held back and yanked my jacket off my shoulders so I could pull my shirt over my head.

The quicker my clothing hit the floor, the faster I'd get to see all of him.

I was panting, and my nipples had formed hard buds. The simple sensation of fabric brushing against them sent sparks flying to my core. Across from me, Xander unbuttoned his shirt and shrugged out of it. This time, I started with his shoulders and moved down. Scars crisscrossed chest and belly, visible even through a thick coating of silver hairs. His shoulders were broad, fluid. Colorful ink depicting a wolf pack began on one forearm, traveled up and across his chest, and down the other arm. Curved against his belly, his cock was magnificent. I couldn't wait to taste him, for him to sink into my vault inch by glorious inch.

"You're beautiful," he rasped. "So much more elegant than I imagined."

"When did you start picturing me naked?"

"The moment I met you."

I smiled, pleased by his admission. For someone who's never taken pains with her appearance, I wanted to be attractive for him.

He held out his arms. I walked into them. The shock of flesh against flesh sent high voltage electricity soaring through me. I clung to him, nails raking a path down his back. Our mouths crashed together. His fingertips left trails of lust running up and down my spine. They kept on zapping me like an out-of-control arcade game even after he gripped my ass to hold me tight against the swell of his erection.

Somehow, we ended up on the bed. I hadn't noticed anything about the room, and I didn't now beyond light filtering through the windows. It added an ethereal element, painting our bodies in shifting colors as we kissed and touched and stroked one another.

He moved away from my mouth and strung kisses down my breastbone before taking a breast into his mouth. I sank my fingers into his thick, curly hair as he traveled from one nipple to the other, biting and lashing his tongue around my ridged flesh. My existence had turned into one continuous blast of ecstasy. Desire intensified, forming paths and trails around and through me. I was still vibrating from his mouth on my breasts when his tongue traveled lower and lower still. When he closed his lips around my distended nub, delight seared me. I jackknifed around and licked the head of his cock. Already coated with droplets of semen, it quivered under my touch.

Fingers thrust inside me, and he swirled his tongue up, down, and around my nub. I didn't think I could go any higher, but I was in the stratosphere before sensation crashed around me. I worked the column of flesh in my mouth with both hands and lips. The hotter I got, the firmer my strokes. I wanted him to come too, needed more of the bitter-salt taste of his semen.

Orgasms cascaded through me, each seeding from the one before and each one driving me higher. I'd never revealed any of myself to my lovers. Once the deed was done, so was I. I'd drawn the line at teleporting away, but I scrambled out of intimate situations damned fast.

This was different, so different it cast lovemaking in a whole new light, one where I couldn't get enough. I swirled my tongue around the head of his cock again and murmured, "You're amazing. Come, goddammit."

He lifted his face from my streaming sex. "On your knees, wench."

The words made me laugh. They sounded positively medieval. I flipped over and got onto my hands and knees. He licked my pussy before moving so his phallus pressed against my entrance. Hot and full, he sank into me ever so slowly. I rocked my hips to hurry things along, desperate for all of him, but he enjoyed torturing me.

My body stretched around him, accommodating his girth. When he hit bottom, he stopped and twitched himself in small teasing motions. Hands settled over my breasts, pinching the sensitive nipples into even stiffer peaks. One moved to my clit, rubbing heat and fire into it.

I came again, and he withdrew slowly before thrusting into me once more. Someone was moaning, crying out for him to fuck me harder and faster. Control has always been my bailiwick. Not with him, and not anymore. The someone squealing like a hussy was me.

He did move faster, and then quicker still. Something scratched first one side of me and then the other as Xander fucked me. I was so lost in lust I figured he'd moved a hand, or maybe he'd done something with magic.

"Hold," he gritted. "Hold and come with me."

We rode the horse together, linked by lust and magic until, "Now," shuddered from him. I loosed the climax that had been pressing for release. It shot me into another dimension as semen painted my vault. The same scratching sensation burned along my flanks, but I barely noticed.

We strained together, wringing every last drop of pleasure

out of our loving. He collapsed on top of me, still buried inside. I lowered us to the bed. Gasping and panting we got turned around until we faced one another, our skin slick with sweat and sex.

I could have sworn his wolf padded around us, but it made me feel safe. I'd only depended on myself forever—and Dorcha. Maybe this wouldn't be as big an adjustment as I'd expected. I wasn't hustling to get away. Far from it, I hugged him tighter, breathing in the clean musk of sex and werewolf.

We must have drifted off because I woke to him sitting next to me on the bed with a carafe of something alcoholic in hand. "Drink," he urged.

I smiled sleepily. "What is it with werewolves and liquor? Grigori forced something down my throat after I brought you back."

"We care about you." His deep voice was a growl.

I took the flagon and drank. It tasted like mead but with more alcohol.

"Before you look at yourself and become concerned, my wolf marked you while we made love."

My eyes opened wider, and I took another sip. "Why?"

"We are mated now. Remember? I told you the sex would be different."

"The sex was amazing, incredible. You've accomplished the impossible."

Xander smiled warmly. "And what is that?"

"I'm still here. Not that I take a man to my bed often, but as soon as we're done, I run for the hills."

"No running, darling. Not this time." He ran a hand gently down the side nearest him. When I twisted to see, a small perfect tattoo of a wolf blinked at me. A quick check of the other three places I'd felt scratching yielded more ink. More wolves in different poses.

"Dorcha will be jealous," I joked. "I'll have to add her to the lineup."

"It would be an honor," Xander said.

"How did your wolf manage it?" I asked, curious. I'd thought werewolves had to take one form or the other, but then I remembered the wolf licking me when we sat by the stream.

"The original magic for the werewolf bond lies with the wolf," Xander explained. "Make sense if you think about it since the wolf's bite is what transforms mortals into werewolves."

"The wolf can operate even when you're in your human shape?"

"The old ones can," he replied.

My smile developed crooked edges. "Seems a given for all magic wielders. Power comes with age."

I set the flagon on the floor and kissed him but only once.

He touched the tip of my nose. "Felt dismissive. Tired of me already?"

"You should get so lucky. I can be a total pain in the rear. Much as I'd love to shut out the world, we need to clean up and get to dinner. It has to be soon. Grigori will want to spend time with you, and I need to check in with Dorcha."

When I looked for the outline of the wolf, it wasn't there. He'd done his job and retreated to wherever wolves went when they weren't in ascendency. It was another question, but I'd ask it later.

Somewhere in the steam of the shower, we found one

another again. This time, we stood face to face under the spray, and he lifted me onto his cock.

Breathless and laughing, I told him I could get used to a steady diet of sex. He growled something and bit my neck. Once he put me back on my feet, he flipped off the taps and handed me a towel, wrapping it around me.

With a courtly flourish, he said, "I plan to make myself so indispensable, you'll wonder how you ever got along without me."

His words both thrilled and terrified me. Being alone had meant never worrying about losing anyone. I'd never worried about Dorcha. She was indestructible. Or maybe I'd only told myself that. Xander should have been bombproof too, and look what nearly happened to him.

Being immortal was all well and good, but immortality only extended so far. Apparently, I'd been lying to myself all along about my emotional cocoon providing full protection from everything. It had let me do whatever I damn well pleased without worrying the consequences would affect anyone else.

I winced inwardly. That strategy had almost cost me my bondmate. I was smarter than that.

Xander tucked another towel around my hair to soak up the drips. "You're quiet," he observed.

"Thinking, mostly."

"About?"

"I've prided myself on some of the wrong things. It's all I'll say about that, except I'll do better."

He drew me close, holding me against his damp chest. "No matter how that project works out, I'll still love you."

Gods I hoped so. My bitchy arrogant side hadn't yet come

out to play. Maybe if I rode herd on her, she'd tone it down. Expecting she'd magically vanish was stupid. It would never happen.

"Your faith in me is appreciated." Argh. I sounded so formal. Holding people at arm's length had become a way of life. I softened my tone. "Truly, it is."

"Someday, we won't be in the middle of a war."

I raised my gaze to meet his. "Do you have seer mixed in with your werewolf? I've been embroiled in one war after another for most of my life. There've been occasional breaks, but they never lasted more than fifty years or so. Grigori started the Circle because the assassin trade was hopping. If it weren't for war, no one would require our services."

"What I meant was someday the war won't be personal. Events will revert to the way they used to be where you were called out to do a job."

"I hope you're right." And I did. Being caught up in demon crosshairs infuriated me. Add in my renegade kinfolk, a few other fallen-from-grace mages, and perhaps Poseidon, and we had a piss pot of problems.

I wormed out of his embrace and collected my clothes. No reason not to put them on. They weren't dirty. All I'd done since my last wardrobe change was sit vigil over his sickbed.

Leaving was hard. I didn't want to, but shutting out the rest of the world wasn't practical. "See you at dinner," I said.

He smothered me in a hug. "I could come with you."

"Next time, you can. I want to find Dorcha and tell her about us."

"What makes you think she doesn't already know?" He arched a brow. "I talked with her before I courted you."

The admission made me laugh. "Like she was my father, and you needed her permission?"

"She is your other half." His tone was serious. "If my wolf had objected, it would have been the end of things. Likewise, for your unicorn."

"They must have wanted for us to be happy." My words were muffled against his shoulder.

"Either that, or they were relieved as hell to have someone else to take up the slack. Being half of an animal bond can be challenging."

"I vote for the former." Narrowing my eyes in thought, I added, "I've come to know a lot of bond animals. Some never bond again if their human half dies, but most move forward and seek another bondmate. It enriches their lives as much as it does ours."

After a quick nuzzle, I strode from the room. I felt different, more alive than I had in ages. I found Dorcha in the grove, almost as if she'd been waiting for me. At her invitation, I swung onto her back, and we ambled through lush countryside.

"I want to tell you about Xander and me," I began.

"I approve."

"That's it? No questions?"

She turned her head and nipped at one of my feet. "You've needed someone like him. I was worried you'd shut him out. You're good at that."

"I almost did," I admitted.

"Almost doesn't count."

We trotted across the creek he and I had sat next to. "What if something else happens to him?"

"What if something happens to me?" she asked.

"I'd never get over it."

"You would," she said firmly. "And now I don't have to worry as much about inadvertently leaving you alone."

"Keep worrying," I told her. "We're a team."

"Neither of us are doomsday seekers," she replied. "It's why we've made such good friends."

Swathed in a companionable silence, we headed toward the guild house. I slid from her back in the courtyard, and we trooped up the stairs. "Will the other unicorns remain?" I asked her.

"For now."

"What are their names?"

Dorcha shook her head. "Names hold power. If they wish you to know, they'll tell you."

The rich smells of dinner surrounded me as soon as we were inside. I hadn't been aware how hungry I was until the scents of onion soup, fresh-baked bread, and roast wafted our way. The dining room was about half full, and mages were helping themselves from the long tables in the back of the room.

Dorcha left my side and circulated through the room, stopping to visit here and there. Of the two of us, she's always been the social butterfly. Xander and Grigori were chatting animatedly on the dais. I headed their way to tell Xander I'd make up a plate for him and find us seats.

Grigori caught sight of me and smiled wider than I'd ever seen him. Next, he caught me up in an embrace. He's as undemonstrative as I am, so we ended up letting go fast and exchanging an uncomfortable look.

Smile still in place, he retreated to a far more common

method of communication between us as he punched my upper arm lightly. "Welcome to the pack, sister."

I laughed. Damn I was doing a lot of that lately. "From one werewolf to three plus an honorary one," I joked.

"Something like that. Xander is simply stellar. You couldn't have made a more solid choice."

"Actually, he chose me, but I'm glad he did."

"Enough mutual admiration." Xander took my arm. "Shall we fill a couple of plates? I'm starving?"

"Best offer I've had all day. Eh, maybe the second best."

We were both chuckling when we left Grigori.

Dinner was festive with many toasts and well wishes on our mating. At some point, Grigori dropped my harp into my lap. Someone found another for Xander, and we made music with something other than our bodies.

The Circle felt welcoming, more so than it ever had, but perhaps I was viewing it through fresh eyes. I'd changed, so it made sense my worldview would have shifted along with everything else.

People sang to the beat of our music. Happiness filled me. No longer an emotion for everyone except me, it cuddled by my side, warm and inviting.

Dorcha cantered across the room. I glanced up, and my fingers stilled on the pulsing strings. I know all her expressions, and this one did not bode well. "Tell everyone," I said, "not just me."

A piercing whinny cut through conversation, song, and laughter. "Remember that trap we set?" She stamped her hoofs. "It's been sprung. They're almost upon us."

Grigori bolted into action, leaping across the room to the

dais. "We planned for this," he thundered. "To your battle stations. This ends tonight."

"You and Dorcha are with me." Xander was on his feet. "This way."

Glad he'd been paying attention to Grigori's earlier tactical session, when I obviously hadn't, I kept pace next to him. Along the way, we collected Ciara and Quinn and the birds. Loren and his wolf joined us too.

I might have wasted a few minutes mourning the transition from joy to readying myself to fight. Feeling sorry for myself isn't my style, though. I got over it fast.

This was my life, the life I'd chosen. I could have left everything behind along with the other elemental mages, but I'd opted to remain.

Dorcha neighed. The birds cawed. Loren's wolf snarled.

"We've got this." Quinn fist-pumped the air.

"Yeah, we do," Ciara seconded.

I'd moved beyond my pity party; battle lust caught me up. By the time we made it to the far side of the courtyard, I was ready.

For damn near anything. Grigori had said we'd end this. I gathered power around me, determined to make it so.

19

"Lie low, everyone," Quinn cautioned. "The whole point of luring the enemy was to make sure they're well and truly through whatever portals they used. Once they are, we'll turn earth against them and seal off their exit routes."

"I'll add water," Ciara said.

Someone would need to be beneath everything checking we didn't miss any channels. I was the logical choice. "I'll ensure they can't get away," I murmured and reined in my power. It burned so brightly, it could be seen for a long way.

"May I accompany you?" Loren asked.

His question was so unexpected, and his tone so deferential, I said, "Sure." Maybe he was going to try harder to be a team player. It wasn't exactly one of my strengths, either.

"My magic is the outlier here," Xander said. "How can I help?"

"Since Rhi and Loren will be managing the escape hatches, it frees us up to kill." Quinn beamed at me. "Thanks. You handed me my favorite part."

"I will remain above ground," Dorcha said, "unless you have need for me in the channels beneath."

"Your strengths are here," I told her and redirected my power to encompass Loren and his wolf. If the bond animal didn't wish to accompany us, he'd speak up.

"I'll ward us," Loren said quietly.

"Do it," I told him as my spell carried us downward. The ward was a good idea since tunnels sprouted all around us. One was so close I had to scramble to get us out of the path of mages intent on what they'd encounter above.

Elements are the same, no matter which world I'm on, and the Earth recognized me here. Loren too. I felt her outrage at being used as a conduit for darkness. That our guests came from a different world doubled the insult. I reached for her, soothing, reassuring.

We'd get rid of the enemy sullying her, but she had to be patient, let them through before we blocked their way. She'd been intent on trapping them to drain their power and redirect it for her own purposes.

"No reason we can't do both," Loren agreed and helped her seal two large pockets containing eight mages each. I sprayed the same spell I use to wipe memories except I didn't pinpoint anything. By the time I was done, they wouldn't even know their names. It would allow Earth time to set up siphons without pushback from mages frantic to escape.

Mixed magics can be a crapshoot. I had no idea if they'd have found a way out if I hadn't intervened.

Wolf by his side, Loren was working his way through

closing off channels when I joined him. We split the remaining ones between us. "You've done this before," I commented.

He smiled. "Aye, and recently."

"It shows."

"They can always build new portal systems," he said.

"Yeah, but it takes time. While their power is diverted to crafting tunnels, we'll swoop in and annihilate them."

"This is why I've stayed." His message was simple.

"Why's that?"

"To make a difference. To make my magic count." His wolf rubbed against his side, and he scratched between its ears.

Because we coordinated our efforts, and two tunnels were already shuttered, it didn't take long to finish. Loren had dismissed the original ward. He pulled it into place again as I retraced our steps upward. The stamp and din of battle reached us long before we broke through the surface.

A whole lot of demons and mages had been part of this supposedly stealth operation. Maybe as many as a hundred, but the odds were wildly in our favor. They'd assumed we were leaderless and diminished. They were in for a hell of a surprise. We needed a definitive win. One where they'd at least back off for a few years and let the Circle return to doing what it did best: knocking out evil wherever it reared its head.

I wouldn't mind a few months settling in with my new mate, either. We could go on assignments where it was the two of us—and Dorcha—dealing with something reasonable. A single problem rather than turncoat mages who wanted the Circle crushed to dust.

We oozed through into a thicket at the far side of the courtyard. Competing magic turned the air thick with the smells of the natural world running up against rot and decay.

"See you." Loren clapped me across the shoulders before he and his wolf dove into a pile of mages slugging it out a few feet away.

Blood ran into the ground adding its particular coppery stench to all the other scents. So much enchantment thundered around me, no one would even notice my tracking spells. I hunted for Dorcha and Xander. Lucky for me, they were together, so I didn't have to choose.

They'd set up a line in front of the grove with Quinn and Ciara. I'd always known the white oaks held power, but damn if they hadn't turned into something resembling Ents complete with crooked branch fingers and eyes lighting the night with green fire.

Any mage who came too near ended up with a branch through an eye or embedded in their chest. Xander sidled close. "All done?"

"Yes. No one will leave. Not easily."

"You're assuming any will be left," Quinn cackled, having moved near enough to listen in.

"You're having way too good a time." I elbowed him.

"I am. The best days are when I kill something."

"Whole lot of somethings today." Xander looked as stoked as Quinn.

Dorcha swept me onto her back with magic. Twisting midair, she gored a Dark Fae and galloped toward a pack of demons.

"Leave some for me," I shouted and let power spool within me until javelins shot from both hands. I immobilized our targets. Dorcha killed them. We made a fantastic team, efficient and effective.

Grigori raced past in werewolf form with Rhea by his side. Xander joined them, sleekly silver with his tail pluming. They piled into a mixed bag of demons and mages. I spat on the ground in disgust. When the day came that any mage would fight side by side with a demon, it was time for the mage to die.

Demons are challenging to kill, but there's never been a mage I couldn't end. Fury drove me off Dorcha's back. I leapt into the midst of the sack of shit mages who'd teamed up with demons.

"Where's your pride?" I shouted. "You should choose death over your current companions." My comments were rhetorical. I didn't wait around for answers before I carved heads from bodies with bands of fire-infused magic.

The werewolves mowed through demons. I started to yell for them to watch out for the same poison blood that had nearly killed Xander but didn't. They knew about it without me coming off as an overprotective mother.

I'd expected the enemy to make a run for the gates long before they did. Only about twenty remained when they set teleport spells in motion, assuming they'd leave the same way they arrived.

Ha! Wrong.

"Got you," I shouted, augmenting my voice with magic. "Your only choices are fighting or running like the cowards you are."

Dorcha and the unicorns closed on small groups intent on flight. I jinxed their transport spells. The unicorns gored with speed and efficiency. In some ways the battle was anticlimactic, over almost before it had begun. I looked around, hoping for one more mage to kill, but there weren't any.

The werewolves were back in their human bodies. We whooped and hollered and offered high fives all around. Once we got over the first flush of victory, we piled bodies and purged the world of their taint with magefire.

Dawn was well-established as everyone trooped toward the guild house. The enemy may have had plans to take it over, but they'd never come close enough to walk inside.

Grigori held us in the great room. Once everyone was present and accounted for—we'd sustained two injuries but no losses—he said, "You did a fantastic job today. Made me proud of the Circle and all of you."

Cheers rose. When they died down, he went on. "I can't take credit for today. This particular trap was Quinn's idea. Rhiana's too. They have a diabolical streak, and their ideas were brilliantly executed by all of you."

With Gwaihir riding on his shoulders, Quinn took a bow. "Why thank you, oh fearless leader."

Grigori crossed to where the unicorns stood. "Your assistance was appreciated. Will you remain?"

The silver-white male lowered his head until his horn rested on Grigori's shoulder leaving a rust-colored stain. "Aye, we will. Perhaps mages in need of a bondmate will surface. Most powers are a complement to ours."

"Woohoo!" I shouted, and then whistled and ran across the room to hug the other unicorns. "Thank you. It will be great for Dorcha to have company."

Aidyrth stomped forward. "Next thing you know I'll have to talk a couple more dragons into signing up." Fire plumed from her mouth and circled around the unicorns' heads. "See what you've begun?"

"Our seers predicted this day," the silver-white male told her solemnly.

Aidyrth snorted ash and smoke. "Means ours did too, but conveniently neglected to mention it to me."

"You have to ask the right questions," Grigori reminded her. "Seers can be downright opaque when they choose."

The dragon trumpeted, but then she puffed steam, the dragon equivalent of love, around Grigori.

Someone broke out bottles of assorted liquors. Trays materialized from the kitchens. We sat on chairs and couches and the floor eating and drinking and chatting and visiting.

"It's like a wolf pack," Xander observed, "except considerably larger."

I leaned against him. "Feel like getting out of here?"

"Thought you'd never ask."

Dorcha and the unicorns had left. Presumably, they were outside killing something they could eat.

Xander and I bid Grigori and the others farewell and walked out into the new day. Smoke from the various magefires still stained the air, but they burned clean. Eventually, no traces of today's carnage would remain.

"This won't be the end of it," Xander said.

"No, it won't, but it will buy Grigori time. Satan and his crew will probably think twice about infiltrating the Circle again."

"Do you agree with Ciara about Poseidon being involved?"

I shrugged. "Hard to say. Dorcha and I did a grand job pissing him off."

"Looks like we have a spot of time. Where would you like to go?" Xander asked.

I turned and smiled at him. "What makes you think I want to go anywhere? We could retire to one of our rooms—or both of them—and not surface for a month."

"We could do that a whole lot of places." He laced his fingers with mine. "If we stay here, someone will roust us out for a strategy meeting or to run a training camp or to research something."

Laughing, I said, "You've never lived here. How could you know that?"

"Because I've been the alpha for a werewolf pack forever, and on our council. Idle hands are the devil's workshop, so I've always kept everyone busy."

"You and Grigori graduated from the same school." I turned his question back on him. "Where would you like to go?"

"Not necessarily right away, but I want you to come home with me so my pack can meet you. Me mating is a big deal. Huge, actually."

My lighthearted mood fled. What if they resented me for not being one of them? "Um, yeah, let's get that part over with," I said.

"You make it sound like they'll draw and quarter you."

"They might." I aimed for joking, but it fell flat.

He squeezed my hand tighter. "I wouldn't take you somewhere you'd be mistreated."

"Let's go there first," I insisted. If they hated me, it wasn't too late to enjoy what Xander and I had had and move on without him. "We should bring Dorcha."

"We will," he agreed. "Many of my pack have never met such as her."

Not bothering with my mind voice, I whistled. Dorcha came at a gallop, something bloody hanging from her jaws.

"We're going to meet Xander's pack," I told her, aiming for neutral so she wouldn't pick up on how worried I was.

She whinnied amiably around whatever she was chewing. I took it as assent and waited for Xander to pull a journey spell together. I knew roughly where we were going, but these were his people, and I wanted the feel of his power to alert them they were about to have visitors.

He tried reassuring me as we traveled. When I didn't respond, he switched to telling me folk stories about werewolves. Fenrir had created the first werewolf to share the glory of wolfhood with a worthy mortal. The idea caught on. Over time, Fenrir altered the magic so he didn't have to bless every pairing. If werewolves had a personal god, it was him.

I'd been so caught up in Xander's story, I didn't notice the telltale signs his spell was winding down until the last moment. I had no idea what I was expecting, other than a circle of wolves all spitting in my face. We traded Xander's travel spell for a small village. It appeared untouched from 1700s Europe with neatly spaced houses facing cobblestone streets. They should be under snow, but something must warm the stones from beneath.

"Are there mortals here?" I asked.

"Nay. Only wolves. Mortals cannot find this place. It's separated from their world by veils."

"I love magical spots like this." Dorcha pranced next to us, excitement spilling from her.

Xander took my hand and led me down this street and

that to a central square. A fire burned in its center. Maybe a hundred people stood around it. The moment Xander came into view, they shouted greetings and cheered. I caught snatches of, "It's about time," and ribald suggestions about arcane sexual positions.

In her element, Dorcha cantered forward and worked the crowd, touching this werewolf and that with her horn that trailed magical streamers.

"You called ahead," I murmured.

Xander shook his head. "My mating was felt throughout my pack. No telepathy needed."

Werewolves closed on us. Everyone wanted to shake my hand or kiss my cheek. At first, I was filled with bewilderment, but it ceded to pure joy. "I was certain you'd hate me because I'm not like you," I sputtered, too overcome to take care with my words.

A woman with long, silver braids hurried forward. "How could we feel aught but love for our alpha's mate?" she asked.

"We thought he would never select one," a man called.

"A pack with an unmated alpha is bad luck," another told me.

I turned to Xander. "They must really love you to have stuck with you, even unmated."

He grinned sheepishly. "Never thought about it."

"We prepared a feast," the woman with braids said. "Please, join us and share our joy. Many of us will take wolf form."

Dorcha neighed. "Means meat is on the menu. I prefer mine raw."

Raucous laughter rose from many throats. "You'll fit right in." The woman patted Dorcha's coal-black neck.

Xander wove an arm around my shoulders, and we walked toward a two-story building with the front door standing open. Wolves flowed around us as his pack formed an honor guard. Some hurried inside.

"How did you know?" I asked him.

"That they'd accept you?" When I nodded, he went on, "I love you, Rhiana. My pack loves me and wants nothing beyond my happiness. Since we're here, might we remain for a while?"

"Of course."

We walked up the stairs and beneath the lintel. Xander stopped, turned me to face him, and closed his mouth over mine amid whoops and hollers and cheers. I even thought I heard Dorcha's neighs mingling with wolfy howls.

I'm a lucky woman. In the blink of an eye, I've gone from being convinced my bondmate had abandoned me to having not one family but two. It would take getting used to, but I'd have plenty of help. Throwing my arms around Xander's neck, I returned his kiss with everything in me.

You've reached the end of *Rhiana*. Read on for a sample from *Kylian*, next in this series. Once a part of the Circle of Assassins, he focused his power inward determined to hone his seer talents. But psychic ability cuts both ways. Grigori needs him. Will he upset his carefully structured life to answer the call?

BOOK DESCRIPTION, KYLIAN

Power is intoxicating. Anyone who says you can overdo it is either incompetent or a very good liar. I've chased down every scrap of additional magic that crossed my path, drained it, and started the hunt anew. My obsession hasn't made me much of a companion. I wouldn't have blamed my bondmate for leaving, but the snow leopard has stuck by my side.

It pains me to admit he's my sole connection to my better nature. He tempers my penchant for blowing holes in the world and asking questions later. Not that he has a soft side. He doesn't, but we've taken care of each other for all the years in my memory.

Information just fell into my lap. Critical material I should have picked up on if I'd been paying attention. My next stop is Grigori, the werewolf who heads up a gang of paranormal assassins. Once I was part his Circle, but I left to sharpen my seer skills. No matter how adept I became, scrying the future—or the past—didn't augment my power, so I moved on. Flitting from this to that to the other has been the story of my obscenely long life.

No more. It's back to the Circle for the leopard and me. We'll remain as long as we're needed.

KYLIAN, PROLOGUE

Ice cracked ominously. Another epic chunk peeled off from the glacier above and divebombed our position. A surreptitious shot of magic diverted it, not so far away as to cause suspicion, though. The thousand-pound missile thumped to the ground narrowly missing one of our precious snowmobiles. We used them to ferry supplies, and I'd be damned if I'd leave shit for the Russians to steal parts from.

"Dame Fortune loves us," one of my companions shrieked and fist-pumped the air.

I stifled a wry grin, amused at how quickly mortals attribute random events to some special intervention. Would he still be hanging his hat on Dame Fortune, who doesn't exist, if the block of ice had landed on his helmet?

My earpiece crackled with instructions to move out. The falling seracs suggested the day had grown too warm for maneuvers on Ellesmere Island, a scrap of rocky land next to Baffin Island north of the Arctic Circle. The Russians had snuck in an outpost here, violating of a bunch of international treaties. Because it was so remote, they refused to admit it existed.

My group of mercenaries had been dispatched to take it out. So far, we hadn't made a hell of a lot of progress.

I try not to lead expeditions like this one. Too much temptation to toss magic about and out myself. But I'm not shy about voicing opinions. I located Frank, our *de facto* team leader, with a thread of seeking magic and hustled to his side before anyone acted on his pull-the-plug command.

A big man with a full black beard and the build of a linebacker, he shot me an annoyed glance. "We're pulling out," he said. "Something wrong with your communicator?"

Because I could, I scraped the surface of his mind to see what was really going on. Surprise, surprise. He wasn't annoyed, he was scared. The last batch of falling ice must have gotten to him.

"We can finish this," I said, holding to a neutral, non-confrontational tone. Before he ginned up a reply, I went on. "Then we won't have to keep coming back."

No need to point out we were going on two weeks and so far hadn't gotten near enough to the Russian installation to be much more than a nuisance. They'd wisely sunk their building deep in the ice with its foundations resting on bedrock. It protected them from avalanches, and damn near everything else. It was how they'd gotten away with denying its existence. The only thing that stuck up above ground—or in this case, ice—level was their com machinery.

The satellite apparatus protruding from the roof was all we'd managed to destroy. Since I was certain they had a duplicate inside, we hadn't made a dent in their defenses.

Frank wasn't all that swift on the uptake, but he did manage to grunt, "How?" in response to my comment about finishing things.

I considered it a win. He could have told me to shut up and get moving. Line of command and all that shit. "So far, the problem has been we can't get inside."

"Tell me something I don't know," he growled.

Time to lie my fucking head off. "I did some poking around," I told him. "I believe I can breach the barrier, and then the rest of you can follow. We'll finish whoever we find, and then we can go home."

"Not seeing it. We've been around and around the target ten times."

Another volley of automatic weapon fire split the eerie quiet of the Arctic. We returned fire. Waste of good ammo if you ask me. The rattle of weaponry was the only noise other than the perpetual pounding of the ocean on ice that rimmed the shore. We had a ship moored quite a way out in Baffin Bay. Danish troops were keeping an eye on it for us. Amazingly, our fleet of Zodiac rafts still lined the ice, untouched.

But then, we had our target pinned in their building. It might be considered an accomplishment, but the Russians are masters at stonewalling enemies. They barricaded themselves into Leningrad during World War Two and beat the Germans by default.

"Let me worry about the where part," I told Frank seeding my words with enough calming magic to, hopefully, settle him down. I could launch my plan without his blessing, but I try to be a team player on these missions. I only sign up to amuse myself. If I got a rep for being tough to work with, no one would tap me for anything. It was hard enough keeping all my various aliases straight.

Most mercenaries keep go bags stashed in key locations. I craft what I need on the spot with magic.

"What are we doing, boss?" hissed through my headset.

It made sense. After Frank's pronouncement we were leaving, he hadn't fleshed out any details. The troops were growing restless, all fifteen of us. Including me.

I made a decision, one that might cost me, but I was tired of dicking around. Dropping a hand onto his shoulder, I said, "Maybe you were right the first time. Fall back to the rafts. Don't wait on me." Along with my persuasive suggestion, I did some rearranging so he wouldn't remember our conversation.

Or me, until I materialized.

Hopefully, when I saw him next aboard the ship, he'd go along with my version of reality, the one where I reminded him he'd assigned me to go in solo. A secret mission only the two of us knew about. As fact-planting went, it should be simple enough to accomplish.

Frank keyed his mic. "Pack up. Move out."

Excellent. My wee bit of compulsion had taken root. I didn't wait around for him to ask questions. Our team was on the move, revving up the snowmobiles and packing gear. Drawing invisibility around myself, I headed for the Russian installation. Ione joined me well out of sight of the others. He's a snow leopard and my bondmate. He's always along on these expeditions, but he knows to stay out of sight. His kind aren't exactly native to this area, but that's not the worst of it. He's easily double the size of a normal snow leopard, and would draw the wrong kind of attention.

Wind had been brisk since daybreak; it picked up still more. Bits of ice thwacked my face, the only place I had exposed skin. Ione sported bloody smears near his mouth. "What'd you kill?" I asked.

He licked his whiskers, but it didn't obliterate the evidence. "Seal," he mumbled.

I muffled a snort. "You ate a whole seal? That's going to slow you down."

"Only half." He sounded miffed. "Saved the rest for our next trip here."

"Ha! You may have to do battle with a polar bear."

Ione growled. He and I both knew he was more than a match for any polar bear, but not many were left. Seals were ubiquitous. "What are we doing?" he asked.

"We're teleporting inside and killing everyone. Then I'll dismantle everything useful, and we'll return to the ship."

"You'll return to the ship. I'll wait...elsewhere."

"Not here. We'll be done here."

He rolled his big shoulders as he trotted next to me. "Fine. I'll go home. Which one?"

I'd been thinking about it. "Maybe you will want to remain here if the hunting is plentiful. I have to stop by the villa. Haven't been there in years."

Ione made a snarly face. He hated the villa by the Adriatic; the climate was far too warm for his taste. Mine too, truth be known, but I couldn't abandon it. Someone had to ensure the warding was still intact.

We reached the perimeter of the Russian installation. A muted electronic whirring suggested someone knew we were here. Guessing at the interior layout, I snatched a spell out of my bag of tricks and teleported to the lowest level of the building, making certain Ione and I were well concealed.

In stark contrast to the outside, the building was overheated. At least the small room forming around us was deserted. As I'd hoped, it contained banks of computer equipment. Ione padded toward the door.

"Wait," I told him and redirected power to assess exactly what we faced. I scanned once, and then again with the same results. Eighteen men, two women, and one Dark Fae. What in the hell was a magic-wielder doing here? Was he passing for human? They were capable of that if they employed a glamour to hide their wings—and their ears.

Until I shot my wad, the mortals would remain oblivious to my presence. But the Fae could find me the same way I located him. I'd been going back and forth on a strategy, but the Fae's presence decided things. I wouldn't have nearly as much fun, but I'd be efficient.

I hustled to Ione and consolidated our ability. Once I had both magics well in hand, I sent lethal power in a wide arc. It would seek out life and destroy whatever crossed its path. Except the Dark Fae. He'd require a direct approach. Lab animals were one floor up. They'd die too, but weeding them out would take more time. Lots more.

Besides, once the humans were gone, there'd be no one to take care of them. The rats, mice, cats, and monkeys wouldn't have a chance at survival if I loosed them. Maybe death was a backhanded favor.

"You're ruining the fun," Ione groused.

"I know. I'll make it up to you."

"How?"

I nudged him. "Wait for it." Untangling our power, I

formed small lightning bolts and contained them as they arced between my hands.

"Fae?" Ione snarled. Hackles shot up the length of his back. "How'd he get here?"

It was the question of the hour, but one I lacked an answer to.

The door to our cramped quarters blew open, carried by a gust of magic. Interesting. This must be one of the stronger Fae. Usually, their White counterparts were the ones with the most magic.

Pinning him and draining his power was tempting, but I wanted information. He probably wouldn't volunteer jack, but I have ways of getting around that. Power poured from him, pelting Ione and me.

"Is that the best you can muster?" I asked. "Hell, blowing ice chunks were worse."

The Fae grunted and swept long white hair over broad shoulders. He was tall for his kind and naked from the waist up. Silver wings mottled with jewel tones were folded against his shoulders. His skin held a coppery tint, which was odd. Most of his kinsmen were fair to the point of looking bleached out. At least his pointed chin and sculpted cheekbones looked like they should. His legs were encased in khaki pants, and he wore shiny leather boots. Another oddity. All the Fae I've known preferred to go barefoot. It amplifies their connection with the earth.

"You killed my beasties," he gritted and hurled more power our way. Had he figured out what I am? If he did, he'd have conserved his resources. Or maybe he already knew he was a dead mage.

I tried to place his accent and pegged him for one of

Faery's residents. Even more curious. What in the hell was he doing here?

"Stand down." I infused command into my words. A shocked look crossed his face, eyes wide, fair eyebrows raised. But he dropped his hands and stared at me.

Yup. Thrall works damned well, especially for those with weaker magic than mine, which is damn near everyone.

Ione padded closer, his amber eyes brimming with disgust. "What were you doing with those beasties?"

The Fae averted his silver eyes. Not many can stare Ione down and live to tell about it.

"Making them better," he mumbled.

I could play twenty questions, or I could hurry things up. He was the last loose end. Nothing alive stirred on the floors above. If I'd been feeling generous, I might have opted for something that wouldn't hurt him, but he was on his way out anyway.

Shaping a spell, I shoved it into his memories as I mined for all the details I could come up with. He groaned and grabbed his head. My estimation of him shot up a few notches. He wasn't squealing or begging for mercy.

Ione trotted through the door. Good. He'd check on the rest of the facility and make damn good and sure no one was left. Where there was one Fae, there might be others who'd been hidden to my probing.

I passed through surface layers of the Fae's mind and was trolling deeper. Once I was convinced I'd moved past his association with the Russians, I cut the connection. The Fae dropped to his knees, keening softly. He knew the jig was up. It was only a matter of how I chose to drain his power.

Not much shocks me, but this mess held a worrisome

sophistication. "You violated our covenant," I shouted. The Fae didn't even bother to look up.

Ione was back, furry face twisted in disgust. "His beasties are unnatural monsters." He swiped a paw down the side of the Fae's face leaving bloody tracks.

"I know. I saw everything in his mind," I told my bondmate. "Keep an eye on him. I'll have a look for myself, and then we'll blow this place up."

I hadn't planned on taking out the installation, but I wasn't about to leave the twisted specimens I figured I'd find above. A crafty scientist could probably harvest their DNA and save themselves a whole lot of steps recreating this Frankenstein's palace.

Crap. No wonder the Ruskies had denied all knowledge of the place. I hurried down a concrete corridor and up the first set of stairs I came to. The next floor up was one big room with cages of varying sizes. I'd picked up on the animals when I scanned. But I'd missed the hybrids because they didn't pigeonhole neatly into any categories.

How long had this project been underway? More importantly, was it the only one? The Russians were clearly breeding soldiers by splicing animal DNA in with human, with obvious advantages. They'd grow to fighting size in less than half the time humans took, and they'd have cunning and strength and more of an animal intelligence than a human one. It might mean warriors who obeyed without question.

Or not.

I'd seen things like this before, and the results usually backfired. Animals rely on instinct. Unlike men, they have principles. The comparison amused me, which was a relief after the bleakness of the lab. Draping everything with protoplasm with the unmaking spell, I kindled it and watched bodies turn to dust.

To be on the safe side, I ran through the upper two floors. Other than dead bodies and a greenhouse, I didn't find anything noteworthy. On my way back to Ione and the Fae, I congratulated myself for making a sound decision. Frank and the troops wouldn't have added anything. This was definitely a one-man operation. The sounds of chewing reached me before I bolted back into the computer room. Ione was crouched over the Fae working on one of his legs.

"Time to go," I said cheerily.

The snow leopard offered a bloody grin and trotted to my side.

The Fae was clinging to life. I took pity on him and drilled a hole in his magic center. Brilliant light spilled into the dingy space as his essence bled out. This had almost been too easy, but then very little challenges me. It's a curse in a way. I'd really love to sink my teeth into a situation where the outcome's not a foregone conclusion.

"Why?" Ione asked once we were outside in what had turned into a raging blizzard.

I understood what he wanted to know. "They did those experiments to breed a race of warriors."

"Not fair to the animals."

"Not fair to anyone." I set a good pace. When we were a hundred yards away, I called on the sea. It's never far away on these Arctic islands. Its answer was instantaneous. Flowing through bedrock, it crashed through the remains of the Russian installation and annihilating it.

Being Poseidon's son has a few perks. That's one of them.

All in all, a good day's work.

"Still going to the villa?" Ione asked.

"I don't want to, but yes."

"Find me when you need me." My bondmate swiped my face with a bloody sandpaper tongue that smelled of Fae. Power sheeted from him, and he was gone. Guess what we'd found had disturbed him enough he wanted to put space between himself and Ellesmere Island.

I girded myself to return to the ship. My first stop would be Frank, where I'd convince him our super-secret mission had been a total success. I'd have skipped it, but if I didn't do something, the team would suit up and show up.

And find the installation gone, a crater leading to the sea in its stead. Tough to explain shit like that.

First, I built a ward, and then I set a course for the ship and the corridor right outside Frank's quarters. Hopefully, he'd be there and not shooting the breeze with the Danes in the bar. I wouldn't bother mentioning the human experimentation side of the equation. Frank would run to his bosses in the CIA, and it would spawn an international incident. I'd stymied the DNA lab efforts for now; it would have to be good enough.

The cramped corridor formed around me. A sailor bumped into my shoulder and stumbled off mumbling about having had too much to drink. I waited until the corridor was empty. It took a while. In one fluid motion, I dropped my ward and knocked on Frank's door.

"Come."

I turned the latch and walked inside, miming a jaunty salute. "Mission accomplished."

"Huh?"

I tossed believe-me magic all over the place and said, "You know."

"Know what? For Christ's sake, spit it out, man."

I pushed the door shut. "The installation is gone. Very few were manning it. They're all dead. We can go home." I pushed more power his way, rearranging a few brain cells and hoped for the best.

His mystified expression yielded to a broad grin. He high-fived me. Then he slapped me across the back. "Strong work. Find anything inside?"

"Nah. People. A greenhouse. Computers."

A sly look crossed his face. "We'll split the bonus."

If money mattered to me, I'd have stopped his heart for being a dick. Lucky for him, it doesn't. "Generous of you," I mumbled and walked out of the cabin. Teleporting away from here was tempting, but I had to stick it out until we made port. I'd catch a flight from Reykjavik, and then I'd be free.

If I cared a twit about mortals, I'd have hunted for additional clone labs. I didn't. Let mortals solve their own damned problems.

One of the team ran toward me. "Frank gave us the good news. Come to the bar, man. We all want to buy you a drink."

Breath hissed from me. I hadn't expected Frank to finger me, but then he was focused on the bonus, money that should rightfully be divided among the entire team. Maybe there'd be a way to guilt trip him into doing just that.

"On my way," I said. "Right after I change into something that doesn't stink of blood and cordite."

"Take your time," he said. "Booze will still be there."

Laughing, I ducked into my cabin and plotted how I could manipulate Frank into sharing the bounty.

ABOUT THE AUTHOR

Ann Gimpel is a USA Today bestselling author. A lifelong aficionado of the unusual, she began writing speculative fiction a few years ago. Since then her short fiction has appeared in many webzines and anthologies. Her longer books run the gamut from urban fantasy to paranormal romance. Once upon a time, she nurtured clients. Now she nurtures dark, gritty fantasy stories that push hard against reality. When she's not writing, she's in the backcountry getting down and dirty with her camera. She's published over 90 books to date, with several more planned for 2021 and beyond. A husband, grown children, grandchildren, and wolf hybrids round out her family.

Keep up with her at www.anngimpel.com or http://anngimpel.blogspot.com

If you enjoyed what you read, get in line for special offers and pre-release special reads. Newsletter Signup!

Grigori

Coven Enforcers

Blood and Magic

Blood and Sorcery

Blood and Illusion

Demon Assassins

Witch's Bounty

Witch's Bane

Witches Rule

Dragon Heir

Dragon's Call

Dragon's Blood

Dragon's Heir

Dragon Lore

Highland Secrets

To Love a Highland Dragon

Dragon Maid

Dragon's Dare

Dragon Fury

Earth Reclaimed

Earth's Requiem

Earth's Blood

Earth's Hope

Elemental Witch

Timespell

Time's Curse

Time's Hostage

Gatekeeper

Shadow Reaper

Rebel Reaper

Untamed Reaper

GenTech Rebellion

Winning Glory

Honor Bound

Claiming Charity

Loving Hope

Keeping Faith

Ice Dragon

Feral Ice

Cursed Ice

Primal Ice

Magick and Misfits (Fall and Winter 2020)

Court of Rogues

Midnight Court

Court of the Fallen

Court of Destiny

Rubicon International

Garen

Lars

Soul Dance

Tarnished Beginnings

Tarnished Legacy

Tarnished Prophecy

Tarnished Journey

Soul Storm

Dark Prophecy

Dark Pursuit

Dark Promise

Underground Heat

Roman's Gold

Wolf Born

Blood Bond

Wolf Clan Shifters

Alice's Alphas

Megan's Mates

Sophie's Shifters

Wylde Magick

Gemstone

Lion's Lair

Unbalanced

STANDALONE BOOKS

Branded, That Old Black Magic Romance (paranormal romance)

Edge of Night (short story collection, paranormal and horror)

Grit is a 4-Letter Word (nonfiction)

Heart's Flame (post-apocalyptic romance)

Icy Passage (science fiction romance)

Marked by Fortune (post-apocalyptic coming of age story)

Melis's Gambit (historical paranormal romance)

Midnight Magic (paranormal romance)

Red Dawn (post-apocalyptic paranormal romance)

Shadow Play (historical paranormal romance)

Shadows in Time (Highland time travel romance)

Since We Fell (contemporary romance)

Warin's War (paranormal romance)